THE RED MONK OF ROHA

Kwamu

Raven Rider Books
www.RavenRiderBooks.com
TikTok: @HistoryFellow
Twitter: @kwamu22
Instagram: @HistoryFellow
ISBN: 979-8-9856238-0-2

For

My son, Rohan, the toughest kid I know.

ACKNOWLEDGMENTS

To my amazing wife, Esda, for putting up with my late nights and early mornings, reading early drafts and keeping me partially sane during the writing of this book. Without her, this book would still be nothing but an idea wasting in my mind.

I also wish to express my gratitude to my little sister, Setche, for her continuing encouragement and steadfast support as I continue to take steps towards this journey of creating stories.

Last but not least, I give thanks to my late grandfather, former Senior Divisional Officer, David Abunaw, who in the summer of 1990 at his residence along the historic dusty John Holt Road in Mamfe, Cameroon, first introduced me to Ethiopia's rich history and its monastic legacy, when I was 12 years old. You are dearly missed, sir.

AUTHOR'S NOTE

This book is inspired by the true story of St. Moses, who lived during the 4th century and is also known to history as Moses the Ethiopian. Although the main storyline of this book is largely fictionalized and takes place about 800 years after the death of St. Moses, the setting and narratives are historically accurate and portray a rich part of African history that is mostly unknown outside of Ethiopia.

PROLOGUE

By AD 333, Ethiopia, then known as Axum, had become one of the first two nations in the world to officially adopt Christianity as a state religion, along with Armenia. Ethiopia called its church the Tewahedo Church. For 300 years the kingdom maintained extensive links with many Christian lands of the world, exchanging ideas, pilgrims, monks, priests, and ambassadors with places as far away as Egypt, Byzantium, Tyre, and Jerusalem.

With the emergence of Islam in the seventh century, and its eventual spread across Eastern Europe, Asia, the Middle East, and North Africa, Ethiopia's connection with the rest of the Christian world became severely diminished. Isolated and constantly facing attacks on all sides—from Muslim kingdoms to its north and east, and from "pagan" lands to its south and west, Ethiopia became the last standing major Christian bastion in the southern hemisphere. With the fall of Jerusalem in 1187 and the withdrawal of European Crusaders from the city, Ethiopia's contact with the wider Christian world was effectively cut off, sealing its isolation. It then became known as the Outpost of the Cross.

CHAPTER 1

Shire, Ethiopia, AD 1203

Lord Kiros had once survived the bite of a black mamba, yet few things terrified him as much as the increasing possibility of losing the affections of his wife. He downed a small cup of mountain coffee she had brewed for him, then stood up and approached her from behind as she painted a portrait of St. George on the wall next to the fireplace. He gently ran his fingers through her long, braided hair that flowed gracefully down to her shoulders. She turned around to face him, her large bright eyes that contrasted deeply with her smooth coal-black skin meeting his intense gaze. He leaned in to kiss her but she turned her head away. He was about to make a second attempt when his horse neighed outside.

"Hyenas?" she wondered aloud, seizing the moment to pull back and avoid his kiss.

"No," Lord Kiros said, his ears perked. "Something worse—people."

Lord Kiros could smell danger. It was his job. He was a tracker and a scout commander in the king's army.

"You stay here," he whispered.

He hurriedly slipped on his sandals and rushed to the wooden shelf where he had placed his sword that evening, fresh from being sharpened and polished by the best blacksmith in Shire. He was to assemble with a local detachment of the king's Army the following day for its scheduled deployment to the frontlines. But now it seemed he would put his sword to use for the first time in months, in chasing off horse thieves instead of clashing with the kingdom's enemies on the battlefield.

Having no time to put on his tunic, he stepped outside, with the cool night breeze slapping against his bare chiseled chest and blowing against his baggy cotton trousers. But who he saw outside were not some mere vagrants sneaking about in the dark from the enclosure where he kept his horse. Instead, he saw three men dressed in dark robes and standing before his two-story stone home, waiting for someone. Two were armed with swords and one with a short stabbing spear. Those men were not horse thieves, he quickly realized. They were hired mercenaries—desert nomads who would do anything for the right price. They were here to kill someone. Lord Kiros could not think of why anyone would want him dead. Or was it his wife they were after? She had no enemies he could think of.

As Lord Kiros's eyes caught the glare of the moon's reflection against the iron head of the stabbing spear, he realized he did not have time for questions just yet. He had to act. He had to neutralize the threat before him and protect his wife and his home, which sat on the last piece of his land that had not been seized from his family. But could he fight three armed men by himself? He had been trained to fence by his father from an early age. He was also a veteran of many battles, but so were the mercenaries most likely. They must have been hired because of their skill and experience. Regardless, Lord Kiros was going to have to fight. He had no choice. Being a lord, his home in the rugged landscape was somewhat isolated, the nearest buildings being a cluster of dwellings in a valley some distance away. Even if his wife screamed, no one else could hear her and come to their aid.

"Are you Lord Kiros?" the man with the spear asked.

"State your business with him," Lord Kiros demanded.

Lord Kiros heard a swoosh as the two men with swords unsheathed them while the man with the spear tilted it forward.

"This is our business with him," the man with the spear said, stroking its shaft.

Lord Kiros watched as the men stepped forward, positioning themselves to his front and flanks. He slowly closed the door behind him, ensuring his wife remained safely indoors. Deciding to do the unexpected and thwart whatever strategy the men had in mind, he suddenly darted forward, towards the spear man. Taken off-guard, the man swiftly raised his weapon and thrust it forward. Lord Kiros grabbed it just below the tip and swung his sword, slicing the spear's wooden shaft in half and instantly jabbing his sword into the thigh of the man, who let out a loud piercing scream as he dropped, incapacitated. His scream muffled the gurgle of the attacker from Lord Kiros's left flank, who had inadvertently sprang into the deadly half of the spear, having been rapidly placed in position for just that purpose by Lord Kiros, without even looking. With the spear man grievously wounded and the attacker from the left flank dead, Lord Kiros quickly turned his full attention to the attacker from his right. Lord Kiros quickly dodged the man's sword blow, blocked a rapidly delivered successive one, then took a step back to reassess his opponent. Lord Kiros could hear his own heart beating above the chirping of crickets as he understood that the man was a good fighter who posed a real threat to his health. One false move and he would be dead without ever knowing why.

He suddenly caught sight of his wife, who had just emerged from their home, standing in the doorway, terrified at the scene unfolding before her. He quickly turned his attention back towards his opponent. The attacker sprang towards him, but he stood his ground, blocked the man's blow, and shot forward with his sword, finding a landing spot on the man's chest and into his heart. The man made no sound. He simply collapsed almost as silently as the instant Lord Kiros pulled out his sword from his body.

Lord Kiros then turned towards the wounded and screaming spear man on the ground, who had his hands pressed over his wound in a fruitless effort to stop the bleeding. Lord Kiros walked over to the man and stood over him. It was then that he noticed a medallion of St. Aboli dangling from a necklace around the man's neck. The man was likely an ex-soldier—a cavalryman, who had chosen one of the equestrian saints as his inspiration and spiritual protector, like many horse soldiers in the king's army did. It had not worked for him this time. At that moment, Lord Kiros thought he may have seen the man before, but he could not remember where.

"Why?" Lord Kiros asked. "Do I know you?"

"It does not matter," the man groaned. "You will kill me anyway."

"No, I will take you before the town judge."

"No judge can help you," the man said with a pained smile.

Before Lord Kiros could say anything else, the man swiped a dagger from within his robes and lunged for Lord Kiros. But Lord Kiros had been quicker. He had been in the killing business for a long time and knew every trick. The man's forward thrust only pushed him deeper towards Lord Kiros's already waiting sword. The mercenary's demise was instant.

Lord Kiros sighed. Now he would not know why the men had wanted him dead. Worst of all he would not know who else lurked in the shadows waiting for an opportunity to strike at him. He turned towards his wife. He had to live in order to protect her, save his marriage, his home, and regain his family's lost lands. That is why he was assembling with the army the following day. The fate of the kingdom was at stake. That fate partly depended on how well his commander performed his duties in battle. His commander's performance depended on how well, he, Lord Kiros served him. His commander was the man he blamed for all his troubles.

CHAPTER 2

Lord Kiros's family was once one of the wealthiest in Shire, owing to his father's skill as a horse merchant with a reputation for absolute honesty. However, after his father reported to the town's Head of Merchants on Lord Groda's tendency of using his position as town judge to obtain bribes in order to render partial judgements on cases brought before him, the family's luck took a downturn. That was because in retaliation, Lord Groda used his position to file false charges of treason against Lord Kiros's father, causing the Kiros family to lose favor with the reigning king at the time. As a result, not only was Lord Kiros's father briefly jailed, but most of his lands and properties were seized and offered for sale to the highest bidder. And of course, Lord Groda very conveniently found himself in the best position to purchase the lands, and for almost next to nothing. Although Lord Kiros's father was allowed to retain his title, the family became destitute, with the elder Kiros vowing to do all in his power to reclaim his properties and family's honor, and swearing his son to the same commitment.

To this end, in the year 1185 at age 19, Lord Kiros had joined Lord Groda's forces when experienced trackers and soldiers were needed to accompany a new king and an entourage of priests and monks to Jerusalem. It was a royal mission to visit and render support to the Ethiopian resident monks at the Church of the Holy Sepulcher, where the Ethiopian church had maintained a presence for centuries. Known for his tracking abilities honed through years of hunting deer, ostriches, jackals, and wolves in the Ethiopian highlands, and his potential usefulness as a scout for the long and treacherous journey, the young Lord Kiros had hoped to curry favor with Lord Groda, the man who had destroyed his family, but also, the one man who had the power to restore it to its former glory. Lord Groda readily accepted him into the army, fully recognizing the young scout's value to him.

However, after 15 years of serving Lord Groda faithfully, little had changed. Instead, Lord Groda's greed had seen him ruin the lives and reputations of more nobles in Shire, and concocting devious schemes to seize their lands. To make matters worse, Lord Groda even confiscated land granted by the current king to Lord Kiros's family as a reward for his father organizing the building of wells for the use by trade caravans along the routes to Shire. Lord Groda achieved this by using his power as a town judge to seize the documents certifying the land grant. As long as he held those documents and those of the many others he had swindled, he was the rightful owner of the lands and all they produced. Yet, Lord Kiros continued to serve the man devotedly. He had made a promise on his father's death bed to restore his family's good name and lands, and if that meant serving Lord Groda unquestionably, then that is what he was determined to do.

So seven months after he had departed for the frontlines after being attacked at his home by unknown men, he was with Lord Groda's army, riding through the dry and dusty territory of imposing mountains and plateaued hills that were dotted with small batches of juniper and acacia trees. They were at war against the Islamic Shewa Sultanate, one of the many enemies that threatened the kingdom of Ethiopia. Approaching from the southern borders, Shewa troops had crossed the Gugu Mountains and swept down like a swarm of ravenous locusts deep into the Christian kingdom, hoping to absorb it in one striking blow. However, it was a task that had proven more difficult than the Shewa sultan had expected. Now he was on the retreat, pursued by the king of Ethiopia and 60,000 troops harassing his army at every hilltop, every valley, every pass, and every crossing.

Lord Groda and a hundred of his men, all horse soldiers, were among the many smaller elements of the king's army that had been dispatched to locate and destroy roving bands of the sultan's stragglers and patrols that were still ravaging the countryside.

"The sultan's main army will be marching through here in three days, my lord," Lord Kiros warned as Lord Groda and his staff debated their next move.

"Then we ambush them there—at the pass," Iskander, Lord Groda's nephew said, pointing towards some hills. "We kill as many of them as we can, then disappear into the hills again before they can organize a pursuit."

"No," Lord Kiros countered, "We let them keep moving."

"You are a just a coward, Commander Kiros!" Iskander accused the scout commander.

"Ears that fail to listen to advice often accompany the head when it is chopped off," Lord Kiros responded calmly, quoting a proverb he had learned as a boy growing up in Shire, and dismissing the man whom he had always regarded as having about as much worth as a fly. He had always thought of Iskander as a pathetic lifeform who couldn't even lead an army to fight goats, but whose presence as an officer in his unit was simply because his uncle was Lord Groda.

"You—" Iskander began an angry response.

Lord Groda held up his hand, silencing his young nephew and giving his scout commander the opportunity to explain himself.

"My lord," Lord Kiros continued, "the sultan's men have come this way before. There's a gap beyond those hills that you can't see from here. His scouts know the territory. If we try to ambush them at the pass, they will simply send men through the gap and attack us from the rear, trapping us in the middle. We simply do not have the numbers to fight them."

Just like during the journey to and from Jerusalem, and in numerous battles since, Lord Kiros had served Lord Groda well as a scout leader, saving his life and his small army from annihilation countless times. Lord Groda trusted him.

"Rider!" one of Lord Groda'a men suddenly yelled out. "From the east!"

Lord Groda and his men turned their gazes east.

"It's Yohannis," Lord Kiros said.

Yohannis was Lord Kiros's second-in-command of the scouts. He raced towards the body of soldiers, his horse kicking up the dust behind him. He came to a halt before Lord Groda and Lord Kiros.

"It's not good, Commander," Yohannis addressed Lord Kiros. "We have secured the village, but we arrived there too late. The sultan's patrols had been there before us."

Moments later, Lord Groda and his men arrived at the village of Bodera, where their small force had hoped to rest, water their horses, and obtain supplies before riding back to their base of operations in Shire after many months of hard fighting.

"They slaughtered everyone," Lord Kiros lamented, dismounting his horse and staring aghast at the bodies of men, women, and children that lay scattered across the village.

One of Lord Kiros's scouts who was already on the ground in the village approached Lord Kiros and handed him some water in a wooden cup.

"At least the well was not poisoned, Commander," the scout addressed Lord Kiros, who took a sip of the water and licked his lips. "We can water the horses."

"How do they know it was not poisoned?" Iskander quietly asked Lord Groda.

"They drank it," Lord Groda responded.

"They drank it?" Iskander scoffed. "Why didn't they test it on the horses first?"

"Commander Kiros and his men belong to that breed of soldiers who care more about their horses than they care among themselves," Lord Groda responded.

Iskander rolled his eyes. There were certain things he could never understand.

Lord Kiros, after examining the surroundings, stepped towards Lord Groda, who remained mounted on his horse.

"How many riders?" Lord Groda asked him.

"At least a hundred, my lord," he responded, observing the tracks left behind. "Maybe 120. They have not gone far."

"What is done is done," Lord Groda declared. "We cannot bring back the dead."

"The sultan's men took prisoners, my lord," Lord Kiros pointed out, picking up an arrow from the ground and presenting it to Lord Groda. "There was resistance."

"From who?" Lord Groda asked.

"Not sure," Lord Kiros confessed. "But this arrow is made from the branch of the myrrh tree."

"And?" Lord Groda asked.

"The myrrh is not found in these parts," Lord Kiros explained. "It comes from the east. Whoever fought back may have been part of the king's army, which may explain why they have been taken as prisoners."

"How many prisoners?" Lord Groda asked.

"Four men," Lord Kiros said, again observing the tracks. "They are on foot and being led by the horses. It should slow down the riders."

"Which way are they headed?" Lord Groda asked.

"South."

"We ride south then," Lord Groda declared. "We rescue our Christian brethren from the sultan's men, and then we return home to Shire."

"The church," Yohannis said, pointing at a small patch of forest in the middle of the village. "It is a disaster."

Amidst the sea of dust and dryland that seemed to have swallowed up the entire area, was a neat cluster of greenery in the middle of the village that presented a glaring divergence from the surrounding landscape.

Lord Kiros, Lord Groda, Iskander, Yohannis, and some of the scouts rode through a well-beaten path into the miniature forest, until they arrived at a smoldering rectangular stone building with a cross at the top. Several bodies of priests, deacons, and worshippers lay scattered outside, where they had been slain.

"Shoo!" one the scouts chased away hyenas and wolves that were gnawing on the bodies.

"This is the church of St. Gabriel, my lord," Lord Kiros pointed out to Lord Groda, anger rising in his throat. "It has stood here for 500 years."

The highlands were dotted with churches, many commissioned and built by Ethiopian kings over the centuries to mark the territory of the Christian kingdom. Some had been built to blend in with the environment in order to keep them hidden from enemies of the Church, especially during the scourge and eventual reign of the tenth century rebel Queen Gudit. She had ravaged the land in her futile attempt to rid it of its nobles and Christian heritage by destroying every church and monastery she could find. But there were also those churches that were anything but hidden, like the church of St. Gabriel, which was situated in a prominent and conspicuous patch of green forest located in a vast sea of brown earth.

"Why?" Iskander muttered under his breath.

"Why what?" Lord Groda asked.

"Why not hide this church on a hilltop, or build it into rocks like is the case with many others?" Iskander wondered.

"In the land that is dying," Lord Groda responded, "the people ensure that the forest around the church stays green and alive. It is like the Garden of Eden. The forest represents life itself. If it lives, life goes on."

"Well, it didn't save these lives," Iskander chuckled, pointing at the bodies before them.

Everyone ignored him.

The soldiers buried all the dead in a mass grave and placed a cross marker over it.

Their horses already watered, Lord Kiros and his scouts mounted them and rode out as the advance column to seek those responsible for the massacre.

CHAPTER 3

Several hours later, Lord Kiros and six of his scouts lay on a hill, watching 120 Muslim soldiers from the Shewa Sultanate camped in a valley below them. The Muslims were roasting several goats on an open fire, spoils looted from the village they had just laid waste to. Their prisoners were tied to an acacia tree and kept under close guard. Relaxed in a false sense of safety, the Muslims had no idea their lookouts had been permanently neutralized by Lord Kiros and his scouts just moments before.

"Lord Groda approaches," Yohannis notified Lord Kiros as clouds of dust rose across the horizon.

Leaving the rest of his small force about 300 meters away, Lord Groda, Iskander, and some of the commanders soon drew closer, dismounted their horses, and crawled towards Lord Kiros and his scouts, making as little noise as possible lest they alarm the Muslims.

"There," Lord Kiros said to Lord Groda, "pointing at the prisoners."

"They should not have taken the Christians," Iskander remarked.

"Get your men and block the south end of the valley," Lord Groda instructed one of his commanders, then turned to Lord Kiros. "On my signal, sweep down from here with your scouts and the second column, and hit those cursed barbarians as hard as you can. The rest of the men and I will attack them from the north end of the valley."

"Mengesha and I will stay back to prevent any of our men from falling back," Iskander declared.

Mengesha was a seasoned soldier tasked by Lord Groda with personally protecting Iskander. Always by Iskander's side, the man was effectively his bodyguard.

None of the men were going to fall back. Lord Groda and Lord Kiros knew that, but completely ignored Iskander. After many years of combat,

Lord Groda's commanders had learned to simply allow Iskander to back out of every fight at every opportunity. He was as much a danger to the enemy as he was to friendly forces, so it was safer for him and everyone else if he just stayed out of the way. Once, for example, during fighting against a Funj army on the retreat after a failed attacked on the Nubian kingdom of Alodia, he had somehow succeeded in the near-impossible task of setting his own camp on fire during a rainstorm while attempting to shoot a flaming arrow. And that was just one of his many accomplishments. Although he fancied himself to be a fine commander, he was no more a soldier than a fish was a biblical scholar. He always talked about yearning for combat, but he had perfected the art of avoiding one when actually faced with it. The only enemy he ever killed was a prisoner he accidentally trampled on after he lost control of his horse just before a river crossing. So when Iskander volunteered to stay behind, no one had expected any less from him.

Lord Groda had practically surrounded the Muslims, from the north, south, and east. They could not flee west unless they could fly, for that was bordered by a vertical cliff higher than any man could scale.

Lord Kiros and his men performed one final quality control check on each other, making sure their swords, lances, spears, and daggers remained serviceable. Unlike most of the soldiers in the king's army, who carried shotels, the backwards curved sabers popular with the army, Lord Kiros carried a kaskara, a straight sword with a cross-shaped hilt, popular with the small Nubian kingdoms across the northern border. Although the backwards curved design of the shotel was designed to wrap behind an opponent's shield to inflict injury and hook the shield when struck diagonally, Lord Kiros thought it made a sloppy weapon for fighting from horseback.

Yohannis reached for the straps behind Lord Kiros's vest and tightened them, after which the commander did the same for his second-in-command. Even though many higher ranking and wealthier officers in the king's army wore vests of light chainmail produced in the iron forges of Axum, the soldiers of Lord Groda's patrol wore none. They had to travel light on their horses, where speed was crucial for launching lightning-quick hit-and-run attacks against larger forces. This was especially true of Lord Kiros and his scouts, who were usually the advance guard and the messengers of the battlefield, always vanishing as speedily as they appeared, informing on enemy locations quickly and efficiently. Instead, Lord Groda and his men wrapped themselves in vests of thick cotton fabric padded with seasoned leather to help protect them from light sword blows. This avoidance of heavy chainmail meant greater maneuverability and flexibility on the battlefield. While in Jerusalem, Lord Kiros had been impressed with the ornate and heavy armor worn by European Crusader knights. However, he had been grossly disappointed after witnessing many of the knights ride into battle only to be hauled down from their horses and cut to pieces by their very lightly armored Saracen opponents, who nimbly pranced around the knights almost as easily as a leopard around a wounded deer.

A moment later, at the sound of a horn, Lord Kiros, his six scouts, and 15 other men assigned to him sprang from their hiding positions and darted towards the Muslims, screaming like ravenous vultures swooping down unto a desert carcass.

"Christians!" one of the Muslim officers screamed.

Taken completely by surprise, the Muslims began to scramble for their weapons and horses.

Several of them grabbed their bows while the others, with not enough time to mount their horses, quickly formed a line to halt the enemy charge. But before they could fully rally to face Lord Kiros and his men, they were again completely taken aback when Lord Groda and his horsemen charged into them from the north end of the valley, howling like a rampaging pack of highland wolves. The horsemen tore into the Muslims with horrific effectiveness, crushing men under the hooves of their horses and completely throwing the defenders into disorder as many fell under the swords and spears of the attackers.

Meanwhile Lord Kiros and his men delved into the thick of the Muslims in what seemed almost like suicidal fearlessness. Entirely confused and unprepared, some of the Muslims turned to flee north, but were met by Lord Groda's men attacking from that direction, even before those who had stood their ground could let fly a single arrow. The Muslims were trapped. Lord Groda and his men had found and fixed their enemy. Now it was time to finish them. The Muslim archers had been the first to be cut down, having hurriedly stepped ahead of their men in order to get clear fields of fire.

Lord Kiros dove into the enemy, slashing and hacking his way through with unholy vengeance.

"The prisoners!" he screamed at his men as he engaged a big man with an equally big scimitar who attacked him with the fury of a lion in his eyes.

Yohannis immediately disengaged from the main fight and led two of his men towards the prisoners, who had been completely ignored by the Muslims as they fought desperately to save their own lives. Yohannis slashed the bonds of the four prisoners, who immediately, and without hesitation, sprang into action by picking up bows and arrows from slain Muslim archers and began unleashing wave after wave of deadly volleys into the rapidly dwindling mass of their former captors.

Lord Kiros struggled with the big man, his kaskara against the scimitar, parrying and thrusting with steady intensity and vying for the upper hand. The man had a shield, which made Lord Kiros's task much harder. This was because unlike most Ethiopian soldiers, who carried a standard round cone-shaped shield made of seasoned crocodile skin complete with a leather padding behind it to make it more comfortable for the user, Lord Kiros never carried one. But he was skilled enough to do without one. He knew how to fight and how to trick the enemy. As his opponent took a step back to mount his next move, Lord Kiros raised his sword high above his head, ready to slash down towards his opponent, but at the same time exposing himself, a fatal flaw most experienced fighters knew must be avoided. The big man saw his chance and wasted no time in taking it. He instantly raised his scimitar to his shoulder level, preparing to swipe from left to right in order to slash Lord Kiros's chest open. But Lord Kiros was one step ahead. He collapsed to his knees while at the same time unleashing a dagger from its sheath with his left hand and thrusting it forward, burying it into the man's side. The man let fly a ferocious roar, then collapsed to his knees too. Lord Kiros quickly stood up and finished off the man by delivering a crushing blow to his head using the hilt of his sword.

A few moments later, it was all over. The Muslim patrol had been completely annihilated.

"My lord, the enemy is slain and the prisoners rescued," Lord Kiros reported to Lord Groda, who remained mounted. "We lost five men."

"Good work, Commander," Lord Groda commended his scout leader. "Give the prisoners some supplies and send them home. We've spent many months in this miserable, godforsaken place and I'm ready to return to Shire."

Iskander, accompanied by Mengesha, then came trotting towards Lord Groda and Lord Kiros, battle-hardened after his immense task of preventing a non-existent retreat.

"Not one of our men fell back," Iskander announced, satisfied with himself.

He expected a pat on the back from his uncle, but like all the other commanders, he ignored his nephew. Iskander was about to say more, but a stern look from his uncle signaled that it was best for him to shut up.

Yohannis then walked the now-freed prisoners to Lord Groda.

"My lord," Yohannis introduced the leader of the prisoners. "This man wishes to thank you and express his regrets for the loss of some of our men."

A smile disappeared from Lord Groda's face the moment he laid eyes on the prisoner. It had to do with something protruding from a pocket in the prisoner's garments.

"What is that?" Lord Groda asked.

The prisoner pulled it out and held it in his hand.

"Just my prayer beads, my lord," the prisoner responded casually.

"You are a Muslim?" Lord Groda asked incredulously. "Those are Muslim prayer beads."

"Yes, my lord," the prisoner replied.

To many others, the prisoner's prayer beads looked not much different from the mequteria, the prayer rope carried by Ethiopian Christians.

The mequteria had 64 beads depicting the number of prayers to be said, which represented the number of lashes Jesus received and Mary's age upon her assumption to heaven. But to seasoned eyes like Lord Groda's, he instantly recognized the Muslim prayer rope, which had 99 beads of two different sizes.

"So you are indeed a Muslim?" Lord Groda reiterated.

"I am, my lord," the prisoner proudly acknowledged, then pointed towards his fellow prisoners. "These are my companions. We are all Muslims. We come from Harar. Most of the people there have been Muslims as far as anyone can remember."

Lord Kiros knew Harar, the City of Saints. Located within the eastern corner of the Ethiopia, it was the fourth holiest city in Islam after Mecca, Medina, and Jerusalem. An Islamic stronghold within the Christian kingdom, it was often a no-go zone for the king's troops, given the difficulty in subjecting its people under the king's will. Lord Kiros had been there with the king's army several years earlier, when they had rescued it from a notorious Somali brigand who had successfully scaled the city's massive protective walls in order to rob and pillage its people.

"You are Muslim, and yet you fought against the sultan's men?" Iskander addressed the prisoners.

"We escort salt caravans across the desert from the salt mines in Danakil," the lead prisoner responded. "We were returning home and were simply defending the people of Bodera. They had always shown us great hospitality. We may worship in a different way, but we are people of this land, same as you. We men from Harar are good with the bow, so we have always fought as archers for armies of Ethiopian kings long before my father and his father before him were even born."

Lord Groda stood silent for a brief moment. He had spent the previous seven months of his life chasing the armies of a Muslim sultan who had ravaged and heaped horrors of volcanic proportions across the countryside. He could not possibly imagine for a moment breaking bread with a Muslim, Ethiopian or not.

"Seize them," he ordered his soldiers. "Hang them!"

"Wait! What?" a confused Lord Kiros stepped in front of the Muslims and faced Lord Groda. "My lord?"

"These men are traitors to the kingdom," Lord Groda declared. "They and their kind made it possible for the sultan's men to advance this far."

"No, my lord!" Lord Kiros protested. "You do not have that right! There has been enough killing of our people today. Enemies we may sometimes be with Muslims, but there is no law against the presence of Muslims in the kingdom! These men are subjects of the king, same as you and I!"

"Seize them!" Lord Groda repeated.

Lord Kiros instantly drew his sword, making clear his intentions to face any man who stepped forward to seize the Muslims.

CHAPTER 4

Lord Groda wanted to hang the Muslim prisoners they had just rescued even though they were all on the same side in the ongoing war and had committed no crime. Lord Kiros was no saint himself and desperately wanted to stay within the good graces of his commander, but there were certain lines he would not cross.

"These prisoners are now my responsibility!" he insisted, sword in hand and ready to fight any man who approached the prisoners. "We lost good men rescuing them. Any man among you who raises a hand against them raises it against me!"

Several soldiers who had been about to seize the Muslims backed off slightly, unsure of how to proceed. Most had fought with Commander Kiros for many years, and owed their survival to his scouting abilities. And they knew better than to engage him in a sword fight. He was deadly with the weapon.

"You dare to oppose Lord Groda?" Iskander snarled at Lord Kiros, safely postured behind Mengesha. "You are a traitor to the kingdom."

Lord Groda fired a penetrating look at Lord Kiros, then spoke coldly. "A hundred pieces of gold for the man who brings me the head of Commander Kiros," he announced.

Without hesitation, Lord Kiros's scouts drew their swords and jumped in front of their commander.

"My lord," Yohannis addressed Lord Groda, "we stand with Commander Kiros. Please, I ask you to reconsider."

"I warn you to step aside or you will meet the fate of the traitor," Lord Groda warned the scouts.

"We will do no such thing, my lord," Yohannis shot back, his grip tightening around his sword.

Few of the soldiers were willing to fight Lord Kiros, for aside from him being a respected commander, engaging him risked losing one's life. But it slowly began to dawn on them that a worse fate awaited those who challenged Lord Groda or failed to bend to his will. They could lose not only their lives, but those of their relatives and even and their families' fortunes as well. Lord Kiros weighed the prospect of him and his six scouts fighting the more than 40 soldiers who were now slowly beginning to close in on them. His odds of survival, if he chose to fight, were fairly low.

"Yohannis," Lord Kiros called softly. "Put your swords away."

"Commander?" Yohannis asked with a quizzical look.

"All of you," he addressed his scouts. "Sheath your swords. You should not be harmed on my account. I will make Lord Groda answer for this before the king."

The scouts reluctantly sheathed their swords, as did Lord Kiros himself. Then four of Lord Groda's men approached, seized him, disarmed him, and quickly bound him in ropes as the other soldiers watched, unsure of what to do.

"The king's court will hear of this, Lord Groda!" Yohannis warned angrily.

"And who is going to report him to the king?" Iskander asked mockingly. He had a permanent smirk on his face.

"Seize the scouts!" Lord Groda ordered his men.

"My lord, I ask you to stop this!" Lord Kiros protested as soldiers surrounded the scouts, who were all dismounted. "My actions are mine alone. My men bear no responsibility."

His pleas went unheeded.

"You are all traitors to our cause," Iskander said.

"Lord Groda, I have served you well and without complaint despite the injustice you have done to my family," Lord Kiros continued to plead. "I have never once complained. If it is my lands you want to keep, I yield. But keep my men out of this."

Lord Kiros knew it was Lord Groda's greed that was getting the better of him. Lord Groda had sworn to return Lord Kiros's family lands upon their return to Shire, if he was pleased with the scout commander's performance. But in a stunning reversal of fortune, it seemed Lord Groda intended to kill him instead.

"I know what you are doing, Lord Groda," Lord Kiros continued. "You have no intention of returning what you stole."

Lord Groda took a deep breath, then smiled.

"Do you know the story of the leopard and the antelope?" he asked Lord Kiros.

Lord Kiros said nothing. He fixed a steady gaze upon Lord Groda, a deep hatred rising in him for the man.

"Well," Lord Groda proceeded, "I will tell you. There was this very hungry leopard that had tried and failed for many days to catch an antelope. The antelope was smart and avoided every trap the leopard set. So the leopard called the antelope one day and said, 'Hey, you should not run away from me. We live in the land together. There is no reason why we cannot be friends. So let's be friends so you may never fear me again. Let's make an oath to our friendship.' The antelope thought about it, and then asked, 'What shall the oath be, Leopard?' The leopard said, 'If either of us breaks this oath, may God kill his child.' The antelope agreed to the oath, and they became friends, spending their time together. The leopard slept on top of the tree while the antelope slept under the tree. Because the antelope no longer had to run from the leopard, it became fat and more attractive to the hungry leopard. But you see, the leopard had no child, so breaking the oath meant nothing to it. One day it decided to make its move. It leapt down from the tree to catch the antelope, but got stuck on a branch, which went through its belly. The antelope sprang to its feet and saw its friend about to die, but it did nothing to help. 'Why, my friend, do you leave me here to die?' the leopard asked. 'Didn't we make an oath that God would kill our child if the oath is broken?' And the antelope said, 'Yes, my friend, we did. But I think your father also made the same oath, and perhaps he broke it. And now you, his son, pays the price.'"

Lord Groda paused for a moment to let Lord Kiros dissect the meaning of the story. Iskander looked confused.

"My lord," Lord Kiros said. "This is not right."

"Do you know what the meaning of that story is?" Lord Groda asked.

"Leopards should not climb trees," Iskander said confidently, smiling from ear to ear.

Lord Groda turned his head towards his nephew. That one is about as smart as a bowl of beans, he thought. But he quickly thought better of saying anything to him, and instead returned his focus to Lord Kiros.

"Surprisingly, I am the antelope in that story and you are the leopard, Commander Kiros," Lord Groda said. "Perhaps you are just paying for the sins of your father."

"Do what you must to me, my lord," Lord Kiros pleaded. "But please spare my men. They too look forward to seeing their families in Shire in a few days."

"Your men have chosen their fate, Commander Kiros," Lord Groda declared. "There is nothing I can do for them."

Lord Groda turned to Gebre, one of his commanders, and nodded.

Gebre was a ruthless character who had been transferred from a post in Axum to Lord Groda's unit in order to escape charges of theft, looting, and murder. Those close to him called him Raw Meat. It was said that was because he kept a pack of wolves and sometimes joined them to feed on raw meat in order to increase his bond with them and intensify his ferocity.

Gebre approached Yohannis, pulled out a dagger from a sheath hanging from his waist, looked the scout dead in the eyes, and plunged it deep into his side, between his ribs. Lord Kiros gasped in horror as he watched the body of his close friend and second-in-command collapse lifelessly on the ground. Yohannis had been a good friend. They had met ten years prior after Yohannis had helped a small group of the king's soldiers track down and kill two deadly man-eating hippos that were terrorizing some villages along the western shores of Lake Tsana. Now, there he was, lying there like the carcass of a wild animal. His wife and children back in Shire would never see him again.

Before Lord Kiros could fully bring himself together upon witnessing the murder, Mengesha and several other soldiers, with Iskander's encouragement, crowded the remaining five scouts and hacked them to death with their swords and spears. Lord Kiros stood completely bewildered, his anger giving way to frozen silence.

"As traitors to the kingdom and to the army entrusted to me by the king," Lord Groda announced, "these men have lost their rights. Their lands and property will therefore be forfeited and placed in my control on behalf of the kingdom."

Lord Kiros was furious. Lord Groda's greed and treachery knew no bounds. Not only had these men been lost, but their families were also going to lose their holdings. Several of the scouts were Oromo tribesmen from the south. Known for their horse-riding prowess, many Oromo had moved north and settled in its towns, making a living as horse traders and soldiers. The oldest of his scouts was almost 50 years old, a peasant who had joined the army at the tender age of 17 and had risen through the ranks due to his own merits. Now he was gone, just like that. The scouts had fought valiantly for years for the kingdom. They were due rewards by the king's court upon their return to Shire in a few days. Furthermore, two of them had completed their contractual 12 years of military service and were due to retire upon their return to Shire. But on Lord Groda's whim, just because the war with the Shewas was almost over and his need for the scouts was no longer as critical, all that had been lost. As a judge and important official in Shire, he would confiscate their benefits for himself.

"No one defies me, Commander Kiros," Lord Groda hissed.

Having been focused on Lord Kiros and his scouts, Lord Groda's men had briefly ignored the Muslim prisoners. Taking advantage of this, the prisoners seized their moment and immediately sprang on the horses of some of the slain scouts. Lord Groda's men quickly rallied and scrambled to stop them. Three of the Muslims were hauled down from the horses and hacked to death, while the fourth, the lead prisoner, managed to break through the lines, shooting out of there like Satan himself was after him. Some of Lord Groda's mounted men were about to give chase.

"No," Lord Groda ordered the men. "Let him go. Let him warn his people and those like him about what we do to enemies of the kingdom."

The men backed down as the prisoner disappeared in a cloud of dust beyond the hills.

Lord Groda's focus returned to Lord Kiros.

"Let me kill him," Iskander begged his uncle, his dislike for Lord Kiros never having been hidden.

"Watch and learn, Nephew," Lord Groda instructed Iskander. "When someone defies you, you don't just kill him. You teach him a lesson, as a warning to others."

"But we can't let him live," Iskander insisted.

"Oh, he won't live," Lord Groda reassured his nephew. "But first, I have a fate worse than death for him."

"What do you have in mind, Uncle?" Iskander inquired, glee in his voice.

"The Shewa sultan himself is coming this way in three days," Lord Groda said. "And they will find Commander Kiros, a Christian soldier, alive—not so well, but alive, among the bodies of their comrades. The sultan's men will then do the rest."

Iskander smiled. He was pleased. He knew exactly what the sultan and his men were capable of. The mere thought of being captured alive by the sultan's men often sent shivers of terror through the bodies of Ethiopian soldiers—even Lord Kiros. This was largely because of the stories that circulated about how the sultan treated captured Christian soldiers. Having lost his wife and four daughters to Christian soldiers just a few years before, the sultan had invaded Ethiopia with vengeance on his mind. In an epic display of barbarism during his initial onslaught, he was said to have boiled Christian captives alive and fed some to cheetahs while other prisoners and their families watched. Some captives were said to have been skinned and flailed alive, with some being killed by the pouring of boiling water down their throats. Whether any of these stories were true or not, Lord Kiros now faced the grim fate of finding out the truth of the matter first-hand.

Two soldiers marched Lord Kiros towards a dried-out warka tree and began to bind him to the tree with twine ropes.

"No one else will come this way, especially after what happened here," Lord Groda said to Lord Kiros. "You have a chance to slowly die of thirst as you smell, watch, and feel every moment as you are picked to your bones by vultures. If I were you, I would try to take advantage of that opportunity and die before the sultan arrives."

"Lord Groda," Lord Kiros called as the midday sun began to bake into his forehead, the dry, leafless warka tree offering no shade. "If it is what is left of my land that you want, take it. Just don't kill my wife. I ask that you spare her."

Lord Kiros knew Lord Groda well. When he went after people, especially if his intentions were to seize their property, he had the terrifying penchant of not only destroying them, but also their families, through jailing, execution, or murder, in order to reduce the number of surviving family members who could possibly challenge or bring claims against him in the future.

Lord Kiros could not believe that Lord Groda had actually once wanted to become a priest. Lord Groda had indeed started out as a deacon in Shire in his younger years, but had been relieved of his duties shortly after, and banned from ever seeking a church position after having been declared to be no longer ritually pure. That was because the day before his ordination, he was found to have had a forbidden relationship of a carnal nature with a local woman. He blamed the poor woman for the whole thing, even publicly praying and asking God to forgive her, for the Devil had used her to tempt him, he claimed. The church leaders did not buy it and dismissed him anyway. She was found strangled to death two days later, with Groda nowhere to be found. But he returned to Shire ten years later, at the head of a small army, having joined the king's forces and been made a commander and a lord. Apparently, his ruthlessness in helping to expand the kingdom's borders and subduing pagan tribes had impressed the king. Now a lord, Groda made himself the leader of Shire, with his first act being to lay false charges of treason against the family of the woman whom he had very likely murdered and blamed for disgracing him. He had her family exiled, and of course had their lands and properties seized. Then he went after the priests who had dismissed him, forcing the local bishop to transfer them to dioceses located in the most hostile, remote, and inhospitable outposts of the realm. All that was 30 years earlier. Lord Groda remained the same hostile, vengeful, and greedy scoundrel he had always been.

"Have fun with them, Commander Kiros," Iskander mocked, pointing at the vultures circling overhead, along with the few that were already picking on the bodies of the slain.

Iskander then rode closer to Lord Kiros, unsheathed his sword, raised it above the scout commander's head, and slashed downward. Always razor-sharp and extremely potent due to lack of use, it easily tore Lord Kiros's thick, padded vest open, revealing a necklace with a brass cross that hung from his neck. Such neck crosses were popular with the soldiers, as it gave them protection and a little tinge of the hand of God while engaged in battle.

"That is just to make sure the sultan's men really know what you are," he said with a derisive smile. "He will see his dead men lying around here and won't take kindly at all to the Christians who did this to them."

Lord Kiros looked at the imbecile's silly face for a short moment, and then blurted, "Boo!"

Iskander jerked and stumbled back in fright, nearly falling from his horse, with the smile instantly vanishing from his face.

Lord Groda shook his head, embarrassed at his nephew.

"May they choke you to death!" Iskander hissed at Lord Kiros after pulling himself together.

The scout commander smiled.

"Smile all you want," Iskander scoffed. "But my friends you killed are also smiling from their graves at you now."

His friends? Lord Kiros pondered. What was Iskander talking about? Then Lord Kiros noticed the disapproving glare from Lord Groda towards his nephew. Now he understood. The men who had tried to kill him seven months before at his home had been sent by the jealous, greedy, and impatient Iskander, eager to please his uncle by getting rid of Lord Kiros, obviously without the knowledge of his uncle. That is why Lord Kiros thought he had recognized the man wearing the medallion of St. Aboli, one of the equestrian saints. He had seen the man with Iskander before.

"Let's get out of here," Lord Groda ordered his men. "Home awaits the rest of us."

Lord Groda and the rest of his men rode away, disappearing into the hills and leaving behind a hapless Lord Kiros stranded among the dead and awaiting a fate worse than death. He thought of his wife, and prayed she would at least be able to escape Lord Groda's treachery and find some help from the king's court.

CHAPTER 5

Lord Groda and 13 of his men rode towards Lord Kiros's modest home nestled within beautiful ponds and lushly green rolling hills in the outskirts of Shire. Having seized most of his lands, this home and the small parcel of land on which it stood was the last piece of property left to Lord Kiros that Lord Groda had not confiscated. The only occupant of the house was Lord Kiros's wife, Tiki. There were no guards or servants, as Lord Groda had deprived Lord Kiros of all his wealth and the means to employ any help.

"You wait here," Lord Groda instructed his men, posting them outside the home.

Several peasants walking by quickly scurried out of the area. They recognized Lord Groda. He was back. Whatever he was about to do, they wanted to be as far away from it and from him as possible, lest the same fate befall them.

Lord Groda dismounted his horse and began walking towards the door of the two-story stone building. It had been three days since he had abandoned Lord Kiros to the fate of the sultan's men. He thought of Lord Kiros's pleas to him that his wife at least be spared. He chuckled. He paused in front of the heavy wooden door and placed a hand on the hilt of his sword. He was not surprised to find the door was slightly ajar, something many did to let in the cool, refreshing highland breeze. He slowly nudged the door open and gingerly stepped into the house.

Inside the window-lit home, Lord Kiros's wife, Tiki, sat on a stool, facing the door, and weaving some cloth. A petite and beautiful woman, who even seated, carried an air of charm and respectability, she did not flinch when Lord Groda walked into her home. Her eyes locked with his. They stared at each other for a moment. Lord Groda moved his hand away from his sword.

"Is he dead?" she asked.

"He is," Lord Groda responded.

"Did he suffer?"

"It is best I spare you the details, Tiki."

"I loved him, you know," she responded softly, a hint of sadness in her voice. "When did it happen?"

"It's been three days," Lord Groda responded.

"So it happened close to his home," she pondered uneasily. "Now his spirit will wander close by, tormenting me."

"Dead men always stay dead," Lord Groda assured her. "Believe me. I've slain many a man, and unless they were Jesus Christ with the power of resurrection, I have yet to have any of them rise from the dead in any form to torment me."

"You were supposed to have taken care of this far from home—months ago," Tiki scolded. "Why wait until you were close to his home?"

Lord Groda took a deep breath and sat down on a stool next to Tiki.

"Let me tell you something about Commander Kiros, your dead husband," he began. "I never liked him or that godforsaken father of his, or anyone in his family. But I learned from him. Have you ever heard of a place called Gondar?"

"No," Tiki responded.

"It is a small, little-known village near the Semien mountains," Lord Groda continued. "We were tracking down some of the sultan's men one day. They were hiding out in a valley, well defended and protected. I thought we could not get through to them. But your husband, he found a way. I insisted on him showing it to me. To make things quick, I insisted on going with just him and two of my other commanders. He said it was dangerous, but I insisted. Perhaps I should have listened to him. It turns out there was a heavy rainstorm that night. It flooded the area and our path, even killing many of the sultan's men. The rest evacuated the area. For two days we remained lost and were starving. There was nothing to eat in the area. To make matters worse, there were these massive lions stalking us—two of them. I suppose they needed to eat too. A gruesome death awaited us. That is when I learned something from your husband: it is not what you look at; it is what you see that matters. While the rest of us looked at the lions and saw death, your husband looked at them and saw life—food. So we became the hunters. We hunted down and killed the lions, then used their flesh for food."

Tiki looked away from Lord Groda. She had always loved that fearless nature in her husband.

"So you see, Tiki," Lord Groda continued, "a blind man does not pick a fight with his guide."

"He was always resourceful," she said, looking down, "except when it came to getting ahead."

"He was a boy in man's world," Lord Groda laughed. "You need a man who knows what he is doing."

He inched closer to Tiki, put his arms around her, and attempted to kiss her, but she moved her head away, took a step back, looked towards the window, and remembered her life with Lord Kiros.

They had been married for five years. They had somewhat been attracted to each other due to the uncanny similarities of their families' situations. Like Lord Kiros, her family had also once been among the wealthiest in Shire. But while Lord Kiros's family had lost its fortune due to false treason charges against his father, her family had lost its fortune due to actual acts of treason committed by her father. He had been caught smuggling weapons to rebels in the pagan lands of the western territories. He was executed and his lands seized by the king, leaving his daughter a noble with no wealth. Finding common ground, she and Lord Kiros developed a relationship and were quickly married to each other.

What had started out as an endearing bond soon descended into a nightmare. Despite his steadfast efforts to regain his family's lands from Lord Groda, she remained deeply unhappy with him as a result of her unchanging station in life. She did not believe he was working hard enough to change their fortunes. Soon losing all faith in her husband's ability to regain his family's lost lands and enhance their fortune, she began to see herself as being forever condemned to that most dreaded status of being wealth-less nobility. Better if one had simply just been born a peasant.

They had married in the Church, where as nobles, divorce was not permitted. Lord Kiros knew this and used it as an excuse to stay in the marriage, although in reality she knew it was because his love for her remained true.

"What now?" she asked, turning back to Lord Groda, "Where do we go from here?"

"I will see that you get back everything your family lost, like I promised," he responded. "That can only happen if you are my wife. Your husband is dead. Nothing stops us now. Together, you and I will achieve what we have only dreamed of these many years past."

Tiki turned and looked at Lord Groda without saying a word. He attempted to kiss her again, this time planting a wet kiss on her lips as she threw her arms around his large muscular frame.

Lord Groda was happy. His ultimate dream was finally about to be realized. In a society where familial lineage and titles determined success, respect, and lasting fortune, he was a man of low birth who through his cunning, shear ruthlessness, and a stroke of luck, had been made a lord in his own right and gathered a fortune. However, despite his wealth and title, to other nobles in the kingdom, he was still just a lowborn peasant. He wanted to be respected. But everyone knew he was the son of a poor goat herder, as was his father and his father before him. But he could fix that. If he could marry a true noble, like Tiki, then his children would be the children of Lord Groda and Tiki Tewolde, daughter of a noble Tigrayan chieftain. Their marriage would give Lord Groda the respectability he had always wanted, and his wealth would return to Tiki the fortune her family had lost. It was a match forged in hell.

CHAPTER 6

Noah should have squished those two mosquitoes, Lord Kiros thought, as the annoying tiny critters buzzed over his face and inflicted irritatingly punishing bites which he was unable to scratch. It had been four days since Lord Groda and his men had abandoned him, tied to a warka tree. The Shewa sultan and his retreating army were supposed to have passed through the area the day before. But repeated attacks from harassing Ethiopian forces must have slowed them down.

Lord Kiros had been in and out of consciousness several times, and each time he returned, he wished he had died instead. He dreaded the idea of meeting the sultan's men under his current circumstances, literally with his hands tied behind his back.

There was no sign of life in the area, other than the vultures that continued to feast on the corpses of the Muslims they had slain—and his scouts who had been treacherously murdered. An occasional curious vulture dropped in from time to time to investigate him, but scurried off each time he moaned. He secretly wished one of the buzzards would pluck out his eyes so he wouldn't have to watch his dead scouts being fed upon.

The sun was high overhead when he awoke from one of his frequent fainting spells. He opened his eyes to see that it was a sword point that had pricked and awoken him, delivering a jolting pain to his shoulder. It was a curved saber, the kind used by the sultan's soldiers. His eyes followed the weapon to its owner. He was a tired-looking and disheveled man on a horse, with a turban around his head. Behind him were thousands of other men on foot and on horseback, marching along. Next to the man were several others. He recognized one of them instantly—the sultan!

With bronze-colored skin covered in dust, a narrow face and deep intense eyes, the sultan looked as ferocious as Lord Kiros had imagined him. And with squinted eyes that seemed to be on fire, a broad scimitar by his side, and two curved daggers hanging from his chest that complemented the scar that ran diagonally across his forehead, he looked like a human warzone with a ferocious appetite for combat. Having launched his invasion of Ethiopia with the eagerness of a lion setting upon an antelope, now it seemed the sultan wanted nothing more than to get himself and his men out of Ethiopia, his invasion having simply ground to a miserable halt and fizzled away.

The man with the sword spoke to the sultan in Arabic. Lord Kiros was not fluent in Arabic, but after his time in the Jerusalem, he could pick out a few words here and there. He was therefore able to put a sentence or two together of what the fellow black men who spoke Arabic were saying.

"They killed Ahmed and his men," the man with the sword said, referring to Lord Kiros.

Ahmed and his men must have been the Muslims Lord Kiros and his army had killed in order to avenge the slaughter at Bodera village and rescue the captives, Lord Kiros reasoned. He had to think quickly, to avoid the repercussions that were sure to follow.

The sultan said some words to the man, then rode away. The man raised his sword high above Lord Kiros's face and slashed downwards. Lord Kiros did not even flinch. He had such loathing for the sultan and his men that he did not want to give them the slightest gratification that he feared them. He found himself crashing to the ground as his bonds broke, then quickly picked himself up and looked at the man with the sword. Their eyes locked for a second, then the man re-sheathed his sword and rode off behind the sultan, not having exchanged a single word with Lord Kiros. Lord Kiros looked towards the bodies of the Muslims they had slain. That was when he realized that some of the sultan's men had been burying them, as well as those of his murdered scouts.

Lord Kiros did not understand why the sultan had spared him. Perhaps, just like him, the sultan was getting tired of the killing. Or perhaps the sultan felt sorry for him? He did not know, and he was not going to conduct an interview with the sultan to find out why. A life he had been certain just moments before would be extinguished in a most agonizing manner imaginable had now been given a new lease. His energy and resolve strengthened, he knew he had to get to Shire quickly to save his wife from Lord Groda. Deprived of his horse, it would take him at least ten days to walk to Shire.

Exhausted, he took a knee, partly to rest, but mainly to pick up his sword and two daggers, which had been abandoned beneath him after he was bound to the tree. He took a deep breath, then stood up and sheathed his weapons just as what was left of the sultan's bedraggled army slogged on, probably praying to make it back to Shewa before the king's main army caught up with them.

Lord Kiros began to walk in the opposite direction of the soldiers, most of whom barely paid any attention to him despite the fact that he was clearly an enemy soldier. After all, he was still dressed in his uniform and armed with his sword and dagger, with his cross clearly exposed and dangling below his neck. The soldiers marched in silence, barely a word passing through their lips. Like Lord Kiros, they seemed to be weary of all the fighting and just wanted to return home to their families.

During his trek to Shire, he discarded his uniform by selling it to a farmer in a roadside village. The thick and heavily-padded cotton fetched a handsome price of dried meat and fresh fruit, enough to last him for several days. He also obtained some peasant garments so he would not be mistaken by any passing Ethiopian troops for a deserter—especially since he knew Lord Groda, true to his nature, must have spread false rumors about him and his scouts. Lord Kiros took no chances. Deserters were frequently hanged. He and his men had even actually hanged three deserters several months before, after a hasty field tribunal conducted by Lord Groda.

Despite shedding his uniform, Lord Kiros kept his sword and daggers, which he wrapped up and hid in a bundle tied to a stick that he carried across his shoulder. However, to protect himself from the biting cold that attacked at night in the highlands like the sting of a wasp, he exchanged one of his daggers for some thick, dark-red robes from a cloth merchant who was on his way to Axum to trade his wares.

Lord Kiros arrived at the hill above his home twelve days after being rescued by the Muslims. It was during an early morning. He paused, surprised at what he was seeing. It was a scene unfamiliar to him, something he had not seen in the many years since Lord Groda had cheated his family out of its lands. It was the presence of about 15 servants, working on the field of teff, the highland cereal used to make flour. Several armed guards also patrolled the field. This land had not been farmed in years. How had his wife suddenly been able to hire enough servants to work the land? He wanted to believe that his family lands had been restored while he was away fighting, but he knew that to be impossible, for Lord Groda still held the deeds to almost all their lands. Now he feared the worst. Had Tiki been killed? Were those Lord Groda's servants working on the farm?

"No!" he muttered to himself. "Not Tiki, no!"

He ran down the hill towards the farm, making sure that the turban around his head still concealed his face. It was not unusual for travelers to dress that way to protect themselves from the sun and highland dust, so Lord Kiros attracted little attention. At the bottom of the hill, he stopped to speak to one of the workers.

"Greetings, friend," Lord Kiros greeted the man. "Are you well?"

"I am well, friend," the man returned the greeting, standing erect to meet Lord Kiros eye-to-eye.

"Who is the lord of this land?" Lord Kiros asked.

"It was the wife of Lord Kiros, they say," the man responded. "But not anymore. The place now belongs to Lord Groda."

"Did she die?" Lord Kiros asked, fearful of the what the answer would be.

"Die?" the man chuckled. "Her husband, Lord Kiros, betrayed Ethiopia and joined the Muslims. Fortunately, he was killed in battle anyway. But now there are rumors that he may still live. So says some who returned from the battles. But it makes no difference. If he is alive and ever shows himself around Shire again, he won't live long after that. He will be hunted down by every official and soldier until he pays the price for his betrayal—with his head."

Lord Kiros was right about Lord Groda. The man had wanted Lord Kiros to suffer and die, that was why he had not killed him outright. But he had discredited his name and made plans to ensure he died anyway on the slimmest chance that he escaped. Clever reptilian devil!

"What happened to Lord Kiros's wife?" Lord Kiros asked eagerly.

"She is with Lord Groda now," the man said. "They have been married for two days."

Lord Kiros stood silent for a brief moment, stunned. She had married Lord Groda? The man they had both blamed for so long as the cause of so many of their problems? Why?

"Are you well, traveler?" the peasant asked the bewildered Lord Kiros.

"I am," Lord Kiros responded. "I thank you for your time."

Lord Kiros slowly walked away from the man and sat under a mango tree where he and Tiki had sat many times, relaxing, sharing stories, and watching travelers along the road that ran by their home. Despite everything he had done to curry favor with Lord Groda in accordance with his father's wishes, it had all come to nothing. The only thing that he, Lord Kiros, had gained from it was losing the last piece of land that his family had, and a betrayal from a wife that sliced deeper than any wound he had ever sustained in battle.

CHAPTER 7

Despite the betrayal, Lord Kiros, sitting under that mango tree on his land, was surprised that he still loved his wife deeply, for he realized he would have no objections should she return to him. But he knew that was not going to happen. His wife had seen an opportunity in Lord Groda and had seized it. There was no return from this. Lord Kiros's thoughts turned to what he had heard a priest say in church one day to a man whose wife had taken off with another. "When a man takes off with your wife, let him keep her. It is the best revenge."

What was done was done. Lord Kiros quickly pulled himself together as one thing now became clear: he was now a dead man walking. It was only a matter of time before someone recognized him. He had to disappear. He had to become forgotten until an appropriate moment to re-emerge. But when would that moment be? And where would he go? How would he stay forgotten?

"You there!" a farm guard yelled at Lord Kiros. "Get away from here. We don't serve beggars here. Move on!"

Lord Kiros looked up at the guard but did not budge.

"I said get out of here!" the guard repeated, this time marching threateningly towards Lord Kiros and pulling his sword out of its sheath.

Still, Lord Kiros did not budge. He remained calmly seated, fixing a death-defying stare at the guard, a man with the gumption to send him away from what had been his family's land and home for generations. The guard got to within five feet of Lord Kiros and stopped, hoping to intimidate Lord Kiros into submission. Still, Lord Kiros did not budge, his gaze remaining fixed on the guard. The guard suddenly lifted his sword and pointed it directly at Lord Kiros.

"You must want to die today, peasant!" the guard threatened the scout commander.

Lord Kiros still did not move. He continued to stare intensely at the man, his right eye twitching with fury. The guard, expecting to see fear in Lord Kiros's eyes, saw nothing but anger and a deep and growing rage that seemed to be coming from a man who had decided that he had nothing else to lose. Lord Kiros was daring the guard to strike at him, while imagining all sorts of creative ways to carve him up as well. Exercising good judgement, a sense of self-preservation suddenly dawned on the guard. He took a few steps back, lowered his sword slightly, and wondered to himself whether facing down the man sitting under the tree was worth risking severe bodily injury to himself.

"Anything for the poor?" a loud voice suddenly came from the road, followed by three rings from a bell. "Anything for the poor?"

Lord Kiros slowly turned his head towards the road and looked, as did the guard. It was a monk riding a mule cart. Dressed in the customary, loose yellow robes worn by many monks, with his neck cross hanging around his neck, he was collecting charity for the needy, as was the duty of the monks of his order. A cross of Mary, the monk's hand cross, was also perched on his cart, which the faithful could kiss to be blessed by God upon a donation.

"Anything for the poor?" the monk continued to announce.

Lord Kiros slowly and deliberately turned his head back towards the guard, who upon noticing, instantly took another nervous step back, as if he thought Lord Kiros was about to spring up on him like a cheetah on the hunt. Keeping his gaze fixed on the guard, Lord Kiros slowly stood up, turned his head to the side, and spat on the ground. He then bent down, picked up the bundle that contained and concealed his weapons, and walked away towards the monk.

The guard breathed a sigh of relief, with sweat rolling down his face as he watched Lord Kiros walk away, thankful that the encounter had not ended badly for him. Then he noticed that the farm workers he was guarding had watched his entire encounter with Lord Kiros.

"What are you looking at?" he screeched at them. "Back to work!"

Lord Kiros approached the monk as a man dropped a bound goat in the cart, which already contained some fruit and bags of crops and clothing, all donated by the faithful. The monk offered his hand cross and the man kissed it. The monk placed a hand on the man's head and said a small prayer for him as the man prayerfully put his hands together.

"Go with God," the monk ended his prayer. The man made the sign of the cross, thanked the monk, and walked away, grateful for having earned the Lord's grace.

"Are you fine, friend?" the monk greeted Lord Kiros.

"Better days have come and gone, my friend," Lord Kiros responded.

"Each day is what you make of it, my friend," the monk said with a smile worthy of a biblical verse.

Lord Kiros was taken aback at how youthful the monk was, for he had known most monks to be old men who had chosen that path in life only after many years of experiencing the world and its joys and troubles. But this one seemed no more than 20 years old, much younger than his own 36 years.

"Where are you going, man?" Lord Kiros asked the monk.

"To Roha, my friend," the monk responded, his broad smile still gracing his face. "To the House of St. Verena. That is my monastery."

Lord Kiros thought hard before uttering his next words.

"Will they accept me in your order?" he asked. "I am but a simple peasant with nothing to offer the House of St. Verena."

Upon seeing the monk, it had instantly dawned on Lord Kiros that acceptance into a monastery was the perfect way for him to retreat and hide until things died down. Then perhaps he could reemerge at a suitable moment and try to reclaim his life, or even safely flee the kingdom if it came to that.

The monk also thought hard before responding, his smile never leaving his face.

"Can you sing?" the young monk asked.

"Can I sing?" Lord Kiros asked, puzzled.

"The House of St. Verena needs monks who can deliver a good chant on feast days," the young monk explained. "I am a debtara, and all I am left with are aging monks who have lost their voices."

Debtaras were clerics who composed songs and poetry for the church. Often involved in intense studies of church literature and hymnals, they were sometimes the prime authority on the life of Holy Mary, for Tawahedo music often focused on praise of the Virgin Mary.

Lord Kiros wondered if he should lie about his singing abilities, which were practically non-existent. But he wanted to be honest, for if he were to succeed at pretending to be a monk, he had to at least get into character.

"A frog has better melody than I do," he confessed.

The monk chuckled.

"We wouldn't want to insult Saint Yared by having you sing then," the monk said, invoking the father of Ethiopian liturgical music.

"I doubt he would care," Lord Kiros said. "The man has been dead for 800 years."

The monk chuckled again.

"Can you play genna then?" the monk asked.

There was no hesitation here.

"You are looking at a master champion of genna," Lord Kiros proclaimed. "I have played it since I was but a boy."

In addition to playing genna as a boy, Lord Kiros had often engaged in the sport with his fellow soldiers during the occasional lull in the fighting and patrolling when they could find some time for rest and relaxation. Genna was a team sport played with ten players on each team and a goal post on each end of a field. A goalkeeper stood guard at each goal post as each player used a curved wooden club to hit and dribble around a small round ball with the aim of getting it through the opposing team's goal post. Round, hard, and made from hard tree root, the ball was painted with bright green lines to enable players and spectators to easily see it. Whether true or not, the Tewahedo Church always maintained that this game developed in the highlands of Ethiopia, and was first played to celebrate Genna, the feast day that commemorates the birth of Christ on the 7th day of January. It is said when Christ was born, in celebration, local shepherds used their crooks to start hitting a wooden ball around, something that Ethiopians started doing as well around AD 330 to celebrate the feast day of Genna.

"But what has my skill in playing genna to do with me becoming a monk?" Lord Kiros asked the young monk.

"Nothing," the young monk replied with a shrug. "All you need to become a monk is to be willing to denounce the wicked ways of the world and serve people and God."

"Then why genna?" Lord Kiros asked again.

"On every Genna feast day, the of monastery of St. Verena plays a match against the monastery of Debre Damo. The goal of the game is to raise donations for the poor. It draws huge crowds. Whoever loses the game has to send a representative to make the four-day journey to work on the farms of the winners for ten days. It's a small, insignificant task, but it is significant for the monk who has to be that representative of the losing side, especially one who has had to do it every year for the last four years."

Lord Kiros smiled. He could guess now why the young monk wanted a genna player. Considering the Genna feast day had just passed about 14 days before, and that this young monk was travelling from the direction of Debre Damo, he knew what was on his mind.

"So, St. Verena has been losing lately, and you are the fortunate soul who has to make that journey," Lord Kiros chuckled.

"You are correct, my friend," the monk acknowledged, his smile suddenly disappearing. "I am tired of being that representative. I have been a monk there for four years and I am told we have not won a game in ten years."

"Really," Lord Kiros asked, somewhat surprised. "How bad is your genna team?"

"Many of the monks are ageing and can't wield a genna stick or dribble the ball as much as they once used to," the monk said.

"Okay," Lord Kiros assured the young monk. "You are in luck. Allow me to join your order, and you will win your first game in ten years."

"Will you pledge to serve God and obey his wishes?" the monk asked.

"I've never been really close to the man," Lord Kiros confessed, "but I can obey his wishes if I judge them to be worthy."

"The Lord's wishes are always worthy and right, my friend," the monk said softly and with a warm smile.

"Perhaps," Lord Kiros responded. "His ideas of what is right are sometimes a very big mystery to me. But I will serve him, if you will take me with you."

The monk took another hard look at the poor peasant standing before him, requesting to join his monastic order. Could he be transformed into a valuable servant for the Church? At least he was willing to try. After all, the monk knew, most people wanted the graces and charity and help from the Church, but very few were willing to work to serve the Church and the needy in return.

"We will teach you to obey and understand the Lord and all his graces," the monk said. "They call me, Tafari."

"I am—" Kiros began to introduce himself, but stopped short before proceeding. "I am Robel."

Lord Kiros had just adopted a false name. It was the name of one of his soldiers murdered by Lord Groda and his men. He could not use his real name of Giorgis Kiros, lest someone recognize the name and start asking questions. Also, he felt he had let down Saint George, the slayer of the dragon, for whom he had been named. After everything that had happened, Giorgis Kiros hardly saw himself as a dragon slayer. He was nowhere close to being the gallant Saint George on a majestic white horse slaying a dragon with his lance as depicted on paintings that adorned numerous church walls in his beloved Shire. He had watched as his men were murdered right before his eyes, and he had been completely unable to do anything about it. And now, like a coward, he was trying to escape and save his own life by pretending to be a monk. No, he was no Saint George. He would be Robel from now on.

"Hop in the cart," Tafari said to Robel.

Robel threw his belongings in the cart and hopped in the back next to the goat as Tafari started driving.

Tafari was about to resume driving when he heard something. It was Robel's stomach grumbling.

"I take it you haven't eaten, Robel," he said.

"It's been two days," Robel acknowledged.

Holding onto the reins of his mule with his right hand, Tafari turned around and retrieved a small bag from a sack in the back of the cart. He opened the bag, revealing some ripe, delicious-looking figs.

"Pardon my left," he excused himself, handing the fugitive soldier the bag using his left hand—it was rude to give, receive, or interact with another individual using one's left hand, after all. "Have your fill."

Left hand or right hand, the starving Robel did not care. He eagerly dove into the bag, but Tafari stopped him.

"Aren't you forgetting something?" the monk asked.

Robel froze for a moment, his head spinning about what he could have possibly forgotten.

"Forgotten something?" he asked.

"You want to be a monk, don't you?" Tafari reminded him.

Then it clicked. Robel withdrew, made a quick sign of the cross, mumbled something that only he could understand but which in his mind passed for prayer, and quickly made the sign of the cross again.

"Was that a real prayer?" Tafari asked, almost amused.

"That's between me and God," Robel responded.

Tafari laughed.

Robel was about to place his hand into the bag of figs, when yet again, he stopped. He looked around, as if someone was watching him.

"It's okay," Tafari said as he resumed driving the mule cart. "There isn't anyone close enough who can see you eat."

"Ah, good." Robel smiled, for it was rude for one to eat in public unless the food was being shared. He dove into the bag and gulped down the figs so fast that it seemed he had practically inhaled them.

Tafari smiled at his older protégé's manners, turned around, and resumed ringing his bell that hung next to him from the cart.

"Anything for the poor?" he called after every three rings.

As the cart drove away, Robel's old life, his home, the last of his lands, and his beloved Shire became just a speck above the horizon behind him. He could not yet bring himself to think of what the future held for him. He had escorted the king, priests, and Christian pilgrims to Jerusalem

many years before, had fought for almost twenty long years for the kingdom, and told by his commanders and their accompanying priests that
they were fighting for God against the Muslims, who interestingly also
claimed to have been fighting for God against Christians. But despite it
all, he had lost everything, even his wife. Now here he was again, em-
barking on another journey he had just been told would serve God. The
experience was surreal to him, but if serving in a monastery was how he
was going to survive, then he was going to do it, and be as good at it as
he was at soldiering.

CHAPTER 8

It was a three-day ride to Roha. Even though Robel knew a lot about Roha, the capital of the kingdom, he had never been there. The 19th day of January, the celebration of Timkat or Epiphany, was fast approaching. It marked the day Jesus was baptized by John the Baptist. As a result, there were countless pilgrims on the road to Roha and to sacred churches along the way, travelling to obtain blessings and redemption.

Robel's lessons on becoming a monk began during the ride to Roha, with his much younger mentor sparing no moment to implant early lessons. As a monk, Robel was going to be expected to be learned, so that he could read and teach. He could already write and read in Ge'ez script, which he had learned as a boy in the Church school his father had enrolled him into in Shire, as was customary with all noble families. But his knowledge of Church history was limited. He could use some assistance there.

"In the Book of Acts in the Bible," Tafari said, "during the resurrection of Christ, Philip the Evangelist encountered an Ethiopian on the road from Jerusalem and baptized him. When the Ethiopian returned to Ethiopia, he began to spread the word of Christ, until King Ezana himself became a Christian and declared Christianity the religion of the kingdom 900 years ago. As far as I know, we were the first to become a Christian country."

Robel was fascinated. He had never thought more about the Church than it being just a tedious chore he had to do by attending Mass on Saturdays and Sundays for devilishly long hours.

But now Robel wanted to know more about the Church, monasticism, and the monastery of St. Verena. What would his new life be like? How could he exploit it until it was time for him to emerge to reclaim his honor and lands, or to safely flee the country? Tafari filled him with lots of details.

"Have you heard of the Nine?" Tafari asked.

"Of course," Robel responded. "Everyone has heard of the Nine—the nine saints."

"But did you know that they started the first monasteries in the kingdom?" Tafari asked. "Without the Nine, there would be no monasteries here. Without the monasteries, our Tewahedo Church as we know it today would not exist. We monks are the backbone of the Church and the kingdom. The Ethiopian converted in Jerusalem was one man. The Nine spread his teachings to all the corners of the kingdom. Without the Nine, we would be no Christian kingdom."

"I never knew they were monks," Robel said.

"The Nine Saints set up the monastic rules in the fifth century," Tafari continued. "They based them on the monastic rules of Saint Antony and Saint Pachomius, which were already in use in different parts of the Christian world."

Tafari went on to explain that even though monastic rules had the same basis, each monastery was accorded freedoms to slightly deviate from the established rules. They often implemented different practices as long as they fell within the scope of the rules established by the Nine: of maintaining selfless service and detaching oneself from worldly desires and possessions.

"It is freedom like no other," Tafari stressed. "For us, monasticism liberates us from the chains of the material world."

In some monasteries, the monks lived in a commune, sharing everything and keeping nothing as personal property, while in others each monk was more independent, eating and working alone, but praying together. And in other monasteries, both lifestyles were practiced side by side.

"What about the House of St. Verena?" Robel asked.

"We like the side by-side-thing," Tafari said. "Like all monasteries, we sustain ourselves by producing everything we need and accepting donations from the faithful. But there is something that makes us different."

"And what is that?" Robel asked.

"You see," Tafari continued, "most monasteries are located in remote places that no one can easily find or get to. The reasons for this are so that monks can devote themselves to a life of prayer and stay hidden from enemies. Some of these monasteries rest at the top of the highest cliffs and some are even at the bottom of the deepest ravines. But we, in the Order of St. Verena, are located in the middle of Roha, a big city with tens of thousands of people."

"I wondered about that," Robel said. "Why is that?"

"Since the Franks lost the Christian lands in Jerusalem, the king wants to make Roha his new Jerusalem," Tafari said. "He wants a city free of the poor and impoverished. So he gave the Church a land grant to build our monastery. We exist to devote ourselves to helping the poor and the needy, producing and taking donations from the faithful in order to provide that help."

Tafari had wanted to make it back to Roha before Timkat, but because they had to stop many times to rest, accept donations, and bless pilgrims and the faithful, they were significantly delayed. When Timkat arrived, they were one day away from Roha. They had to stop at a church in a small village to celebrate the festival.

"This church is 600 years old," Tafari said to Robel as they took off their shoes to step into the church.

The church was chiseled out of the side of a mountain, and would have been difficult to see from a distance, made that way because of the many threats that churches had faced over the centuries from invaders and usurpers. Although it looked modest from the outside, inside it was a magnificent work of art, filled with colorful frescoes and paintings depicting biblical and historic scenes.

Tafari noticed Robel staring at the blackened image of the Virgin Mary carrying the baby Jesus.

"That is soot from when the church was burned down by Queen Gudit's soldiers," Tafari explained. "The priests leave it there as a reminder of what may happen when we do not take a stand for what we believe in."

Queen Gudit was a woman who had the last king of Axum killed around the year 950, after which she usurped the throne and embarked on a massive killing spree of nobles and church leaders in a terrifyingly bold attempt to eradicate Christianity in Ethiopia. Countless churches and monasteries were razed to the ground, and Christians were even crucified in public. But this only resolved the will of the people, with the Church and the faithful only growing stronger. They believed her time would be short as they awaited the return of the true king, the last descendant of the Axumite kings whom they believed were descended from King Solomon and the Queen of Sheba. But Gudit ruled for 40 years, effectively ending the First Solomonic Age of Ethiopia, until she was overthrown by the Zagwes, the current line of kings.

Robel and Tafari experienced Timkat at this church that served as a reminder of those dark times following the First Solomonic Age. Along with hundreds of pilgrims and worshippers, they awaited the removal of the Tabot from the church. Always hidden beneath richly embroidered cloth, the Tabot was a replica of the original Ark of the Covenant—the sacred box which held the Ten Commandments—which the Church believed was housed in the kingdom, inside the Church of St. Mary of Tsion in the city of Axum. Robel had at certain points in his life been a faithful churchgoer, but he had always had his doubts about all the stories in the Bible and sometimes even questioned the existence of God. His belief in the story about the Tabot was no different.

According to church officials, after God gave Moses the Ten Commandments, the Israelites housed it in the Ark and took it with them to Jerusalem. Many years later, Menelik I, the son that Ethiopia's Queen of Sheba had with King Solomon of the Israelites, brought the Ark to Ethiopia for safekeeping, where it remained in the church of Saint Mary of Tsion. No one had seen it since, except for special monks and priests elected by a council of monks. Not even kings could see it. Even the replicas could not be seen by anyone but the church priests. Anyone who saw them would be instantly incinerated by fire from God. During the massacre at Bodera village many days earlier by Muslim soldiers, the

Tabot in the village church had been left untouched. Either the Muslims had been too terrified of it, or they had not attached enough importance to it to be worthy of their attention. But Robel had always been curious to know what it looked like though—what was really underneath the cloth that wrapped all the Tabots. When he walked into that church that day in Bodera, that was his chance to find out, with no priests to stop him. And although he did not believe in much of the story of the Tabot or that he would meet an instantaneous fiery demise from a wrathful God for simply looking at what lay underneath a piece of cloth, he asked himself a critical question in the end. Why take a chance? And so, like all the soldiers who were with him that day, they left Bodera with its Tabot undisturbed.

Thousands of villagers and people from all over the area had seemingly materialized from out of thin air and congregated around the church to witness the removal of the Tabot from the church. They had come from the neighboring villages and remote outposts to witness this annual event. The Tabot was finally brought out by priests, amidst great chanting, ululating, and dancing. Remaining at the center of the group of priests, it was carried on one of their heads and covered with a splendidly patterned cloth draped in golden threads. The entire congregation, with the priests and Tabot in the middle of them, then began a long walk to the river, amidst more chanting, singing, dancing, and the reading of the scriptures. The large, intricately-designed processional crosses carried by priests—which often depicted biblical figures and events and were made of out pure gold or some other highly polished metal—reflected brightly in the overhead sunlight.

Robel and Tafari followed the sea of thousands of congregants clad in white cotton shammas and loose robes as they marched the Tabot away. Brightly-colored giant parasols that shaded the priests carrying the Tabot and other congregants added to the festive atmosphere and mood. People took turns circulating around the many priests in the procession, kissing their hands and processional crosses. Tafari joined the many debtaras—singers and chanters—as they chanted new and ancient hymns written by Saint Yared hundreds of years before. The sistrums and the large wooden drums combined with the melodic and rhapsodic chants gave Robel an experience that made him feel like he was riding on clouds that were kept afloat by the beauty of the most melodic music he had ever heard.

There were occasional stops for more music and dancing, when men and women put aside their prayer books and stood in long lines according to gender, then faced each other and began engaging in dance movements such as shoulder dancing, accompanied by singing that matched perfectly with the music. The shoulder dancing involved moving and shaking the shoulders, one after the other, symbolizing the constant battle between good and evil, with each shoulder representing each entity. Such scenes at Timkat festivals never ceased to amaze Robel with their sheer visual beauty. He had attended many Timkat festivals before, but each one seemed to be more spectacular and euphoric than the one before it. Even those like him who were not particularly religious found themselves mesmerized by the event.

After many hours of walking, the congregation made of men, women, children, the old, the young, clergy, and lay people, finally arrived at a spot along the river at dusk, where a tent had been erected. The priests took the Tabot inside to be guarded all night by monks and priests. This was followed by more prayers, chanting, and the reading of scriptures late into the night. The following morning, after spending the night sleeping outdoors or in tents, the congregants gathered again to listen to more scripture reading. Then a priest placed a small piece of burning cloth on a leaf, which he then placed into the river. The fire symbolized light, and what remained after the fire burned up symbolized sins, which were then then washed away by the river. That was the moment everyone was waiting for, the moment to be born again and have their sins washed away. It was another of the multiple baptisms that every true Christian had to undergo, the first being 40 days after birth for boys, and 80 days after birth for girls.

The priests then dipped their crosses in the river and started using them to sprinkle water on congregants, baptizing them and giving the go-ahead for all other worshippers to begin the process of symbolically baptizing themselves. Many reached into the river and started sprinkling water over their own heads, while children simply leapt into the river or were briefly submerged into it by their parents.

After the baptism came another moment all were always waiting for—the feasting!

Worshippers started unbundling the food they had brought with them and began to share with others. Those who lived nearby opened their homes and kitchens to complete strangers. Tafari, who had been mingling with fellow clergy, soon located Robel sitting against the wall of a small stone hut.

"There you are," Tafari addressed him. "I worried for a moment you had changed your mind and departed."

Robel chuckled. Hiding out as a monk was the best way to save his life.

Tafari led Robel to a small group of monks who were seated on a mat near a stream, with their prayer sticks and gospels lying next to them. They were engaging in the consumption of a meal of a most delicious-looking injera and goat stew. Tafari and Robel sat down to join them in eating communally from the same large, round metal dish.

"This is sweetened with honey," one of the monks said, inserting a piece of the injera, a flat bread made from teff flour, in his mouth, fully savoring its perfect blend of saltiness and sweetness.

"Eat as much meat as you can, Robel," Tafari said, "for this is one of three times during the year that you will be allowed to eat meat in St. Verena."

"Are you serious?" Robel asked.

"The monks in our order eat meat just three times a year: on Timkat, Easter, and Genna."

"That's why you St. Verena boys can't win a single genna game," one of the other monks joked. "You don't have the energy that comes from eating good, strong meat. We eat meat whenever we want and we beat our rivals at genna all the time."

"Is it too late to change my mind and join his monastery instead?" Robel asked Tafari jokingly.

The monks soon finished eating, leaving a small piece of injera on the plate to show that they had had their fill and had eaten to their satisfaction—otherwise the woman who had prepared the meal for them may have thought that they were not full and pressed on them to eat more food than they would have liked to.

After all the feasting, the entire procession began the journey back to the church, with the priests carrying the Tabot as the chanting, drumming, and ululating resumed.

CHAPTER 9

After spending the night in their cart, Robel and Tafari continued their journey to Roha at dawn. They arrived at the gates of city in the middle of the day. This was Robel's first time in Roha. The city was bustling with people and activities. There were pilgrims flowing into the city and pilgrims returning home after Timkat. There were tradesmen and craftsmen of all types engaging in all kinds of transactions ranging from fruit selling to letter writing and reading on behalf of those who could neither read nor write. What impressed Robel most as they rode their mule cart through the city was how the market areas were separated from the residential areas, unlike in Shire, where people mostly lived where they conducted their crafts and businesses, and where residential and market areas were one and the same. The houses in Roha were made of stone and mortar as they were in Shire and most parts of the kingdom, but in Roha what really amazed Robel was the relatively large number of buildings that were two and three stories high. People sat on the flat rooftops of many of the tallest buildings, simply relaxing and watching the hustle and bustle below.

"Forty thousand people live in this city," Tafari said. "Many others come from afar—some from places I have never even heard of, to trade their wares."

Then something caught Robel's eye.

"Elephants?" he gasped.

"Never seen one before?" Tafari asked.

"No, and I certainly have never heard of anyone riding them," Robel said, gesturing on the two people riding on the elephant closest to them.

"People from all over the kingdom come to Roha to seek their fortune, even elephant riders," Tafari said. "There used to be lots of elephants around here, the old people say. Now there are only a few. And there are even fewer elephant riders. Many, many years before my time or yours. King Kaleb—that's how he launched his Christian crusade in Arabia. He had hundreds of war elephants, trained here in the highlands. The Muslims even call the year his army marched into their holy city, Mecca, the Year of the Elephant, because they say it was the same year their prophet Mohammed was born, almost 600 years ago."

Robel remembered learning about King Kaleb from monks who had taught him in school when he was a boy. When Robel encountered the Franks from Europe in Jerusalem, all he remembered was that about 600 years before their European crusade, King Kaleb of Axum had launched a Christian crusade of his own into Arabia. It had been to protect Christians from being persecuted there and to protect Ethiopian pilgrims who were traveling through there on their way to visit Jerusalem for Easter.

"Who is that?" Robel asked, noticing a splendidly-dressed and armed man riding at the head of about ten other riders. They were all in the uniforms of soldiers, but not in the traditional white colors of the king's forces. They wore a dark yellow and some light chainmail over their padded cotton fabric, with sabers dangling from their hips.

"That is Berhan," Tafari responded. "Commander of the Rohan Riders."

"The Riders of Roha?" Robel noted, partly impressed.

He knew of the legendary Riders of Roha. Often also referred to as the Rohan Horse Guard, the fame of these horsemen who guarded the king preceded them. Robel had even worked with some of them many years before when he was still a very young soldier. He had been attached to them as a tracker during a raid on a remote pagan enclave to rescue a missionary priest. The priest had been taken hostage by a superstitious tribe after he tried to intervene on behalf of a woman about to be stoned to death on suspicion of using witchcraft to inflict bad luck on her niece. Robel helped the Rohan Riders rescue the priest and the woman, and was so marveled by their ability to use the sword and bow while mounted, that in order to boost his young ego among his own men, he challenged one of the Riders to a game of guk. Guk was a jousting horse game in which riders used stick lances to try to unhorse each other. Although it was only mock fighting, it was a violent and sometimes deadly serious sport in which accidental fatalities were not uncommon. Fortunately for Robel, his guk fight with the Rider he challenged only led to him being thoroughly thrashed over and over again, never lasting more than a few seconds on his horse before being brutally thrown off each time. It was one of those moments where one always learned a lot more when he lost than when he won, and it only made Robel a better soldier—and earned him the lasting respect for the Rohan Horse Guard. But as he was about to learn, things with the Rohan Riders he was looking at now were significantly different.

"Everyone knows the king and his army of 60,000 are away in the frontiers fighting what's left of the Shewa Muslims and their allies," Tafari said. "He left Commander Berhan in charge of maintaining security in the city. But he has no more than 24 men to maintain order. They have no control of anything. The city is now run by ruffians and criminals who have the free will to rob and take from the people as they please. Commander Berhan won't stop them."

"Does he even try?" Robel asked.

"No. He allows them to do what they want. If you ask me, he is in league with them, getting a portion of their ill-gotten gains."

"Does he bother the Church?"

"The criminals sometimes do, but Commander Berhan himself does not, at least not directly," Tafari responded. "You see, he is Jewish. If he goes against the Church, the few men the king left with him will rebel against him and he will have even more problems on his hands."

Robel had met people who practiced the Jewish religion in Jerusalem during his brief time there. He had always known there were some in Ethiopia who practiced it too, but he had not met any before.

"I know little about the Jewish religion," Robel said.

"Before this land was Christian, it was Jewish," Tafari explained. "Many Jewish communities remain scattered within the realm. They call themselves the Beta Israel. Some of the books and teachers say they are descendants of Jewish worshippers who came with the son of King Solomon and Sheba, King Menelik I, when he brought the Ark of the

Covenant here a thousand years before Christ was born. Other books say they are descendants of those Ethiopians who converted from paganism to the Jewish religion after Sheba's visit to Solomon. And other books say they are descendants of the lost tribes of the Israelites who made their way to Ethiopia many thousands of years ago—do you know the Israelites, Robel?"

"I'm no monk yet," Robel said, "but I do know a thing or two about the Bible. There was a time when I went to church every Saturday and Sunday, you know."

"There, you see," Tafari said. "Our liturgy and ways of the Church still follow some Jewish traditions."

"Like what?" a curious Robel asked, for this was all part of his education as a monk. He now not only had to be a worshipper, but he also had to be an authority on all things liturgical and historical about the Tewahedo Church.

"Like keeping the Sabbath holy on Saturdays as well," Tafari said. "Also, most of us do not eat pork or shellfish, we use only freshly baked bread for communion, and we circumcise all male children, just to name a few."

"I see," Robel said, understanding now why the Christians and European Crusaders he had met in the Holy Land only maintained the Sabbath on Sundays.

Tafari soon brought the mule cart to a halt in front of a small house on a dark street. He dismounted and turned to Robel.

"Bring the goat," he said.

Robel dismounted, lifted the goat by its feet, and threw it over his head and onto his shoulders. He secured it with both hands by holding onto the poor creature's hooves.

Robel followed Tafari to the door. The monk knocked on it, and a little boy with large eyes opened it up, followed by six other children and a woman who looked to be no younger than 50.

"Tafari," the woman greeted, happy to see him.

"Saba," Tafari responded as they bowed to each other. "This is for you." He pointed at the goat across Robel's shoulders.

Robel placed the goat on the ground inside the woman's home. One of the children immediately untied the goat, which took off running in all directions. The children scurried after it playfully, delighted with the gift. It was some sort of edible toy, Robel thought. Saba smiled, seeing the joy the animal brought to the children.

"May God continue to bless you, Tafari," the woman thanked him.

A few moments later, Robel and Tafari were again riding in the mule cart.

"Saba took in some orphans some months ago," Tafari explained. "So we continue to support her. It is what we do in our order. We ask for help so that we can in turn help those who need it."

"Where were you when I was in need of wine?" Robel joked.

They continued riding through the city, with Robel taking in the sights and sounds.

"What are they digging for, surrounded by priests?" Robel asked, referring to a large group of about 20 workmen who were digging into the ground at various spots while a crowd of about 40 priests and worshippers stood and sat on the ground around them, silently reading from their prayer books.

"They're building a church," Tafari said.

"Looks more like they are digging graves," Robel joked. "The trenches seemed deeper than could be needed for any foundations for buildings."

"These are different sort of churches, Robel," Tafari said. "These churches are being built into the ground."

"Into the ground?"

"Yes, if you can believe it. The king provided the land grant for building our monastery, and has provided land grants for the building of many of these underground churches around the city. Some have been completed. Others, like this, are still being built. They are all connected by a series of trenches."

"Is there a reason for building them into the ground?" Robel asked.

"The Book of Zephaniah in the Old Testament, chapter three, verse 10," Tafari said.

"What does it say?"

"'From beyond the rivers of Ethiopia, my worshipers, my dispersed ones, will bring my offerings,'" Tafari quoted.

"I remember that verse from learning it as a boy," Robel said. "But what has it to do with these churches?"

"After the Frankish Crusaders lost Jerusalem to Muslims," Tafari explained, "traveling there on pilgrimage by our people and maintaining contact with our monks at the Church of the Holy Sepulcher became difficult. So now the king wants to make Roha the new Jerusalem, so pilgrims who can no longer travel to Jerusalem will come here instead to worship. He believes that verse is a prophecy naming Ethiopia as the new center of God's children."

"How do churches in the ground help this to become a new Jerusalem?" Robel asked.

He was about to tell Tafari that he did not remember any underground churches in Jerusalem during his visit there years before, but stopped himself, realizing that any such revelation could only invite uncomfortable questions and compromise his safety and disguise.

"The king has been to heaven in spirit," Tafari said. "And these churches are similar to the ones he saw in heaven."

Robel was about to laugh out loud at the ridiculousness of Tafari's statement and also say that he thought it all sounded like nothing but a pile of horse manure. But in the interest of his upcoming career as a monk—or rather, a fugitive—he judged it best to keep his mouth shut.

"I see," was all he then said.

Tafari turned and looked at him.

"I sense some doubt in your mind, my friend," Tafari said.

"Well, I—" Robel began, but stumbled for words.

"It's not a matter of whether this whole thing is true or not," Tafari said. "For me, the work on the churches and the support the king gives to the Church in Roha enables us to continue to serve worshippers, craft good people, and help the needy in these difficult times."

"Okay," Robel acknowledged.

Then Tafari looked around his immediate area, as if to make sure no one else could hear what he was about to say. He inched his head closer to

Robel and whispered, "If it makes you feel any better, I think this king is full of cow dung myself. He is just trying to legitimize his hold on power and that of his Zagwe clan. Since Queen Gudit's overthrow of the last king from the line of Solomon and Menelik almost 300 years ago, everyone has waited for the return of the true king. And Since the Zagwes overthrew Gudit's dynasty more than a hundred years ago, the Church to this day has not recognized them as true kings of Ethiopia because they are not descended from the Solomonic line of kings. The church considers this king and the Zagwes to be merely stewards to the throne of Roha, and that will be the case until the return of the king, one who is descended from Solomon and Menelik."

"I see," Robel said. "So by building churches and his new Jerusalem, this king is just trying to strengthen his recognition from the Church and the people."

"Correct" Tafari said. "He even claimed at one time to be descended from Menelik, but the Church refused to recognize that claim. But he is a good man all the same. He works for the people."

"It's complicated," Robel said.

"I know," Tafari said. "We monks might sometimes speak politics, but we stay out of it. That is the work for priests and the bishops."

As they rode on, they came across a crowd of hundreds of worshippers and priests also standing and sitting—some reading prayer books, and some listening to scripture from the priests.

"Are they digging another church?" Robel asked.

"Not exactly," Tafari said, bringing the cart to a halt. "Come. Let me show you."

They both dismounted and walked towards the crowd. As they approached, Robel realized the people were gathered around something he could not see. It was beneath the ground. Then Robel eventually got a better look as he drew closer.

"Splendid!" he gasped, truly amazed.

"This is the church of St. George," Tafari said. "It is one of the first of the king's underground churches to be completed."

Robel was looking at an architectural marvel. It was an elaborately crafted church the likes of which he had not seen before anywhere in the realm, or even in Jerusalem or the lands between Ethiopia and Jerusalem. The church had been chiseled straight out of the ground by cutting deep trenches into the rocky terrain in order to form its outer walls. Then to create the interior of the church, the builders and architects had painfully hollowed out the free-standing rock, leaving a roof in place which was the original ground level prior to the digging. And then to add to its beauty and religious symbolism, the entire church, when seen from above—from where Robel, Tafari, the worshippers and priests were standing—was in the shape of a cross! Robel was speechless.

"Pilgrims have started coming in from all over the kingdom to worship here," Tafari said. "A few even come from as far away as Alexandria."

"I have never seen anything like this," Robel said, open-mouthed.

"Some of the donations we receive help to build these churches," Tafari said.

"But what prevents the church from getting completely submerged in water when it rains?" Robel asked.

"There is a builder they call Sidi Masqel," Tafari began to explain. "He studied in a school run by the monks of the Ashetan Maryam monastery here in Roha. He built a complex drainage system consisting of connecting trenches that not only trap enough rainwater for drinking wells and baptismal pools, but also channel excess water towards the rivers below the hills. No matter how much it rains, this church and others like it cannot be submerged. Even the roof of the church is designed to channel water away."

After having had his fill of staring down at the church and even walking within its interior and taking in views of the many fine frescoes and paintings that decorated its walls, Robel and Tafari continued their journey within the city.

They soon arrived at a small cluster of buildings in the center of the city.

"Robel," Tafari called to him. "Welcome to your new home, the monastery of St. Verena."

St. Verena was the patron saint of Tafari's monastic order. She was an Egyptian convert to Christianity in the third century AD, who was known for her love and care for the poor and the sick, as well as her strong Christian faith, despite being jailed for her beliefs.

Robel paused to look at the modest cluster buildings, built of rough, dry stones like a very small village to resemble those of the very poor peasants whom he was now going to be serving. He was now going to live a life like that of the Egyptian woman from a thousand years before him. How had it come to this? A scout leader and tracker who had led fearless soldiers in battle for his entire adult life was now going to be working to help the poor and the needy? He had nothing against them, but that was just not his thing. But if he wanted to stay hidden and alive until things calmed down and he found a way to reclaim his lands, property, or leave the kingdom, then he was prepared to do whatever was necessary.

"I need a moment," Robel requested of Tafari.

"Take all the time you need, my friend," Tafari said, "for this is not a life that is easy. But it is a life that is rewarding."

Robel stepped off the cart, grabbed his belongings that were still wrapped in a bundle of cloth, and walked away, disappearing from Tafari's view. The monk said nothing. He did not believe for even a moment that Robel had changed his mind. He believed he saw a troubled but good man in Robel. Robel, for his part, had no intention of changing his mind. Survival was his greatest goal at the moment.

He found a secluded spot at a remote corner of the monastery's cluster of buildings not too far from where the monastery's stables that housed its cows, goats, and sheep were kept. There, Robel was going to bury the bundle that contained his sword, dagger, and red cloak under some rocks. He took one final look at the sword. Forged in the fires of ever-present lava lake atop the black mountain of Eta Ale, he had never parted with it before. It had been bequeathed to him when he first joined the army, by a dying uncle who was the governor of the Wag district. The uncle had received it as a gift from the previous king, Kedus Harbe, after an incident in the Mogadishu Sultanate. While visiting Sultan Sa'id on a peace mission in Mogadishu, his uncle had stopped an assassin who tried to kill both the sultan and the Ethiopian king by seizing his dagger and throwing the man from the fifth story of the building they were in. Somehow the man survived the fall and involuntarily provided the names of his sponsors, for whom peace between the Christian kingdom and the Muslim sultanate was against their business interests.

Robel smiled at the sword, as if he was parting with a dear friend. Then he took in a deep breath and buried the bundle under the rocks. With that, he had at least for the moment also buried his past behind him and was ready to take on a new life. He promised himself to not think about taking up arms again, for it had only led to a miserable life for him that had gained him absolutely nothing.

When Robel returned to the cart, Tafari did not ask questions. Robel could make his peace however he wished, for he was about to immerse himself into a difficult life of servitude.

CHAPTER 10

The monks of the Order of St. Verena existed to serve the community of Roha. But because Robel was new, he had to undergo many months of training, cut off from the outside world and without setting foot outside the monastery grounds. It was an opportunity to study and learn— to become a proper monk. It was going to stay that way for him until the first day of the new year, September 11th, when he would emerge from seclusion, equipped to take on the world and assume his duties to the poor of Roha as a Verenaian monk. Although this all sounded like a challenging lifestyle for Robel to undergo during the following eight months, it all suited him just fine. He saw the bigger picture. It was also an opportunity for him to keep low and avoid prying eyes.

He was given a hut at the eastern edge of the monastic buildings, for each monk had his own. He was to stay in that hut and dedicate his life to studying the scripture and the history of the Tewahedo Church of Ethiopia. Other than the clothes he wore, his only other possessions were a Bible, a neck cross, prayer beads, and a prayer book. These were all the essential tools of every monk, for the center of a monk's life was prayer. In addition, he was given a bowl for food and a drinking gourd for his nutritional needs.

Robel had no intention of staying a monk. But to play his role and appear convincing, he had to take his studies and responsibilities seriously. Life as a monk, especially a new one still learning, was not easy. The monks of the House of St. Verena awoke every single morning even before the cock's crow, assembled in the rectangular church built of cut stone and mortar in the center of the monastery, and chanted and recited each of the psalms of David by heart. They then met in the eating hall for a simple breakfast usually consisting of some sort of combination of yams, chicken eggs, and vegetables, after which they went about their daily chores within the monastery or in the city, carrying out the Lord's work. Those not working in the city gathered in the assembly hall in the afternoon for more prayers, and then returned to their chores. At dusk, all the monks were expected to be back in the monastery, where they gathered in the assembly hall to address any matters of concern and finished off the day with group prayers and chants.

On Saturdays, Sundays, and feast days, the monks welcomed worshippers into their church, where the priests among them led Mass from midnight to dawn, events that often lasted over six hours. In addition to all this, monks had to make time in between the day to find a secluded place to recite the Lord's Prayer and the Canticle of Saint Mary, as well as spend long hours at night in quiet meditation and contemplation.

The House of St. Verena owned enough land granted by the king to grow its own crops and raise cows, goats, chicken, and sheep. They were entirely self-sufficient. During planting and harvest time, which were determined by the long rains and short rains, all able-bodied monks and young students in the monastery's school worked the fields.

Robel took part in the chores of the monastery when not studying, but because the Order of St. Verena consisted mostly of evangelical monks whose sole purpose was to be dispatched to the city of Roha to spread the word and to help the needy, it required the most experienced of monks to perform such tasks. As a result, Robel had to spend those many months almost in seclusion, undergoing intense study in his hut, with the much younger but experienced Tafari as his mentor. Because Robel could already read and write in the Ge'ez script, his course load was a lot easier to handle. He immersed himself in studying the written monastic rules of the Tewahedo Church and other texts such as Book of the Monks, a devotional text that expressed the essence of monastic spirituality and taught how to overcome temptation and attain physical and spiritual purification. Robel had no intention or willingness to ever overcome any of that, but he understood that he at least had to study them in order to be convincing as monk. Most importantly, he had to learn and deeply understand the five mysteries of faith of the Tewahedo

Church: the Mystery of Trinity, the Mystery of Incarnation, the Mystery of Baptism, the Mystery of Holy Communion, and the Mystery of Resurrection—whatever those meant. But again, he studied them. Whether he understood them or not, he himself could not even tell.

"These rules—everything you study," Tafari once advised him, "will transcend physical boundaries and help you to realize God's presence in everyday life."

"Okay," Robel said, trying to suppress the headache he was getting after a long study session with Tafari over things he knew he would never have any concrete understanding of, and which made very little sense to him. "How will I realize this presence?"

"You will know when it is present," Tafari said.

Robel chuckled.

"Like Jesus, I see you, too, have learned to speak only in parables," Robel accused his friend.

"What do you mean?" Tafari asked.

"The man never gave a straight answer in his life," Robel said, pulling out his Bible from its leather pouch and holding it up, which he had read in its entirety during his previous three months in the monastery. "Every time anyone asked him a question, he always responded with a question or some story about seeds, hidden treasure, or something. Even when they asked him the simplest of questions like, 'Are you the son of God?' his reply was, 'It is you who says it.' What does that even mean?"

"But how else should he have answered?" Tafari asked, surprised.

"How about just 'yes' or 'no?'"

Tafari smiled at his friend.

"You are learning indeed, my friend," Tafari said, patting him on the back.

Robel was having a tough time being a monk, but at least he was not a hermit monk, he consoled himself. He had seen hermit Ethiopian monks before, many times during his travels with the army. They lived completely secluded lives, with some even living in underground catacombs, reading and re-reading the Bible for the rest of their lives until they themselves joined the dead in the catacombs, only to be discovered months or years after their deaths. Robel could not imagine reading the

Bible more than once. With the 84 books of the Ethiopian Bible, it had more books and gospels than any Bible in the Christian world, and eleven more than the Roman Catholic Bible that Robel had become nominally familiar with during his brief interactions with European Crusaders in Jerusalem.

When Robel was not studying, he was cleaning in the stables, helping to serve the senior monks, or was helping with the farm. They grew crops and produced meat, most of which they never even consumed themselves but donated to the poor of Roha or sometimes sold in order to raise funds to help the king with the construction of the underground churches.

"Do you regret becoming a monk yet?" Tafari asked Robel one day as they were toiling underneath a baking sun, chopping down plants and flowers that were going be crushed for the production of ink needed by their monastery's scribes and painters.

"It is not an easy life," Robel confessed, resting his sickle on his shoulder. It was a tool he was comfortable using, since it was not that different from the shotel, which he had wielded a few times before his uncle had gifted him the Nubian-style kaskara sword.

"No, it's not," Tafari acknowledged. "It takes great courage and strength to live like we do."

"If Gebre Kristos chose this life over a marriage, then he must have really hated the woman," Robel added.

Gebre Kristos was the son of King Kaleb of Axum. Around AD 525 he chose to become a monk rather than marry the woman his father had chosen for him, vowing to remain that way until the woman married someone else or died. When he re-emerged from the monastery many years later, after the woman had married another man, he had undergone such a drastic physical transformation that only his dogs recognized him. Robel could relate on some level with the prince from 700 years before him. In a way, he, was now a monk because of a woman—his wife, Tiki.

With that sobering thought, Robel couldn't say much. But he had one observation to voice.

"One thing I have noticed," he said. "We junior monks do all the work. All that the senior monks do is just sit around and pray."

September 11th finally arrived, the festive New Year's Day known as Enkutatash, which marked the end of the rainy season and the beginning of the harvest. Pilgrims arrived from all over the realm to worship and seek penance in Roha in celebration. The streets were filled with children picking up the yellow daisies that blanketed the fields during the period, to present as gifts to houses and pilgrims. The flowers symbolized gifts that people presented to the Queen of Sheba upon her return from visiting King Solomon in Jerusalem a thousand years and more before.

Just like the children enjoying their youth, with Robel finally emerging from seclusion, it was like the dawn of a new era for him. He was ready to start a new life on this first day of the new year. During his time in the Holy Land, he remembered celebrating the new year twice. First, it was with their hosts, the Franks, who had invited the Ethiopian king and his delegation to celebrate it on January 1st, based on the 12-month calendar used by the Europeans. Then he had again celebrated another New Year on September 11th, which was the first day of the year in the 13-month Ethiopian calendar. The same had happened for Genna, which the Franks called Christmas. While Robel and the rest of the Ethiopian delegation had celebrated it on January 7th, their hosts had celebrated it two weeks earlier on December 25th. As for when Jesus was actually born, Robel did not really care, but concluded that it must have been somewhere in between.

With Robel's period of study completed, Tafari had petitioned Abba Mikael, the abba of their order, to assign Robel to work with him in his daily duties as one of the many monks collecting donations for the needy and the underground rock-hewn churches. He had heard nothing back yet form the abba. It appeared Robel's assigned monastic duties would be to continue to be as a farm hand and a stable hand.

"I have staked my name with Abba Mikael based on my trust in you," Tafari warned his friend as they harnessed a mule to their cart. "If my petition for you is approved, I pray you will not let me down."

"I am good at whatever I do, my friend," Robel asserted. "As a poor peasant, that's how I have always survived."

Tafari smiled admirably at his friend's confidence.

"Conditions in the town are a lot tougher now than they were before you went into seclusion," Tafari warned.

"How so?" Robel asked.

"The king—" he began.

"You mean the steward," Robel teased, stroking the mule's back.

"King, steward, it doesn't matter to us mere monks. He has still not returned to Roha with his army. The Shewa sultan is defeated, but other enemies of the realm remain. There are pagan chieftains to subject and Muslim incursions from the north he is fighting back. Last we heard, he was with half the army somewhere in the east fighting to stamp out polygamy in the newly-conquered and Christianized lands there."

"So the bandits and criminals are still running the city?"

"Of course," Tafari lamented. "Crime is rampant. Now they have a leader they call the Headman. He has the entire city terrified. There is no limit to what he does. His goons take whatever they want from people. We are even sometimes forced to give a portion of our donations to him as well."

"And Commander Berhan and the Rohan Horse Guard?" Robel asked. "He still does nothing?"

"Nothing at all. I tell you he is in league with them, getting rich off their spoils. I do not know if he is afraid of them or just corrupt. Even if he wanted to do something, he does not have enough men to face the Headman and his goons."

A moment later, a monk informed Robel and Tafari that Abba Mikael had asked to see them immediately.

"At last," Tafari smiled. "The role you will play as a monk in St. Verena is about to be revealed."

CHAPTER 11

"Abba Mikael was a blacksmith before he became a monk," Tafari informed Robel as they walked through their monastery's courtyard to meet the abba. "He devotes his life to God by also serving the people as a blacksmith. He even makes spurs for the Rohan Riders and the king's court."

"What is his story?" Robel asked.

"His brother was a missionary monk, but was martyred in Makuria by Salahadin's forces about 30 years ago," Tafari said. "That was when he decided to become a monk."

Robel knew of Makuria well. It was a small Nubian kingdom north of Ethiopia. He had travelled through it on his way to Jerusalem with his king. It was a Christian kingdom that had churches as magnificent as those he had seen in the Holy Land, and stunning church paintings not very different from those in Ethiopia. Robel had always wondered whether the Nubians had assisted the Europeans in the Crusades against the Muslims in the Holy Land, for he had seen a detachment of Nubian soldiers there, protecting their pilgrims who also went to worship in the Church of the Holy Sepulcher. But whether the Nubians had really assisted the European Crusaders or not, the Muslim sultan, Salahadin, who later became the conqueror of Jerusalem and drove out the Christians, sent a punitive expedition to Nubia in 1173, where they killed, pillaged, and destroyed an untold number of churches and cathedrals. Sensing an easy victory, Salahadin's forces sent an emissary to the Nubian king, Moses Georgios, demanding that he surrender his kingdom and agree to subject it to Islam in order to avoid further bloodshed. King Georgios responded by sending the emissary back with a cross stamped to his hand with a hot iron pole. The king then rallied his troops and successfully drove out Salahadin's forces from Nubia after their commander drowned while crossing a river.

Abba Mikael had been a monk for 30 years, during which time he had also become a priest to continue the work of his martyred brother. He was a man whose devotion to his God and the poor were beyond reproach. He had travelled to the Holy Land of Jerusalem many times. He had also walked bare-footed, the actual Stations of the Cross, in order to endure the same sufferings as Christ did.

Tafari and Robel walked into the blacksmithing workshop, which was bustling with activity. It was also a place of worship for Abba Mikael. On the wall, there was a colorful mural of Daniel in the lion's den, which was partially blackened with soot after years of enduring smoke from the furnace. Abba Mikael and two apprentices from the school run by the monastery were busy hammering and smelting away. They did not stop working on the round processional cross they were forging when Tafari and Robel walked in. These crosses were larger crosses that were often carried by priests and monks during church services and processions on feast days.

"Are you fine?" Abba Mikael greeted the two monks as he repeatedly used a foot to depress a goatskin bellow to pump air through two iron pipes into a blazing-hot charcoal fire.

"We are fine, Abba," Tafari responded.

Abba Mikael went straight to the point, addressing Robel.

"There is some small talk from the other monks, Robel," he began. "You did well in your lessons, and you know the scripture well. Everyone here is really fond of you, but there is a feeling that you harbor many doubts about Christ and his teachings."

Abba Mikael stopped pumping the bellows as one of his apprentices reached into the fire underneath the charcoal with a pair of metal tongs, pulled out a red-hot piece of metal, and placed it on a stone anvil.

"Abba," Robel began to respond, "you have always taught us that anyone who believes in absolutely anything actually believes in nothing."

"Okay Robel," Abba Mikael acknowledged as he began to beat the hot metal into shape with a hammer. "I just wanted to hear from you. Now I want to show you what I showed the monks who raised concerns about you."

Tafari's stomach tightened. He had heard some of the complaints and concerns before, but had dismissed them. He had convinced himself that Robel would cease questioning aspects of Church beliefs openly once his studies were completed. But instead, Robel had only gotten more vocal by raising even more alarming questions. For example, he asked a group of senior monks if Jesus died for our sins, why were people then not allowed to sin at will? After all, it appeared all people had already been pre-forgiven by God. He also once wanted to know why in the world the day Jesus died was called 'Good Friday.' And to make matters worse, he asked that if Jesus and God are the same, then why is it that the day before he was crucified, Jesus was down on his knees in the Garden of Gethsemane, begging himself to spare himself the pain of being crucified? And then when he was hanging from the cross, he asked himself why he had forsaken himself by allowing himself to be crucified. It did not make any sense! While some of the monks had expressed shock and sheer terror at this question, Tafari had thought it quite funny and chuckled.

"I never meant any offense, Abba," Robel said somewhat regretfully. "They were mere attempts to increase my understanding of the scripture."

"Look around this room, Robel," Abba Mikael pressed him. "What do you see?"

Robel looked around the room. Other than the tools of blacksmithing, it was packed with recently forged crosses—neck, hand, and processional crosses of different shapes and sizes, and even a few horseshoes and toe stirrups, all of which were a testament to Abba Mikael's magnificent iron-forging skills.

"Crosses, mostly," Robel responded.

"What do you notice about them?" the head monk asked. "Think shapes."

That was easy.

"Some of the crosses are round," Robel noted, differentiating the round crosses he had often seen only in Ethiopia, but not in Nubia or the Holy Land.

"Do you know why we have round crosses in Ethiopia?" Abba Mikael asked, taking a break from hammering the piece of iron on the anvil.

"No, Abba."

"Before we were a Christian kingdom, even before the Queen of Sheba introduced the Jewish religion to Ethiopia, we were a land of many religions. We worshipped the sun by day and the moon by night. We highlanders were quick to accept Christ when the brother kings made Christianity the religion of the kingdom, making Ethiopia what it is today. But for the southern peoples, it was harder for them to leave behind their sun gods and their moon gods. They could not easily accept the divinity of the cross. So the Church then started making round crosses, to look like the symbols of the moon gods and the sun gods that the southern chieftains and their people worshipped. It worked. It became easier for them to accept Christianity because they could now somehow relate Christ to their earlier forms of worship. We still make round crosses today, usually for the pilgrims who come from the southern lands. Even the Christian names of the brother kings when they made this kingdom Christian were geared towards appeasing the sun and moon worshippers."

"The Christian names?" Tafari asked. Like everyone else, he had known the brother kings who made Ethiopia the first Christian kingdom in AD 330 simply as King Ezana and King Saizana, who jointly ruled the kingdom with equal authority.

"King Ezana, who ruled from the north," Abba Mikael continued, "adopted the Christian name of Abreha, which means 'he illuminates.' Does that remind you of something?"

"The moon," Robel said.

"Good," Abba Mikael said. "And his brother, Saizana, who ruled from the south, adopted the Christian name, Atsbeha, which means—"

"He who brings dawn," Robel finished. "That is the sun."

"Very good," Abba Mikael said. "Now, why do I tell you all this?"

"I do not understand, Abba," Robel confessed.

"I'll let your teacher explain it to you," Abba Mikael said, turning to Tafari.

"What Abba Mikael is saying is that for nearly a thousand years of Christianity in Ethiopia, there have always been Christians who had different beliefs. Christianity has adapted to people's beliefs everywhere. No two Christians are the same. It is okay not to believe everything you see, read, and hear in the Bible. It is all about your faith in the higher power. Make of it all what you will, but serve God and man."

"Even in Jerusalem, the first Christians acknowledged they believed in a sun god," Abba Mikael added.

"They did?" Robel asked, surprised.

"Look at that mural," Abba Mikael said, using the cross in his hand to point at the darkened painting on his wall, before handing the cross to another apprentice to continue hammering. "Do you know what is above Daniel's head?"

"A halo," Robel said.

"Yes," Abba Mikael agreed. "But in reality, halos are the symbols of the sun's rings. Those who worshipped the sun wore wreaths made out of bright flowers and leaves around their heads. The idea was to represent the roundness and light of the sun and bring the wearer closer to the sun gods. So you see, even our early Christian brethren back in the Holy Land appeased and adapted to the beliefs of sun worshipers in order to bring them into the Christian fold, by painting our angels and saints with rings of light over their heads. That is also why many kings wear crowns today."

"I see," Robel said.

All the studying he had done in seclusion had not mentioned this.

"But that is not why I called you both here," Abba Mikael said to Tafari and Robel. He paused, as he received an elaborate and intricately-designed cross from one of the apprentices, the bottom of which was supported by "Adam's Arms," a motif that represented the arms of Adam supporting the world. But this cross was made of wax.

"You may not believe much in the scripture, Robel," Abba Mikael continued, covering the wax cross with soft clay and carefully placing it into a stone oven to bake as his apprentices watched carefully, "but you do believe in what we do and represent here. That is what is more important to me and the people of Roha. We may not be able to stop the Headman, but we can continue to give people hope."

"That is true, Abba," Robel said.

"Tafari," he addressed Robel's mentor, "you have done well with Robel."

"He is dedicated to our cause, Abba," Tafari said. "He only wishes to serve the poor of Roha."

Abba Mikael paused, retrieved the baked clay from the oven, and turned it over, pouring out the now-melted wax that was the cross into a bowl through a small opening that had been bored through the baked clay. He then used a pair of tongs to pick up a stone bowl filled with molten iron, which he poured into the cavity that had been left by the wax model.

"Serving God through serving people is why we are here, Robel," Abba Mikael said as one of his apprentices took the clay mold from him and placed it on a table, waiting for the molten iron within it to cool down and harden.

Tafari and Robel stood patiently, listening to Abba Mikael and watching with intense interest first-hand the beeswax process of blacksmithing. They sensed that Abba Mikael was about to give them some pertinent information. A few moments went by as one of the apprentices used a small hammer to crack the clay mold away, revealing beneath it an elaborate and intricately-designed cross now formed of iron, which had taken the shape and design of the hollow space left by the wax model that had melted away. One of the apprentices poured water over the iron cross, cooling it down completely. Abba Mikael picked it up admiringly and smiled.

"I think you are ready to face the world, Robel," Abba Mikael said, still gushing at the newly-forged cross.

Robel smiled, and Tafari patted him on the back. Robel had waited for this moment for the eight months he had been in the monastery, studying the scripture and monastic rules in near seclusion, and doing the most menial of tasks in order to help strengthen his faith. Tafari doubted his faith had changed much since they first met. Either way, he was ready to leave the confines of the monastery.

"I am honored, Abba," Robel said softly, struggling to conceal his excitement.

"Like this cross which is now going to be filed and polished to ensure it is smooth enough to be displayed in a church or carried by a priest," Abba Mikael said, handing it over to one of the apprentices to continue the next step of smoothing out the rough edges, "you will continue to work with Tafari. He will help you be a better monk."

"I could not have asked for anyone better, Abba," Robel conveyed his gratitude.

"The first task that you will have will be to assist your teacher in what I am about to ask him to undertake," Abba Mikael said.

"I will do whatever serves our people best, Abba," Robel said.

"Tafari, you are familiar with the Wazir Quarter, yes?" Abba Mikael asked.

"Of course, Abba," Tafari said. "That is Abba Danyel's area."

"You will take over from Abba Danyel," Abba Mikael declared. "You will assume his duties, and Robel will assist you."

"Did something happen to Abba Danyel?" Tafari asked.

Tafari had been close to Abba Danyel since he had arrived at the monastery. Abba Danyel had been raised in the monastery and was a very pious man. He had never known another life.

"Abba Danyel is well," Abba Mikael said, "Tomorrow some soldiers will arrive from Axum and escort him there."

"What did he do?" Tafari asked, puzzled.

"He has been elected as the guardian monk of the Ark."

Robel and Tafari were stunned with disbelief and excitement. To be chosen as the guardian monk of the Ark of the Covenant was an honor so rare that only the most pious of priests and monks were selected for the sacred duty.

"The other monks do not know of his election yet," Abba Mikael continued, "so keep it to yourselves. I will announce it at supper."

"Of course, Abba," Robel responded.

"Be well," Abba Mikael concluded his meeting with the monks and dismissed them.

Robel and Tafari started for their quarters to begin arrangements for their own duties.

"Congratulations," Tafari commended his much older charge and friend. "You have just received your Holy Orders."

A slight smile slid across Robel's face. In truth, he did not care for monasticism and what he considered the strange beliefs and ways of the monks. For him, the entire experience was just going to be a temporary one that was nothing more than a means to an end. But somehow, receiving his Holy Orders lit up something in him he did not quite understand. He felt proud.

"I have heard before of the monk who guards the Ark," he said to Tafari. "But I had never imagined it to be true."

"It is as true as one can believe," Tafari explained. "It takes better men than us to be chosen as the guardian. A guardian must be strong at heart and have the faith of Christ himself to perform the duties. The guardian appoints his own successor, and if he dies before he can do that, then the monks of St. Mary of Tsion elect a successor to replace him. Once the guardian steps foot inside the church to assume his duties, he serves for life and never leaves the building until the day of his death."

"Have you ever seen it?" Robel challenged his mentor, having serious doubts about the veracity of the Ark's existence.

"I have never gone looking for the Ark, my friend," Tafari said. "for it is in your heart, my heart, everybody's heart, in whatever goodness can be found there."

"But you do believe the Ark exists?" Robel asked.

"Of course, it does," Tafari insisted. "I have been to the Cathedral of St. Mary of Tsion."

"Really?" Robel asked, himself having never been to that most sacred church in the entire realm which was built in the fourth century. "To see the Ark?"

"No, I went there as a boy with my father to see the giant obelisks of Axum and to witness the crowning of the king," Tafari said. "The Ark is there, believe me. When the Agaw usurper Gudit let loose her goons to destroy churches in Axum, the St. Mary of Tsion church was the only one that did not burn to the ground, despite the usurper's army's numerous attempts to set fire to it. Something had to have protected it. I can only think it was the Ark."

CHAPTER 12

After Abba Mikael announced Abba Danyel's election as the Ark's guardian monk later that evening, in their excitement, the monks burst into spontaneous celebratory singing, with some reading from their copies of the Deggua—a hymnal first written in the sixth century by Saint Yared, the monk who institutionalized music in the Tewahedo Church.

Robel tried to sing too, but for everyone's sake, Tafari placed a friendly hand on his shoulder, stopping him. "Maybe not, my friend," Tafari cautioned. "You sound like you swallowed a camel."

"Saint Yared wouldn't mind," he laughed. "He's been dead a long time."

"His spirit lives on in here," Tafari argued, placing a hand on his copy of the Deggua.

Tafari had a high respect for Saint Yared. He had even visited the monk's resting place in the monastery of Saint Qirgos, where the monk had died in 571, just to see the monk's prayer stick, his original Deggua, and the bowl where he mixed his ink. Those items were all still preserved in the monastery's House of Treasures, a room or building every monastery reserved for preserving relics and sacred objects. Tafari had even intimately studied the musical notational system that was used in the Tewahedo church that Saint Yared had invented. Most monks learned to read it, and it had helped to preserve church chants of the Ethiopian Church since around 550 AD. Learning to read the musical notes had not helped Robel sing one bit better, though.

The following day, soldiers arrived and escorted Abba Danyel to his new post in Axum. That same day, Robel and Tafari got on their mule cart and rode to Wazir Quarter to begin their duties together of charity collection. It was a relief for Robel to be out of seclusion.

Among their duties was one of the most important that certain monks and priests were to engage in, and which was often very vital for many monastic orders. It was to become attached to wealthy nobles as spiritual advisors. Such nobles and similar benefactors often lavished the monastic orders with gifts and donations so large and extravagant that they in some cases could alone sustain monastic orders for many months or years. In the Wazir Quarter, the noble Tafari and Robel were going to be attached to, replacing Abba Danyel as her spiritual advisor, was Lady Mariam Tezara.

"What should I know about this Lady Mariam Tezara?" Robel asked Tafari as they rode their mule cart.

"She is the daughter of a wealthy noble and merchant who was killed along with his wife by raiders of the sultan of Zeila after their trade caravan was ambushed as they crossed the Ogaden Desert. Lady Mariam's father, and his father, and grandparents before them had always been great patrons of the Church, and always donated handsomely. Lady Mariam continues to do the same. But like with everyone else, the Headman's goons also threaten and make unreasonable demands from her. But she defies them as best as she can, giving as little as she can."

"She sounds like a tough and defiant woman," Robel stated.

"But you must be careful with her," Tafari warned.

"Why?" Robel asked. "Does she bite?"

"I notice how you sometimes look at the members of the opposite gender," Tafari joked.

"You are a dirty little fellow, young man," Robel said, patting his friend on the back of the head.

"Young man?" Tafari laughed. "I am your teacher."

"Okay," Robel acknowledged. "You are a dirty young teacher, then."

"I sneak a peek every now and then myself, Robel," Tafari laughed. "Nothing wrong with any of that. We are men, and to not have certain feelings would be against the laws of nature."

"Wisely said, my friend," Robel said. "There is some sense left in that skull of yours after all."

"But the important thing is to have the strength to keep your vows to God and not break them because someone in a beautiful gown struts past you," he advised. "You have to have the strength of will, Robel."

"Why are we talking about this?" Robel asked.

"The Lady Mariam, they say, can be quite enchanting," Tafari said seriously.

"Now you've got my attention," Robel said jokingly. "Please, tell me more."

"Suitors line up for her every day," Tafari began to explain. "She has three things that any man in Ethiopia will kill for: wealth, a noble title, and beauty—exquisite beauty. I only tell you so you do not get carried away. Keeping aside the fact that we are monks, she has no place in her heart for the likes of peasants like us."

"I truly appreciate the vote of confidence, child," Robel said, forcing a smile. But in truth, he had suddenly been transported to a sad place, where memories of his past life, marriage, and subsequent betrayal were rekindled. He tried to hide it, but Tafari realized something was wrong.

"I'm sorry, my friend," Tafari apologized. "I did not mean to offend. What I said, I did so mostly in jest."

"Nothing to worry about, my friend, I mean it," Robel said sincerely with a soft smile. "You know you cannot offend anyone even if you try."

Before Tafari could say anything else, Robel picked up the charity bell and started to ring it.

"Help for the poor?" he began to announce, ringing the bell three times after each call. "Help for the poor!"

By the time they arrived at Lady Mariam's place, they had filled out half their cart with vegetables, fruits, some silver, three chickens, and two bowls of rare white honey, which was found only in the highlands and known for its distinctive aroma. Lady Mariam's home was a big two-story house built of finely cut stones and surrounded by a beautiful-ly terraced lawn. Eight servants were busy harvesting from the sorghum fields surrounding the home, a task that had to be completed before the end of the meher harvesting season.

A hefty old man with a bloated face emerged from the home to meet them. His face was covered in so much silver-colored hair that his mouth could barely be seen even when he spoke.

"Tafari!" the old man blurted out excitedly. "It takes the departure of

Abba Danyel for you to visit a friend?"

"Jembere," Tafari blurted back, looking at Jembere's ever-growing stomach. "You still do not miss many meals, I see, my friend."

"If I ever had any intentions of missing any meals, I would have become a monk," he laughed, then rubbed his big, round stomach. "Besides, if I ever fall off a horse, this would cushion the fall."

They both laughed heartily and exchanged a burly hug.

"So how have you been, my friend?" Tafari asked. "Are you fine?"

"We are fine, young friend," Jembere responded. "But there have been better days around here. For three generations my family has served Lady Mariam's family, and things have never looked bleaker than they are now. The Headman and his people do not make it easy. They always demand more and more. It's becoming unbearable to deal with those scum."

"And Commander Berhan?" Tafari asked. "I suspect for Lady Mariam he would at least do something to help."

"He is a terrible man," Jembere scoffed. "He will do nothing to help or call off The Headman's goons unless Lady Mariam agrees to marry him."

"Why does she not marry him?" Tafari asked. "It will end much of her problems."

"I don't know," Jembere lamented. "You know her. She has her ways. Perhaps it is because she fears losing control of her family's fortune to him. Or perhaps it is because he is Jewish. Lady Mariam cannot stand the idea of anyone not holding as high a regard for Christ and his word the way she does."

The men were suddenly interrupted by a voice that came from inside the house.

"Tafari," the voice called, "is that old man bothering your ears with worthless gossip like an old woman with nothing better to do?"

"My lady." Tafari turned and responded to the voice, bowing. "Greetings to you."

Robel stood in stunned silence. He was looking at the most strikingly beautiful woman he had ever seen. Tall and slender, with large round eyes, long hair, a darker than usual complexion, and with eyes and teeth almost as bright as the sun. He was marveled. And her voice, it was like the sound of songbirds on a warm afternoon. Now he understood what Tafari had been trying to tell him. He had not lied. She was quite an enchanting woman. From Ethiopia to the Holy Land, Robel had seen few women who matched her beauty.

Lady Mariam turned towards Robel, noticing his silence.

"Your new monk," she addressed Tafari, "does he have a name?"

"Robel, my lady," Robel introduced himself, bowing slightly. "Just a humble peasant from the western territories."

"Peasant?" she responded, looking him over from head to toe. "Each man is what he makes of himself. I welcome you to my home."

Robel bowed again, but said nothing, his gaze fixed on her like she was a painting being held by the bishop of Alexandria himself.

Lady Mariam turned around to return into her home, but then stopped, turned around, and stole a quick look at Robel. Something about the monk was different. He did not look like others who saw themselves as peasants. She flashed him a slight smile then turned around and stepped into her home.

Jembere quickly pulled Tafari to the side, to speak out of earshot of Robel.

"Who is he, really?" Jembere asked Tafari, referring to Robel.

"Peasant I found in Shire," Tafari whispered. "He only wants to serve God and the Rohan poor."

"I have never seen Lady Mariam react like that with anyone before," Jembere confessed.

"Robel has that effect on people," Tafari conferred. "It is an honesty that comes from his heart. He is strong-headed, but we are very fond of him in St. Verena."

"I understand," Jembere said. "You must warn him then against Commander Berhan. He seems a jealous type and may not take very kindly to him."

"Robel's devotion is to God's work in Roha," Tafari insisted. "He will be no threat to Commander Berhan's aspirations for Lady Mariam."

Jembere walked Tafari and Robel into the home, where Lady Mariam had already instructed a servant to prepare coffee for her new spiritual advisers. As the servant roasted the coffee in front of them, Robel reminisced about his days with his wife, where he had drunk coffee almost every day. He had not had any since the day before the massacre at the Bodera village, when their regimental cooks had brewed a huge pot of the beverage in the field. As they waited in Lady Mariam's living room for the coffee to be ground, Robel tried his best not to stare at or let himself be infatuated by Lady Mariam, the arresting beauty who now sat just across from him. She was looking at him, studying him. Something about him did not seem right as a monk. Robel distracted and busied himself by looking at the many fine paintings that adorned the walls of the home.

"You like that?" Lady Mariam asked, noticing Robel staring at a painting of an Ethiopian-looking soldier standing among what looked like European or Egyptian soldiers. "I painted that myself."

"You are very talented, Lady Mariam," Robel complimented her.

"Do you know who the Ethiopian in the painting is?" she asked.

"I can only imagine that to be Saint Maurice with his legion of Egyptians," Robel said.

"Do you know what happened to Saint Maurice and his soldiers?" she asked.

"He was a general in the Roman army," Robel responded. "He and all the 6,666 men under his command were martyred almost a thousand years ago after they converted to Christianity. He was the cousin of St. Verena, and his spirit visited her while she was in jail for converting to Christianity as well."

"Impressive," Lady Mariam returned his earlier compliment. "You know your Church history."

"I have a good teacher," Robel said, tapping Tafari on the back.

The truth is, he had known that story while studying as a boy in monastery schools. But when he became a soldier and understood the value of men at arms, he began to doubt its truth. He could not understand how any army anywhere could just kill 6,666 of its own men. Even the great Roman army could not have afforded such deliberate and self-inflicted loss. Perhaps they had martyred Saint Maurice and six of his men, but 6,666? No way!

"Before our dear Saint George, there was Saint Maurice," Lady Mariam said.

Saint George was said to have been a general during Roman times, too. He was said to have endured seven years of torture at the hands of his emperor after converting to Christianity and refusing to renounce Christ. He was beaten, stretched on a rack, partially skinned alive, had salt poured into his wounds, was beaten with a hammer, impaled, poisoned, and then immersed in boiling water. Yet he still refused to renounce Christ. He was then executed.

"All these saints who endured horrible tortures and deaths," Jembere said. "I respect them, because if it were me, they wouldn't even have had to threaten me. They would just have had to look towards my direction and I would have quickly and readily become even a leaf worshipper if that is what they wanted."

The coffee was soon ground, brewed, and poured before them in 12 little cups representing the 12 apostles of Christ. When Robel took that first sip of coffee, he smacked his lips and closed his eyes to savor it. It was simply a refreshingly good cup of coffee.

"Not had coffee in a while, I see," Lady Mariam guessed.

"We are not afforded such luxuries in the House of St. Verena, my lady," Robel said.

"This coffee is from Kaffa," Jembere added. "It is still the best. Lady Mariam's merchants buy coffee from there and sell it here in Roha."

Robel thanked God for that goat herder in Kaffa who was said to be the first person ever to brew and drink coffee before spreading its heavenly goodness throughout the world as they knew it.

At the conclusion of their visit, the purpose of which had been mainly for all concerned parties to simply lay eyes and feel at ease with each other rather than to discuss spiritual matters, Jembere and the monks stood outside just before they all parted ways. Robel remained awestruck by Lady Mariam, her dazzling beauty imprinted in his mind.

"How old is she?" Robel asked Jembere.

"Ah," Jembere chuckled. "You know it is rude to ask about a woman's age. Even the Bible only mentions a woman's age once."

"Sarai, Abraham's wife," Robel said. "Lived to be 127 years old. You are a good and loyal man, Jembere. Lady Mariam is lucky to have you at her side."

When it came to women and their ages, Robel was reminded of a woman back home in Shire, who at 40, was still unmarried. Worried, she travelled to the next town and told people she was actually 20 years older, so they would think she was a beautiful older woman who aged very well. It worked, as news quickly spread throughout the town of this blessed woman who did not age. Two weeks later she had a husband.

"Lady Mariam is a good woman," Jembere warned Robel. "Please do not make trouble for her."

CHAPTER 13

During the first week of duties in Wazir Quarter, amidst the fretting of the monks over the next genna game against the Debre Damo monastery that was due in about four months, Tafari and Robel split their time between seeking donations for the poor and providing religious services and spiritual advice to Lady Mariam and her household several days per week. On Saturdays and Sundays, Robel and Tafari accompanied her to church, with Jembere and a servant or two always in tow. Although Tafari, as the senior monk, provided most of the spiritual advice to Lady Mariam, she often requested Robel's presence as well, using the pretext that he needed to observe the sessions of his mentor in order to learn from them.

Lady Mariam's generous donations to the church and the House of St. Verena continued as they had been when Abba Danyel was her spiritual advisor. Besides trading in coffee and growing and selling crops, she also raised livestock, and even purchased iron ore from local smelters, which she sold to the king's armorers and local and non-local blacksmiths who sometimes traveled to Roha from as far as Massawa and the Adabay River area. However, she always made sure she reserved a portion of her produce for the Headman's goons, who demanded a cartload every few weeks. Even though she was protected by the king due to her deceased father's friendship with him, his absence had made it impossible to fully leverage that royal connection. Knowing that, and perhaps hoping for the king's demise in the frontiers, the goons and their mysterious and feared overlord, the Headman, increasingly got bolder and bolder with their demands of Lady Mariam and the people of Roha, nobles and peasants alike.

One Sunday afternoon, Lady Mariam, her spiritual advisers, Jembere, and two female servants were returning to her home from Mass at the St. Verena Church, where she now sometimes utilized instead of the local church, to honor Abba Danyel.

They noticed a magnificent gray horse tied to an olive tree in front of her home.

"You have a guest, my lady," Tafari said.

"It is Commander Berhan," Jembere pointed out.

Lady Mariam said nothing. She had grown accustomed to the regular visits from the commander of the Riders of Roha, a man convinced that Lady Mariam was destined to be his wife.

A moment later, Commander Berhan and Lady Mariam were sitting in her living room, drinking coffee and snacking on olives and figs served by her servants. Always wanting to impress her, this time he was dressed in a brightly-colored cotton tunic, produced by weavers in Teseney.

"I can make you happy," Commander Berhan tried to convince Lady Mariam.

"I am happy," she responded dismissively.

"I hear the harvest is bad this year," the commander said. "But I can help you."

"We will manage with what we can produce," she said. "We sell what we can and keep the rest for ourselves and the families of the workers."

"How will you pay off the Headman?" he asked, standing up and pacing in frustration. "You can barely produce enough for you and your workers. If I become your husband, I can help you with that."

"The king left you in charge of the security of Roha," she said sternly. "Perhaps if you do your job, then no one in Roha would have to worry about the Headman."

"Leave him out of this," Commander Berhan warned.

"How much does he pay you to look the other way while he robs the city blind?" she asked, unmoved.

Commander Berhan laughed.

"I am my own person," the commander argued. "I take nothing from the Headman."

"Then why don't you do something about him? Or do you fear him?"

"Lady Mariam," he said, softening his tone and ignoring her accusation. "When the king returns with his army, I will return to my home in Gondar. Come with me. You will love it there."

Commander Berhan was from the little-known village of Gondar, in the foothills of the Simeon Mountains, just north of Lake Tsana. He thought it was the most beautiful place in the world and had even tried to convince the king to move the capital of the kingdom from Roha to Gondar and build his New Jerusalem there. The king had not been convinced.

Moments later, Tafari, Jembere, and Robel were tending to their mule when Commander Berhan emerged from the home. His eyes met and locked with Robel's briefly. It was as if something in his mind pointed towards Robel as a possible romantic threat. Perhaps it was his chiseled features, lean muscular frame, and rugged good looks. Regardless, something just did not seem right about the new monk. But the Rohan commander quickly dismissed the idea of Lady Mariam ever ignoring a relatively wealthy noble and commander like himself and stoop so low as to engage in any romantic entanglements with someone whom he thought was just a mere monk of peasant stock. The commander released his horse from the olive tree, mounted it, and began to ride away.

Robel wondered if the commander was as good a fighter and horseman as the Rohan Rider who had bested him in the game of guk many years before. It was likely. One did not just become a Rider of Roha, much less a commander, by being soft. The Riders of Roha were usually hand-picked soldiers who had proven their prowess on horseback in combat. Their duty was to help protect the king and Roha from external—and the occasional internal—threat.

"He does not look too happy," Tafari commented.

"Lady Mariam must have declined his offer of marriage yet again," Jembere said. "This has become a ritual for the two every few weeks. Of her many suitors, he is the most persistent."

"Good for her," Tafari said. "He does not deserve her. He is one worthless Rohan Rider."

The following day, with another rejection of marriage to Commander Berhan still on her mind, Lady Mariam and her workers were attending a service in her home chapel being officiated by Tafari, with Robel assisting him. A servant barged in.

"What is it, Birakis?" Lady Mariam asked.

"The Headman's men," he blurted, panting. "They are here."

There was a collective gasp of exasperation, as everyone present knew what that meant. The Headman's goons had come at last to collect. They came at random times like a bad relative, and sometimes went weeks without showing up, arriving only when they needed supplies. And they often took whatever they wanted.

Lady Mariam, the monks, and her servants stepped outside, where four mounted men were waiting on horseback, brandishing shotels and spears. They meant business.

"Mekonnen," Lady Mariam addressed the leader of the group. "You visit at a bad time."

"It is always a bad time for you, Lady Mariam," Mekonnen shot back. "Why don't I see a cart with my supplies waiting?"

"We will have a cart filled for you shortly," she said softly, but with a tint of bitterness.

"Do I sense anger?" Mekonnen asked threateningly.

"Perhaps you and your people should try working for yourselves instead of taking from those doing honest work," Lady Mariam said.

"That is not how this works," Mekonnen chuckled. "You work, we take, you understand? We take from you so that we can protect you. That is all."

"Protect us from yourselves?" Lady Mariam scoffed.

"Woman, you are lucky we don't ask you for more," he snarled. "We take two carts from the Zenawi farm over the hill. The Kidanes across the river give us three. But we only ask you for one. You should thank us. We are good to you."

"Aren't you merciful?" Lady Mariam mocked, rolling her eyes, knowing they only demanded less from her because they feared likely negative repercussions if they pushed her too hard, given the king's possible return from the frontiers. Smarter goons may have simply left her alone, but she was just too wealthy and tempting a target to simply be ignored.

They had to at least get something out of her success.

Visibly irritated, Mekonnen raised his spear, pointed it forward, and nudged his horse towards her.

"Oh no!" Jembere gasped, horrified.

Robel suddenly and calmly stepped in front of Lady Mariam and stood facing Mekonnen, with his arms held together with interlocking fingers below his torso and his feet slightly spread apart. Mekonnen brought his horse to a sudden halt, just a few feet away from Robel.

"Step aside, monk!" Mekonnen warned. "My respect for God only goes so far."

Robel stood still. He simply stared the mounted goon straight in the eyes. Unlike with the farm guard who had driven him away from his own home in Shire about eight months before, this time there was no anger or rage in Robel's eyes. It was just a blank stare that proved extremely threatening in its calmness.

Robel said nothing.

"Do you not hear me, monk?" Mekonnen blurted. "Step aside, I say!"

Robel still did not budge from where he stood. His gaze remained fixed on the horseman, unnerving him.

Everyone stood frozen, unsure of what was happening or what to do. Then another goon rode towards Robel, while another whipped his shotel through the air. Robel noticed them both but remained still and kept his eyes fixed on Mekonnen.

"Look!" Jembere addressed Mekonnen with a broad smile, finding a way to defuse the tension. "Your supplies are here."

From the farm, two servants suddenly wheeled out a cart full of sorghum, milk, olives, and a few chickens.

Mekonnen's attention quickly turned to that, ignoring the insignificant monk and blaming his intransigence on a suicidal devotion to God. He had seen men like him die in what he regarded as needless deaths, because they believed they would find salvation in some kind of an afterlife. This monk was not worth his time. He steered his horse towards the cart.

"You have done well," he said to Lady Mariam as his men hitched the cart unto the back of one of their horses. "I like what I see."

"Take it and leave," Lady Mariam said.

"The next time we send word that we are arriving," Mekonnen continued, "I suggest you have the cart ready and waiting for us, or you will give us double for our time."

Lady Mariam spat on the ground. Mekonnen smiled and turned around to ride away with his men. He then stopped, turned his horse around, and addressed Robel.

"I only spare you because your problem is not with me," he said. "It's with God."

Then Mekonnen and his men rode off, along with the cart full of supplies.

Jembere and Tafari immediately approached Robel.

"A goat has more sense than you, man!" Tafari scolded his friend. "The man could have run you down. What were you thinking?"

"I wasn't thinking," Robel said. "I just could not stand him sitting there on his horse like he owns the world."

"He may not own the world," Tafari said, quite upset, "but him—the Headman, Commander Berhan—they all own us. We have to be careful. Do not do that again!"

Then Lady Mariam, who had not moved from where she stood, spoke.

"Robel," she called softly, "come with me."

Robel followed her into a room in her house where she could speak to him alone.

"Why did you do that?" she asked. "Why did you put yourself before Mekonnen and me? Was it for God, like he suggested?"

"I do not care much for God," Robel admitted. "But I do care about his message—to help those who cannot help themselves."

Lady Mariam looked at Robel intensely, who as usual, looked away, never wanting to lock eyes with her. This peasant monk was like no man she had ever seen. He showed no fear at all in the face of certain danger and a possible gruesome death. Other than her father, he was the only man who had ever willingly put himself in danger for her.

CHAPTER 14

Some weeks later, Robel and Tafari had just finished distributing some donated clothing, milk, and crosses to some families in the Warzir Quarter. Tafari was sitting at the back of their mule cart reading passages from the Gospel of Saint Mark to a small crowd gathered before them. Robel was standing by, collecting more donations and gifts from appreciative listeners who were grateful for the opportunity to hear from the Bible, for many could not read themselves.

It was a hot, bustling, and busy day. Merchants and customers haggled and argued over prices. Some people were just going about their business. All were keeping a vigilant eye on pickpockets and petty thieves, too. But those were the least of their worries. The real crooks were the Headman's goons. Those could not be avoided. They were always present, lurking around and making sure they got their share of everything they never worked for.

Three of them, led by a large muscular man, were talking to an ink maker. He had just handed them a small pouch full of silver. The large man smiled, dropping it in his pocket next to the large sword dangling from his left side.

"You are a sensible man," he said to the ink maker. "If everyone paid on time like you, we would have much less trouble, and we wouldn't have to make an example out of anyone."

The ink maker spat on the ground but said nothing. He wanted to tell them where to shove their gratitude, but he did not feel like getting stuck with the long, intimidating spears the muscular man's companions were carrying along with their swords.

The muscular man and his two companions began to walk away.

"Will you give all the silver to the Headman, Yifter?" one of his companions asked him.

"Of course, I will, Zeru," Yifter, the muscular man stated flatly. "What are you thinking?"

"There is this young girl I've had my eyes on," Zeru said. "The thing is, it takes a lot of silver and plenty of property to marry a woman these days. And the roof of my hut is caving in."

"What Zeru is saying," the third man said, "is that we do all the work, and the Headman does not pay us enough for our troubles. He does not have to know how much silver we just collected."

"If he finds out we cheated him, it won't just be your roof caving in," Yifter argued. "It would also be all our heads getting caved in. You forget what happened to Dawit? I won't risk it."

Dawit was a goon who collected silver and gold from merchants every week on behalf of the Headman. One day the Headman found out that Dawit had collected 41 pieces of silver, but had only turned in 40. The Headman had him roasted to death in front of his family.

"There," the third man said, looking at a man leading two donkeys away from the market. "That is how you get your silver, Zeru."

The man with the donkeys was accompanied by a little girl, about 10 years old. He had just donated a small bag of his wares to Robel and Tafari.

"Yes," Zeru smiled. "Just one of those may fetch me two or three pouches of silver. I'll have enough left even after the Headman gets his cut."

The three goons walked to the man.

"Who are you?" Yifter asked the man.

"Alemayu," the man responded, quaking in fear. "I am a trader. This is my daughter."

"What do you trade?" Zeru asked.

"I buy books from bookmakers here in Roha, and I sell them in Dongolo," he said. "Then I buy goatskin parchment from goat herders in Dongolo and sell them to bookmakers here."

"Goatskin?" Yifter asked, not understanding why they were important to book makers.

"Goatskin is white when dried, sir," the merchant said. "The bookmakers prefer it since it is perfect for writing on."

"Hmm." Yifter nodded, actually appreciating that piece of knowledge. "So what did you give the monks?"

"Some books for their school," the man replied. "It has been a good year."

"What about us?" Zeru asked. "What do we get for our troubles?"

The man sighed, reached for a bag on his donkey, pulled out a poetry book, and handed it to Zeru. Zeru knocked it out of the man's hands without even looking at it. His daughter scrambled to pick it up.

"We deserve better than a book, old man," Zeru teased.

"You want another book?" the man asked, confused and terrified.

"How about a donkey?" Zeru demanded, placing a hand on one of the man's donkeys. "This one. I can tell from its eyes that it wants to come with me."

"Sir," the man pleaded. "I am a trader. Without this donkey I cannot transport my products."

"Without our protection you cannot transport anything," Yifter said. "Just look at it as a donation—a gesture of goodwill, you see? You donated to the monks. Now you have an opportunity to donate to us as well. You see, we are just asking you to be fair."

"Please," the man begged.

The ongoing encounter soon attracted the attention of passersby and nearby traders and customers, many of whom hurriedly shut down their stalls and scrambled to get out of there lest they become the next victims.

Robel and Tafari, who had just shut down their operations and were ready to return to the monastery, were the exception. They stood by, watching the situation unfold.

Zeru seized the donkey he had placed his hand on as the man begged him.

"I pay my dues to the Headman," he pleaded. "I pay my taxes to the city. Please do not take my donkey."

At this point, Zeru pulled out a Nubian-style kaskara sword—straight and narrow with crossed handles like the one Robel used to carry. Zeru then looked down at the man's daughter threateningly. The little girl hid behind her father's leg.

"The donkey is yours," the man acquiesced. "I willingly donate it to you."

"Good," Zeru said with a broad smile. "Thank you. That was very generous of you."

Then the man and his daughter began to walk away, leading their remaining donkey.

"Wait," Yifter called the man, placing a hand on the remaining donkey. "That donation was for him," Yifter said, pointing to Zeru. "What about us?" He indicated towards himself and the other goon. "What do we get? Do we not deserve thanks too?"

"Sir, in the name of Saint Aregawi, I beg you," the man pleaded, invoking one of the Nine Saints. "You already have one donkey."

The man's pleas fell on deaf ears. Those goons were not the type who gave a fiddling fickle about the Nine or any other saints.

Yifter tried to pull the donkey away, but the man held it back. The third goon then landed a solid punch to the man's stomach, causing him to double over in pain as his daughter began to wail wildly. Then Yifter and Zeru jumped into the fray and began pummeling the man with kicks as he curled up in a fetal position on the ground, covering his face and continuing to plead.

And then Tafari and Robel jumped in.

"Stop," Tafari implored the goons. "Please stop this madness!"

"Are you serious, monk?" Yifter rebuked. "It is best you mind your own affairs."

"This is madness!" Tafari repeated. "This poor man has done nothing wrong to you."

At this point, Robel was standing still, saying nothing. He was just staring at the men, his hands before him, feet slightly spread apart—no anger, no rage, just a blank, calm stare.

"You look like good Christian men," Tafari said to the men. "I implore you to treat this man with respect. The Bible bids us to treat one another with compassion."

At this, Yifter slapped Tafari, who fell down with a thud. The goon was about to follow up with a kick when Robel stepped right up to him, reached into his cloak, quickly pulled out a Bible, and presented it to Yifter. Yifter immediately halted. Perhaps it was something about the cross printed on the cover of the Bible, but he and his companions immediately froze for a brief moment. They looked at each other in bewilderment, then backed off and stepped away from the trader and the monks.

"You two clowns better watch it," Yifter warned the monks, calming down. Then he looked at his men and said, "Get the donkeys. Let's get out of here. We'll sell them tomorrow."

The goons led both donkeys away, leaving the trader and Tafari on the ground writhing in pain. The man's daughter continued to wail, and the donkeys brayed wildly as if they understood what was happening. The little girl ran over to her father to help him up. Robel calmly walked over to Tafari and assisted him.

"Are you okay, my friend?" he asked, pulling Tafari to his feet.

"I am fine," he said. "I will be okay."

Robel was deeply saddened. He had always known Tafari to be jovial and happy, and had never seen him this downhearted before. It bothered the older monk deeply.

Tafari's attention immediately turned to the man who had just lost his donkeys. He and Robel helped his daughter stand him up.

"I am sorry we could not do more," Tafari lamented with the man.

"You did a lot," the man expressed his gratitude. "At least I get to go home alive with my daughter."

Robel turned to look towards the goons. He stared at them for a few seconds, watching them march away gleefully with their loot. But this time, Robel was not just blankly staring at the perpetrators like he had done moments before, or the way he had the goons at Lady Mariam's place. This time, the rage and fire in his eyes had returned.

Robel found that night to be restless as a he lay in bed in the monastery. It was late into the night, and the snoring from the nearby huts of other monks was so loud the ground seemed to shake. Robel tried to sleep, but it just was not happening. There was just too much playing around in his mind. He had put his past behind him, but his thoughts ached for something else. He hated how the goons in the market had treated his friend that afternoon. Tafari had not deserved that. He had been doing what he loved most, and was a good person. He could not hurt an ant even if he tried to. Yet the Headman's goons had treated him like he was just little more than a mosquito. That was just was not right. No.

Robel then suddenly leapt out of his bed. He put on his robes, stepped out of his hut, and began to gingerly snake his way through the monastery compound. He passed by Tafari's hut, and for a moment, he worried that that his friend would have been so rattled by the day's events that he would still be awake, also replaying the episode over and over in his mind. But Tafari had long moved past it. He was snoring so loudly that Robel was surprised he didn't wake himself up. Robel smiled. His friend was fine. After everything, as Rohan monks whose main task was to assist the poor, Robel knew they had it better than other monks such as Evangelical monks who were often killed by locals after being deployed to newly Christianized lands. But still, those goons should not have hit his friend. They really should not have.

Robel made his way to an area around the stables. He had buried a bundle there under a pile of rocks about eight months earlier, when he first joined the House of St. Verena. That pile of rocks was still there, undisturbed. He displaced the rocks, one by one, and underneath them still lay the bundle he had left there, untouched. He unwrapped the bundle, revealing his kaskara sword, a dagger, and his red robe. He tested the weapons for sharpness by rubbing the tip of his thumb across their edges. He was not disappointed.

It was a cold night, and he needed to feel warm. He donned the red robe, draping the hood over his head, so that only part of his face was exposed. He then wrapped his belt that held his weapons around his waist. The belt fit snugly over the thick clothing. Then he reached into the robe to his chest and pulled out his neck cross so it hung over the robe, the cross's polished brass surface catching the moonlight and sparkling over his chest like the Star of Bethlehem. He breathed deeply, made the sign of the cross, and disappeared into the darkness.

A short while later, he was standing in the dark again, this time staring at three sleeping men. They were the goons who had seized the merchant's donkeys and assaulted Tafari. Robel was just staring at them. One of the men stirred, and then suddenly woke up with a start, feeling an unwanted presence.

"Who is there?" the goon called out in the dark.

"You must be the one who calls himself Yifter," Robel said calmly, pushing open a window to let in the moonlight and fully exposing himself.

Yifter's companions woke up.

"Hey!" Zeru blurted, recognizing Robel. "You are that monk from the market!"

Yifter made a sudden move for his sword, which was hanging from a wall along with those of his companions. But he froze, noticing to his astonishment that Robel also had a sword hanging from his waist, and realizing that Robel could reach for his own sword much faster than he or any of his two men could reach theirs.

"It's okay," Robel said calmly, his arms folded. "Go ahead. It won't help you, though."

The goons immediately sprang for their swords, while Robel stood still, just watching them. Within moments, they pulled them from their sheaths and turned to face Robel, pleased with the security offered by their weapons in their hands. Like Robel, they too had kaskara swords.

"You have some guts coming here, monk," Yifter threatened Robel, pointing his sword at him. "We spared you once. It won't happen again. I really hate when people disturb my sleep."

"Not to worry then," Robel said. "Where I am about to send you, no one again will ever bother your sleep."

"Uhh?" Yifter gasped.

Then all three goons charged forward towards Robel, itching to chop him to bits. But to their stunned surprise, he very easily parried their sword blows and delivered his own, moving so quickly in the process that he wound up standing on the other side of them—where they had been standing before. They turned around to see him facing them, very calmly, with his sword in hand. He had been so fast they had not even noticed when he had drawn his sword.

"Damn!" Yifter gasped again, completely baffled. He and his goons had thought this was going to be a quick and easy kill.

Before they could launch another attack, Zeru suddenly coughed, staggered, and started bleeding from his neck. He had been cut. Yifter and the other goon stared in horror, watching their friend choke helplessly. An icy chill suddenly ran up their spines. It was then that they suddenly realized that they had grossly underestimated their adversary.

"Who are you?" Yifter demanded. "What do you want from us?"

"You should not have hit my friend," Robel said softly, maintaining his calmness.

"How did you find us?" the other goon demanded.

"I am a scout," Robel responded calmly. "I know how to track down people. For you, all I had to do was follow the stench."

Then Zeru tumbled over. The thud startled Yifter and the other goon, who were now awfully spooked by Robel. Then in a desperate attempt to save their lives, the two goons made a sudden charge at Robel. But it was over before it even started. Within just a few seconds, both goons were lying on the ground, moaning and groaning, with wounds on their torsos. Robel liked it that way—to leave them alive for just long enough so that they could ponder the wisdom of their choices and how it had delivered their fates.

Robel sheathed his sword then stooped over Yifter, staring into his dying eyes.

"Plea—please," Yifter struggled to speak, extending his hand to Robel.

Robel just continued to stare at him, as if enjoying the sight of the life draining out of Yifter's eyes. Then Yifter stopped moving, dying with his eyes open. Robel slowly turned and looked at the other goon. He was already dead. Robel's cuts had been so quick and precise that there was no blood on his sword. It had been the modicum of precision.

Robel stared at the bodies before him. He was a monk who had just broken the sixth commandment—thou shall not kill. He had put three men to the sword in cold blood. How could he justify his actions as a monk? That was easy. He was not a real monk. But even if he were, he could justify the actions. Even Jesus resorted to violence when it suited him, he thought, remembering the story of Timan. The Church said she was a woman who refused to give help to Joseph, Mary, and the baby Jesus during their flight to Egypt. In response, an angry baby Jesus turned her, her husband, and her children into monkeys, then drove them into the desert. Baby Jesus! If baby Jesus could do that to a whole family, then surely killing three pieces of human scum who had assaulted a monk and stolen a man's property was no sin in the eyes of God.

Robel began searching the dead men's belongings. He found two small pouches. He put them inside his robes, exited the room, and disappeared into the darkness.

CHAPTER 15

The following morning, Alemayu—the trader who had been brutalized by Yifter and his goons—was about to wake up earlier than usual. He now had to work longer hours to increase his earnings in order to buy and replace his seized donkeys before travelling season ended. His daughter was already awake. She stepped outside their small stone home, carrying an empty pail, and headed towards a well that had been dug in front of their yard. She stopped suddenly, puzzled at the sight before her.

"Papa, wake up!" she screamed.

Her father flew out of his house and stopped suddenly as well, staring at the sight before them.

"Saint Aregawi be praised," he muttered as his daughter made the sign of the cross.

Before them stood the donkeys Yifter and his goons had seized from him. Someone had brought them back to him and just left them in his yard. There were two small bags dangling by rope across the back of one of the donkeys. Alemayu walked to them and opened one of the bags. It was full of silver, which Robel had taken from the goons. Inside the bag was a note, written in Ge'ez script.

"Here," the man said, handing the note to his daughter. "What does it say?"

"It says 'The silver is for your troubles. I pray you have safe travels to Dongolo,'" the girl read, having been taught to read in a monastery school.

Alemayu and his daughter smiled.

Later that morning, Robel and Tafari were riding in their mule cart through town. Robel was driving as Tafari called out for donations.

"Help for the poor?" his call went out, followed by three rings from the bell each time. "Help for the poor?" Ring, ring, ring.

They rode past two little girls playing kilibosh, a rock-tossing game that, for some reason, was only played by girls.

"I have never understood the object of that game," Tafari wondered.

"It's a display of good reflexes and coordination skills," Robel said. "Whoever has the better of those wins the game."

Robel knew a thing or two about coordination and reflexes. That was what made him an excellent swordsman. That was what had enabled him to fairly easily overcome the goons the night before. The encounter, though, had made him worry. The fight had lasted less than one minute, but he had found himself terribly fatigued at the end. A minute longer of the same intensity and he would have run out of breath and be overcome. He was a long-distance runner, and had won several races across the Shire highlands during racing competitions held on festival days. But he knew what the problem was. It was the eight months he had spent in near seclusion learning to be a monk, just praying, studying the scripture and liturgy, and doing some manual labor, during which time he had added a little here and there to his girth. He had to do something. He had to get back in shape and be ready for the world whenever he thought it safe to leave the monastery.

"When do we start practicing for the genna game?" Robel asked Tafari.

"Practice?" Tafari asked, surprised. "The game is not for another four months. And we do not practice—ever. We just play when Genna Day arrives."

"Without practice?" Robel asked, even more surprised. "No wonder you all lose every single time."

"We rely on God," Tafari said. "If he wants us to win, we will."

"Second Thessalonians, chapter three, verse ten," Robel said.

Tafari chuckled. "'A man who does not work shall not eat,'" he quoted the Bible verse.

"Or to put it in simple terms," Robel stated, "God will only help you if you help yourself."

"You are a smart man, my friend," Tafari said. "I'll bring the idea of practice up with the others. What do you have in mind?"

Before Robel could answer, they noticed a certain excitement through town. People seemed to be gravitating towards a basket-weaving shop.

"What is happening?" Tafari asked a woman carrying her baby on her back, strapped securely with a wide piece of cloth.

"Some people killed three of the Headman's men," the woman said. "Commander Berhan is offering a reward to whoever provides information leading to their capture."

The woman ran away, racing towards the site.

"That can't be good," Tafari said to Robel. "No one touches the Headman's men."

"What will he do now?" Robel asked.

"I don't know," Tafari said. "Such a thing has never happened before. But we should go to where everyone is going if we want to fill this cart today."

Robel then turned the cart to the left, heading towards the site of the gathering.

A crowd had gathered where the bodies of the three men killed by Robel during the night were displayed, with a very angry Commander Berhan and some Rohan Riders standing beside their horses next to them.

Robel and Tafari stood on the cart so they could see over the crowd and get a better look at the scene.

"Good," a blacksmith next to whose shop they were standing said. "Someone needs to start doing something about the Headman's criminals."

"Did anyone see who killed them?" Robel asked.

"Yes," the blacksmith said. Robel's eyebrows raised and his ears perked. "A woman who was outside doing her—you know what, said she saw a man in red."

"A man in red?" Robel asked.

"Yes," the blacksmith said. "Just a man in red. That is all."

"Look," Tafari observed. "It's Lady Mariam."

The arrestingly beautiful Lady Mariam, Jembere, and two of her female servants had just walked out of a building in front of which Commander Berhan was busy addressing the crowd.

"That is the meeting place of the Guild of Coffee Houses," Tafari continued. "She sells her produce to the guild, who sell it to other coffee houses even as far away as Lasta."

"No one is above the law," Commander Berhan announced. "Whoever did this to these men must be caught and brought to justice."

"You are angry at the deaths of these men?" Lady Mariam scolded the commander. "Where is your anger when these men and their friends go around tormenting, stealing, taking, beating, and even killing other people? Where does your anger go then?"

The crowd let out a loud cheer in agreement at her question.

"If it is brought to my attention, I will take action," Commander Berhan said, lowering his voice.

Lady Mariam scoffed dismissively.

"I would love to see that happen, Commander Berhan," she said. "I really would."

Tewodros, Commander Berhan's second-in-command, came riding hastily, then dismounted his horse. A cross of St. George hung around his neck, for the Riders of Roha were all followers of Saint George, the most famous of the equestrian saints. Their Jewish commander, Berhan, had no such cross around his neck. He did not believe in Christian saints. Almost all soldiers who fought from horseback followed one of the warrior equestrian saints such as Saint George, Basilides, Tewoderos Romawi, Fikitor, Gelawdewos, Filotewos, and Susenyos. But these saints had all met the same fate: gruesome torture and death for their Christian beliefs. Because of that, Robel had never really followed any equestrian saint. He was not willing to die for Christianity and had no issues agreeing to worship a tree, moon, serpent, or even a frog if it meant saving himself from having his tongue ripped out of his mouth or his skin flailed and fed to him.

Tewodros had an urgent message.

"What is it, Tewodros?" Commander Berhan asked the messenger.

"The Headman is here," he replied.

Fear suddenly gripped Commander Berhan, and he stood straighter, as if to present a better picture of himself in the presence of the approaching Headman. A murmur of fear also rippled through the crowd. Many were about to disperse when 40 horsemen suddenly galloped in with swords drawn and positioned themselves to surround the crowd. A frightening silence then settled in. No one was going anywhere.

"Who is this Headman?" Robel asked in a whisper to Tafari.

"You are about to find out," Tafari said. "Just keep your head down and do not make any eye contact with him."

After the crowd had been secured, two men rode gallantly and slowly towards Commander Berhan. Robel's eyes widened. He could not believe what he was seeing. He rubbed his eyes and took another look at the two men. No, his eyes were not deceiving him. One of the men rode closer to Commander Berhan, who slightly bowed his head in reverence to him. He looked at Commander Berhan and then at the bodies of the three goons on the ground.

"That is the Headman," Tafari whispered to Robel.

Robel stepped down from the cart. He did not want to be seen. He could not afford to be, for the feared and dreaded Headman was none other than Iskander, the nephew of Lord Groda, the cowardly and pitifully stupid man who had ordered the killing of his fellow scouts and then left him to be tortured to death by the Shewa sultan's men. He still had that annoying permanent smirk on his face. The man next to him was, of course, Mengesha, his companion and bodyguard, who had personally killed some of the scouts with his own hands. Some of the surrounding horsemen were veterans of their campaign to hunt down the sultan's men, and had played a part in the killing of the scouts.

"How did this happen?" Iskander screamed at Commander Berhan. "How did three of my men end up dead?"

"We are still looking into it, my lord," Commander Berhan replied nervously. "We will find the people who did this and we will bring them to you."

"I hope you do, Commander," Iskander warned, loud enough for everyone to hear, "or there will be the devil's behind to pay!"

"My lord," Lady Mariam addressed Iskander, a mixture of defiance and some fear in her voice, "no one from this town did this to your men. It has to be a stranger. But please, this town suffers enough because of your men. Put a leash on them and things like this may not happen again."

Iskander stared at Lady Mariam for a few seconds, anger and disgust in his eyes because the woman had the nerve to address him.

"You," he warned sternly, pointing a finger at her threateningly. "They say you've been talking too much."

"My lord," Lady Mariam responded, "I only want the people in this town to live in peace. Your men do not allow that to happen. With your help, people in Roha might once again feel safe in their homes and on the streets."

Enraged, Iskander placed his hand on his sword and started riding threateningly towards her.

Commander Berhan quickly spoke up.

"My lord," he pleaded. "Please forgive her. She has not learned how to behave herself. There is no man in her house to teach her the ways of the world. I will see to it that she learns to behave herself."

"You better," Iskander said. "Otherwise, she will meet with an accident one of these days and just disappear."

"I will continue to work with her on her manners, my lord," Commander Berhan said, relieved to have averted a potentially dangerous situation.

Iskander then turned to address Lady Mariam.

"The protection you enjoy from the king may not last much longer," he warned. "Sooner or later there will be a new king. And then we will come looking for you. I would be very careful around here if I were you, Lady Mariam."

"Please don't speak back," Tafari muttered to himself, expressing his wish for Lady Mariam to just remain silent, lest she risk further enraging the Headman, which could lead to serious bodily harm to her.

Lady Mariam said nothing back, partly out of fear and out of disgust for the fiery little man. She just stared at him. Iskander then turned his eyes away from her and back to Commander Berhan, then pointed at the bodies of the men lying on the ground.

"Find the people who did this to my men," he warned.

"It will be done, my lord," Commander Berhan promised. "I give you my word."

Iskander then turned his horse to ride away.

"Let's go," Mengesha instructed the horsemen surrounding the crowd, and they all galloped away, allowing the terrified crowd to breathe a sigh of relief. The last time the Headman and his men showed up like this, some months earlier, after someone from a market had thrown a rock towards a convoy of his men, a few heads were left, pinned to stakes as a painful reminder of who was in charge.

Commander Berhan and Lady Mariam immediately turned to face each other. Before Commander Berhan could say anything, Lady Mariam beat him to it.

"You are a coward," she scolded him.

"I saved your life," he shot back.

"I don't need you to save me," she responded. "You should first save yourself."

"The Headman was right," Commander Berhan responded. "You do need someone to teach you manners."

"Certainly not by the likes of you," she fired right back, then turned around and walked away, followed by Jembere and her two female servants.

As Robel watched them walk away, he could not understand for the life of him how Iskander, the same loudmouthed idiot and mosquito who could not fight to save his life, who avoided combat like the plague, and who was about as smart as a coconut, had come to be so feared and perhaps even respected to a degree. How could the Rohan Riders, the most famous horsemen in the realm, stoop so low and be cowed by that obnoxious little worm? And that permanent annoying smirk on his face was still there! Something about him always reminded Robel of an insect.

CHAPTER 16

"Lord Groda will see you now," a soldier informed Iskander and Mengesha, who stood in a courtyard of a huge compound within Lord Groda's fortress in Shire.

That soldier was none other than Daga. He was one of Lord Groda's Commanders and had led a small detachment of men when Lord Groda's forces destroyed the Muslim soldiers who had conducted the massacre at Bodera village. It was his men who attacked them from the south end of the valley. He had also been present when Robel was abandoned to the mercy of the Shewa sultan. Like many of the soldiers that day, he too continued to serve Lord Groda. He had once been a priest, although of questionable benevolence.

Iskander and Mengesha followed Daga into the building, where none other than Lord Groda and Tiki, Robel's former wife, were seated at an intricately-patterned table being served lunch by several servants. A large fresco of Saint Claudius spearing a sebetat—the half-man, half-lion monster with two snakes for a tale and believed to eat people alive—graced the wall behind Lord Groda. Iskander immediately sat down at the table too, grabbed a wooden plate from one of the servants, and began helping himself to some lamb chops. Mengesha followed suit and was about to reach for a plate when Iskander stopped him.

"Who said you could sit?" Iskander hissed.

Mengesha stood up, stepped back, and turned his head away.

"Apologies, my lord," Mengesha said, chastised.

Iskander stared at him for a few seconds, then broke into a broad smile.

"Ha ha ha, Mengesha," Iskander laughed. "I am just joking with you.

Sit down. Help yourself. Learn to take a joke, man."

Mengesha hesitated for a moment, then grabbed a plate and threw himself on a seat across from Iskander.

Lord Groda and Tiki looked at each other, then Lord Groda shook his head, unsure of what to make of his young nephew's childishness.

"So, tell me, Nephew," Lord Groda addressed Iskander. "What's all the trouble in Roha I hear about?"

"Someone killed three of our men," he said, biting into a juicy, roasted lamb thigh. "All we know is that it is someone who wore red."

"You wanted to have Roha," Lord Groda said. "I gave it to you. Now at the first signs of trouble you come crawling to me."

"I just thought you should know," Iskander said. "But we have it under control. Berhan is on our side, and he will deal with it or there will be trouble for him and the town."

"What about Lady Mariam?" Tiki asked. "Why does she still keep her lands? The last time we discussed this, you promised you would have run her out by now."

"She is stubborn," Iskander responded. "We have tried everything possible. She would not give her land deeds to us. Other than continuing to frighten and squeeze, there is not much more I can do. The king may yet return any day now, you know?"

"Or he may not," Tiki blurted.

"It won't be your head pinned on a stake if the king returns," Iskander sneered. "It will be mine! So perhaps you should leave Lady Mariam to me and I should leave the whoring to you."

"Enough, Iskander!" Lord Groda screamed at his nephew. "One more word from you about my wife, and I will have your teeth removed with a cowpoke."

Iskander smiled, put a hand on his chest, and slightly bowed towards a fuming Tiki.

"I apologize, my lady," he smiled. "You are my uncle's wife now. I should be mindful of that."

Tiki calmed down despite the sarcastic tone of Iskander's apology. But that was the most she was going to get out of him. She settled for that. The tension abated, Lord Groda returned to the matter at hand.

"We have to have Lady Mariam's lands, Iskander," Lord Groda insisted. "I have the deeds to the lands of many nobles of Roha and many other towns around here. The revenues they generate is how we pay our people, do you understand? We cannot have her be the only one who stands up to us. If you cannot bring her to submit, I will send someone who can."

"I want her to suffer like her father made my family suffer," Tiki blurted. "I want her to know what it means to lose everything."

"But to be fair," Iskander said with a slight smile, "your father was kind of a jackass."

Tiki's eyes bulged out of her head.

Lord Groda pounded his fist on the table and stood up, staring Iskander square in his eyes. "Careful, Iskander!" he lashed out. "I warned you already!"

All the servants stood terrified. Mengesha froze in place, holding a piece of chicken in midair that he was about to bite into, moving only his eyes between Lord Groda and Iskander to see what would happen next.

"My apologies once again, my lady," Iskander addressed Tiki with that same wry smile. "It appears your father was actually a decent and intelligent man, after all."

Tiki cooled down. Lord Groda breathed in deeply, calmed himself, and sat down. The servants breathed a sigh of relief. Mengesha took the bite out of his chicken and continued devouring his meal like nothing had happened.

"The protection Lady Mariam enjoys from the king won't last long if he doesn't return from the wars," Lord Groda stated. "And we cannot just simply seize her lands. But we can continue to make her life so miserable that she will eventually give it up to us."

"Or we can simply arrange for her to disappear or meet with an accident so no one will suspect us," Iskander suggested. "She was present when I addressed the town about the deaths of our men. I gave her a warning. I think she got the message."

"Really, Iskander?" Lord Groda said apprehensively, leaning forward to hear more clearly. "And what message exactly did you give her? I really want to know."

"Exactly what she deserves to know," Iskander said, shoving a piece of injera into his large mouth. "I told her to be careful or she'd meet with an accident."

Tiki shook her head and looked down in exasperation.

"So, Iskander," Lord Groda addressed his young nephew, sitting upright. "We may have to kill this woman without letting her suspect it or letting anyone think it is connected to us in any way, yet you warn her that we could kill her—in public, in front of hundreds of people?"

"Well—err, well—" Iskander stammered.

"If you weren't my dead sister's son," Lord Groda fumed, "I'd choke you myself with my bare hands right where you stand!"

It was a hot afternoon. Robel and Tafari had just finished reading Bible passages to a crowd of about 70 enthralled listeners in the southern end of the Wazir Quarter. It was their first time coming here. Earlier that day, as they had been doing during the previous three months, Robel and Tafari, along with 11 other monks selected for the genna team, had been training and practicing for the upcoming genna game. Abba Mikael had approved the practice sessions, even though he had not understood why they were necessary. If God wanted them to win, then they would win regardless of what they did. That was how he saw it. But whatever the case, if the monks who were going to be the ones playing wanted to practice, then they could. Whatever it took to finally beat the Debre Damo champions, it had to be done.

For training sessions, prior to their practice games with six players on each side, Robel and his genna players usually began with some long distance running and lifting of weights that consisted of logs and pails filled with dirt. This was to help build strength and endurance. It was part of the training Robel and his scouts had also received in the army. Now Robel and his players had to be equally as tough and as resilient.

Despite feeling sore from the morning's training sessions, Robel and

Tafari were still eager to complete their daily duties. They decided to split up in order to cover more ground and read the Bible to more interested parties. Robel went to a nearby market. He did not find much reception there, but he read from the Bible anyway, hoping to attract a crowd. No one came this time, as often happened. Instead, people crowded around the azmaris—minstrels sitting on street corners, delivering healthy doses of poetry, jokes, and the music they produced from their masenqos, their one-stringed fiddles. Many women also flocked to the multiple stalls that lined the streets, where stylists braided their hair into all sorts of styles imaginable while sharing the latest gossip.

Realizing he was getting nowhere, Robel decided to relocate to the dried fish area of the market, where Gambela tribesmen, with their scarification lines across their faces, had made the seven-day journey from their homes in the south to sell their dried and salted fish caught from the Baro River.

But here Robel saw someone who made him stop in his tracks and hide. Again, he could not afford to be recognized. But this time, it was a woman. She was a vendor, selling himbasha, the tasty round loaves of bread Robel had loved since he was boy. Each loaf was individually designed with intricate patterns on them called "the stamp of God." The woman was talking to a very tall man, definitely one of Iskander's men. She was Fetiya, Yohannis's widow.

Robel and his scouts had fought for a long time together, until their betrayal and murder. Branded traitors by Lord Groda upon his return from the wars, Robel had learned that he had seized the lands of the scouts, as well as the rewards they were due from the king's treasury for their services, depriving their surviving families of a lucrative source of income. There had been nothing Robel could do about it. The last time he had seen Fetiya was just before they had departed for the operation to root out the last of the Shewa sultan's men in the highlands, when they had assembled in Yohannis's village. Robel deduced that Fetiya must have moved to Roha with her children in order to eke out a sustainable living and make do as best as she could.

"I do not have a pouch of silver to give you every time you show up here!" Fetiya pleaded with the man she was talking to, who had a giant sword strapped to his side.

"You were about to close down for the day," the man said.

"I have three children at home," she pleaded. "I have to get to them."

"If you close down your shop later, then you can make more silver for both of us, no?" the man insisted. "Now give me what I ask or I will take everything."

Fetiya reluctantly gave the man the silver he demanded.

"May the devil go with you," the woman cursed him, looking up into his eyes.

"I am the devil, woman," the man said, laughing.

The man then grabbed a loaf of Fetiya's himbasha bread and took a bite out of it.

"Tastes good," the man said.

"That will be half a piece of silver," Fetiya said.

The man smiled, amazed that she had the courage and gumption to charge him for the bread. He reached into the pouch of silver Fetiya had given him, took out a small piece of silver and tossed it on the ground for her, then turned and walked away.

Fetiya put her arms on her waist and spat on the ground.

Robel had watched all this intensely. He secretly followed the man, then waited until the goon was beyond Fetiya's sight. Robel approached him, Bible in hand and cross in the other.

"Are you fine, friend?" Robel greeted the man. "I come to you with a message."

"What do you want, monk?" the man asked him dismissively. "Why don't you go bother some other fool. I am not the donating type."

"I do not seek a donation, friend," Robel said. "I only ask that you show compassion to a fellow person in need."

"Are you serious?" the man laughed giggled.

"I ask you in the name of God," Robel pleaded, then quoted from the Bible, "'Learn to do good; seek justice, correct oppression; bring justice to the fatherless, and please the widow's cause.'"

"The Book of Isaiah," the man said with a smile.

"You know the scriptures, friend," Robel said, rather impressed. "Then you do understand the error of your ways."

"Get out of my sight before I make you wish you hadn't met me," the man fired back and brushed past Robel, pushing him to the ground.

Robel slowly stood up and stared at the man as he walked away.

"That is a big sword you have there, friend," Robel said to the man, looking at the long, curved, heavy sword popular with people from the eastern regions of the kingdom. "It's about as long as you are tall."

The man stopped and turned around. He put his hand on the sword's hilt and smiled.

"I had it specially made in Mogadishu," the man said. "I have fought and killed 20 men with it. If you want, I can show you just how easily it can slice through the neck of a monk."

The man walked threateningly towards Robel, slowly drawing his sword.

"No, sir, please," Robel pleaded, stepping back. "I am but a poor monk who needs to learn his place."

The man stopped, took his hand off his sword, and smiled again.

"You are lucky I am in good spirits, monk," he said, rolling his fingers over the pouch of silver he had taken from Fetiya. "Next time I may not be in such a nice mood, and you may not be so lucky."

He walked away, his tall, lanky frame disappearing into the bustling street. Robel turned around and returned to the marketplace, this time far away from where Fetiya was, to seek listeners for his scripture reading. He found no willing audiences, but did get some donations of yams and cooking pots from some sympathetic vendors who wished to compensate him for his efforts. He soon returned to Tafari.

"How did it go?" Tafari asked Robel when he returned to their mule cart some hours later.

"Not much to show for my efforts," Robel responded with a shrug, although what he really wanted to say was, I think Roha will be safer after tonight.

CHAPTER 17

It was nighttime. The inn that was located not far from the small lake was popular with cutthroats, soldiers, disgraced priests, ex-merchants, ex-officials, ex-soldiers, and lots of other ex-somethings. Tej, the wine made from the sweetest highland honey, flowed cheaply and in abundance. Several loose women also mingled freely, working hard to earn their share of all the silver being passed around by the many shady characters having themselves a grand time in the rowdy establishment. Half of the men were dead drunk, with the other half determined to catch up. What they were not spending on tej or women, they were gambling away over games of mancala. A lone azmari provided some laughter and some poetry and music, using his krar—a six-stringed lyre—to great effect, captivating those who were sober enough to pay any attention to him. Like all azmaris, he was an expert in wax and gold poetry, where the "wax" was the obvious meaning of what he was saying, and the "gold" was the hidden meaning and always delivered with a touch of humor.

At a corner, oblivious to all the rambunctiousness all around him, was one man who seemed to have his wits about him. He had not had a single sip of tej this night. He was engaged in a serious game of mancala with some other characters who also seemed to mean business, but may have had perhaps one too many cups of tej. He was a tall and lanky man with a big sword strapped to his waist. It was the same man who had forced Fetiya to hand him a pouch of silver. He was in good spirits. After all, he had already won several games against his opponents, not quite making many friends among them. He rubbed the mancala beads made out of finely polished cow bones before placing each into the pits on the intricately carved board. Before long, all his beads were in the mancala pits—once again. He had just registered another win, proving himself to be a better strategist than his opponents. He was on a winning streak. The one small bag of silver he had brought to the gambling table had multiplied to four bags. He was pleased. Three of his opponents were not.

"You cheated," one of them accused him.

"Yes," the other two agreed. "No one wins that many times."

"I won fairly," the tall man insisted calmly.

At this point, sensing trouble brewing, everyone around the four quickly moved away to a safer distance as silence settled across the room. Everyone else had stopped whatever they had been doing to see what was about to happen. Even the azmari was frozen in place, his gazed fixed on the four men.

"No one has that much luck in one night," one of the opponents accused the man. "Seven wins in a row? How can you explain that? No man can win at the rate even if he could cure blindness while walking on water."

"You have all been drinking," the tall man said. "I haven't. I can think more clearly than you, so I win more games than you."

"I say you cheat!" one of the opponents shouted.

"Perhaps," the tall men responded. "But the witness of a rat is another rat."

"We want our silver back!" one of the opponents demanded.

The tall man breathed in resignedly. No need to argue with this lot, he thought. But as he expected, all three of his opponents suddenly pulled out their swords from their sheaths and charged towards him with predictable ferocity. In a flash, the man's large sword sprang out from his sheath, parrying the blows sent his way. But he did not stop there. Almost in the same instant, he lunged for the three attackers, unleashing a torrent of thrusts and jabs so quick and vicious in their speed that for a moment he seemed to have four hands and four swords. One of the opponents screamed in terror. His sword was on the ground, along with half his hand. The tall man stood still, silent and calm, directing a piercing glare on his remaining two combat-effective opponents.

"Tej is sweet to the tongue," the azmari suddenly resumed chanting, spinning a note from his krar, delivering the "wax" to his poetry, then finished with the "gold." "But courage for those filled with tej is but empty."

The tall man eyed the azmari and smiled.

His remaining two former gambling opponents did not smile. They were furious. They lunged again at him, their blind and empty courage fueled by tej at full display. This time, they wound up on the floor, gagging and struggling to breathe with their throats sliced. The tall man keenly watched in silence for a few seconds as the two on the ground stopped struggling and died. The man who had lost his hand was still alive, cowering in a corner and whimpering like a scared animal, knowing what was to come.

The tall man then walked over to him and lifted his large sword over the head of the poor half-handed creature.

"Please," the half-handed man begged. He reached into his robe, pulled out a small pouch of silver with his remaining hand, and tossed it on the floor. "Take it. It's yours. You won fair and square. I see that now."

"I know," the tall man said calmly. Then he brought down his sword with a crisp swoosh, slashing his opponent's chest. He reached down and picked up the small pouch of silver as the body collapsed next to him. He returned to the gambling table and collected all his winnings, which no one had dared to touch. He walked to the bodies of the first two men he had killed, searched their robes, and collected their pouches of silver for himself.

"For my troubles," he announced.

He reached into one of the pouches, obtained a small piece of silver, and tossed it towards the azmari, who caught it and smiled.

The tall man exited the inn and disappeared into the darkness.

He carefully followed the path along the small lake that had always led him to his home. He soon noticed a figure before him. It was a person dressed in red. The tall man did not mind. No one who knew him would dare to stand in his path. But as he moved closer, he noticed the person before him did not step out of his way as he had expected.

"Step aside before you get hurt, whoever you are," the tall man warned.

The person in red still did not get out of his way. He stepped forward instead, closer to the tall man. He was startled, but he relaxed when he recognized the person in red.

"It's you, monk," the man jeered. "What do you want this time?"

"Deuteronomy chapter 27, verse 19," Robel said, placing a hand on the cross dangling from his neck.

"'Cursed be he who perverts the judgement of a stranger, orphan or widow,'" the man quoted the Bible phrase. "You came here to give me Bible lessons, monk?"

"I came here to cut you down to size," Robel said calmly.

"Eh, what?" the man smirked.

"I gave you a chance today to change your ways," Robel said. "You turned me down. Now I have come to make sure you no longer take from the defenseless."

"Ha ha ha," the man laughed stepping forward, his hand on his sword. "You run your tongue rather loosely, monk. I warned you that if I ever saw you again, you might not be as lucky. Looks like I am going to have to make good on that promise. You see, I never break my word."

But the man stopped when Robel suddenly reached under his robe, threw back the loose flapping, and exposed the sword and dagger in the sheaths dangling from his waist. He slowly pulled out the sword.

The man chuckled. "That is a small sword you have there," he said.

"Perhaps," Robel said. "But it's sharp enough to slice open a rat like yourself."

"Okay," the man hissed. "You look like someone who wants to go down in a hurry. I will help you with that."

The man unsheathed his large sword and lunged at Robel. Facing a direct frontal assault, Robel simply and effortlessly pivoted left, escaping the man's straight thrust. Then, just as effortlessly, he very quickly and rapidly fired off a few quick thrusts of his own at the man. Surprised, the man stopped, stepped back, and touched his arm. He was bleeding.

"What kind of a monk are you?" the man asked Robel, taken by complete surprise. There was some panic in his voice.

"You should have left the woman alone," Robel said.

"Ah, Fetiya," the man chuckled. "So this is about her. Well, now because of you, starting tomorrow she will have to pay me double what she already does. She will—"

Robel suddenly lunged at the man, giving him no time to complete his sentence.

The man raised his large sword to defend himself but stood no chance. Within a moment, he was on the ground, his stomach sliced open and bleeding. He closed his eyes shortly after.

Robel reached into the man's robes and searched through them. He collected all the pouches of silver the man had with him. He then pulled his body next to the lake, placed some rocks inside the man's robes, and rolled him and his sword into the lake. He watched his body sink to the bottom.

Robel smiled. The entire encounter had seemed quite effortless. All the training with his fellow monks for the genna game had paid off. He was nowhere near as fatigued as he had been when he had fought Yifter and his two goons. Now he was as fit as he had been prior to becoming a monk.

The following morning, Fetiya was talking to her oldest son, a 15-year-old with a rather small head.

"Did you see anyone enter the house during the night?" she asked her son.

"No, Mama," the boy replied. "Is everything okay?"

"Yes—yes," Fetiya stammered. "Everything is fine."

She then smiled, looking back into her room at the pouches of silver, including the one she had been forced to give to the tall man the day before. Someone had had left the pouches next to her bed during the night as she slept.

"There was no one here, Mama," her son repeated.

Then her daughter, 13 years old, having just woken up, walked in holding her brother. He was about four years old.

"Mama," the girl said, yawning, "Haile could not sleep last night. He said he saw a ghost in the house."

"A ghost?" Fetiya asked, stroking Haile's head.

"Yes," the girl said. "A red ghost."

CHAPTER 18

Robel was admiring the ornately crafted hand cross he was holding. With round edges like many in the realm, this one was shaped like an ostrich egg, a very significant symbol in the Tewahedo Church, representing the Holy Spirit. It had this shape because just like the ostrich never left its nest of eggs unattended and always cared for them, the Holy Spirit was always present and always cared for people.

"She's here," Jembere said as he walked into the chapel in Lady Mariam's home, where Robel and Tafari were preparing the room for the next day's service.

"Who is here?" Robel asked.

The answer to that question hit him like a thunderbolt.

"Tiki Tewolde," Jembere said. "Lord Groda's wife."

Robel almost dropped the cross he was holding.

"What is the matter?" Tafari asked Robel. "You seem—"

"My hands are just sweaty," Robel answered. "Nothing to worry about."

"Be careful," Tafari warned. "That cross is older than half the monks in St. Verena put together."

"Are you coming?" Jembere asked the monks.

"What does this woman want with Lady Mariam?" Robel asked.

"Same thing the Headman wants." Jembere said. "This land and all it has."

"And she comes here herself to ask for it?" Robel asked. It did not make sense.

"For lady Tiki, this is a personal matter," Jembere said. "Her family and Lady Mariam's have a history. Not a friendly one at all. Tiki's first husband was Lord Kiros. Ever heard of him?"

Robel froze. Of course, he had heard of himself. But he shook his head.

"No," he simply said.

"Lord Kiros of Shire," Tafari added. "He was a lesser lord from Shire, the town you were travelling through when we first met."

"Hmm," Robel mumbled.

"Anyway," Jembere continued, "the rumor is that he betrayed the kingdom and joined the Muslims while fighting with Lord Groda's army against them. They say he is dead; but there are rumors that he is still alive, fighting with the Muslims somewhere. It is quite unclear. But if he is alive and he ever shows himself in Shire or Ethiopia again, his head will be put on display for all of Shire to see, separated from his shoulders of course."

"And what has Lady Mariam to do with all this?" Robel asked, rubbing his hand around his neck.

"So after Lord Kiros was killed or escaped—whatever the case may be," Jembere continued, "his wife, Tiki, married Lord Groda. That gave her a lot of power. She now uses it to hunt her enemies to the grave. Lady Mariam is the last of her enemies, and she will stop at nothing to destroy her. They have some bad family history, those two."

Robel—or Lord Kiros—and Tiki had been married for five years, and it was possible she had told him of Lady Mariam before. But he did not remember. That was because her list of perceived enemies she ranted and raved about regularly, blaming them for her misfortunes, was long.

"What makes Lady Mariam her enemy?" he asked Jembere.

"We can discuss this another time," Jembere said. "Are you two coming or what? Lord Groda's wife will be here any moment now. And they say that snake, Commander Berhan, is with her."

"You go ahead, Tafari," Robel said. He could not risk being identified by his former wife. "I will finish up here."

"Watch the sweaty hands," Tafari mocked as he and Jembere walked out of the chapel. "We don't want to have to explain to Abba Mikael how we damaged a centuries-old relic."

Shortly after Jembere and Tafari left the chapel, Robel immediately went to the window, from where he could see the courtyard. He saw a small entourage consisting of ten armed men, horsemen, and several servants escorting a covered cart pulled by two horses march into the yard. Commander Berhan and three Rohan Riders, including his second-in-command, Tewodros, were also part of her escort. Lady Mariam, Jembere, Tafari, and several of her servants were standing in line, as if welcoming an important member of the royal family they disliked but were being forced to do so. Yes, they disliked Tiki intensely, but from past experience they knew better than to treat her any less reverently. She had once ordered one of Lady Mariam's servants whipped by her guards simply because the servant had walked by her without expressing a greeting during one of her previous visits.

Robel watched as Tiki stepped out of the cart, her servants cowering before her as they placed a stool for her to step on. She took a look around and liked what she saw—the adulation, what she had always wanted.

Tiki looked at Lady Mariam and spat on the ground. Lady Mariam threw an accusatory glance at Commander Berhan, who caught the look but promptly looked away. With an air of entitlement perhaps worthy only of the Queen of Sheba herself, Tiki strolled into Lady Mariam's home without an invitation, a deliberate move to demonstrate that she really had the upper hand in their current situation.

"Wait here," Commander Berhan instructed Tewodros and his soldiers. Then, like any good servant, he followed Tiki into the home, ready to assist in whatever capacity he was needed. She was the wife of his benefactor, and he had to grovel before her. Tewodros nodded, resisting the urge to run Tiki through with his sword. But that would have brought down the wrath of Lord Groda and his many goons on the less than 30 members of the Rohan Horse Guard left in Roha.

Lady Mariam sighed, shook her head, then followed Tiki and Commander Berhan into her home as well.

"What's with Lady Tiki?" one of Commander Berhan's newest soldiers asked Tewodros.

"She's a bitter woman," Tewodros responded. "She used to be married to the traitor, Lord Kiros."

"I see. I'd be bitter too." After a pause, the soldier asked, "And what's with Commander Berhan? Why do we get assigned to escort someone on a private matter?"

"You are new around here," Tewodros replied. "You will soon learn who really runs things in Roha."

"It is bad enough that we good Christian soldiers have to be put under a Jewish commander, but—"

"Commander Berhan is our leader," Tewodros snapped at the soldier in a raging whisper. "The king left him in charge of us. The king trusts him because his family has served the king's family for four generations. Like it or not, we will follow his orders. Do you understand?"

"Yes, Commander," the soldier responded, humbled.

"Now keep your eyes open," Tewodros stated calmly. "There is a mysterious man in red killing the Headman's men."

Still in the chapel, Robel had its door closed, but stood with his ear close to it. He wanted to hear everything that was being said. He needed to know what his former wife was up to. What an unpleasantly bitter coincidence that he had fled Shire only to wind up in the same home with her, many days' ride from Shire.

"You do not try to send me away like you tried to do last time?" Tiki teased Lady Mariam. "Am I to believe you've had a sudden change of heart about me?"

"Genna will soon be upon us, my lady," Mariam responded. "This is a time when we welcome strangers, friends, and even enemies alike into our homes."

Tiki smiled.

"My family lost everything because of your father," Tiki said. "It feels good to see his daughter grovel at my feet, begging me not to lose everything."

"I will never beg you, my lady," Lady Mariam said softly. "What do you want?"

"My lady?" Tiki teased. "My family called your mother that for years. If only your mother were here to see her precious little daughter quaking before me now. I could end you with a snap of my fingers, you know."

"What is the purpose of your visit?" Lady Mariam asked again, maintaining her calm.

In a sudden fit of rage, Tiki violently seized Lady Mariam by the hair, pulling it and holding her head back so hard that Lady Mariam bent backwards. Lady Mariam grimaced in pain with a moan. A concerned Commander Berhan immediately tried to step forward to calm the situation.

"Stay where you are," Tiki instructed him, not even looking at him, but keeping her eyes fixed on Lady Mariam's face.

Commander Berhan reluctantly but dutifully stood back as instructed, with his hands before him. Robel heard the commotion and Lady Mariam's moaning. He fought himself, resisting the urge to interfere.

"You want to know what I want?" Tiki scolded her. "Leave this land. Give me the deed and go snivel somewhere else. I can get more out of this land in one year than you will in a lifetime!"

Tiki then released Lady Mariam, who stepped back, unfazed.

"I cannot do that, my lady," Lady Mariam responded, panting. "This land belongs to my family and the families of all those people out there working on it."

"And before long it will belong to me," Tiki insisted. "You will suffer for how your father betrayed mine. I was there when they beheaded my father. I watched it all. We lost everything!"

"Your father was an evil, conniving man who cared only for himself," an irritated Lady Mariam fired back. "He tried to kill the governor of Tigray and thousands of people just to satisfy his greed. My father did the right thing by reporting him to the king, and I would have done the same thing if I were him."

"What did you say about my father?" an infuriated Tiki snarled.

"He was a greedy and selfish man, my lady," Lady Mariam repeated softly but decisively, "and as sure as Satan breathes, your father would not be disappointed in you."

Tiki raised her hand to strike Lady Mariam. Lady Mariam did not flinch or try to defend herself. Instead, she stepped forward, her head inches from Tiki, and looked her directly in the eyes, daring her to strike, in a stoic display of defiance. Tiki suddenly stopped with her hand in mid-air. She cooled down, dropped her hand, and smiled. Commander Berhan breathed in deeply, relieved.

"You have a lot to learn about the world, Mariam," Tiki said. "You only have one life to live, yet you concern yourself too much with these thieving little peasants and their problems. That is why you will never be richer than you are now."

"Riches do not make people happy, Tiki," Lady Mariam said.

"It doesn't make people sad either, does it?" Tiki shot back.

"My lady," Commander Berhan notified her, "we have to leave now, before it gets dark."

"Enjoy the king's protection while it lasts, Lady Mariam," Tiki said. "And pray he returns from the wars alive. If he does not, well, we will be seeing a lot of more each other."

Lady Mariam turned to leave, then noticed the cross on the door of the home chapel, where Robel was hiding and listening.

"Look," Tiki said with a smile. "You even have your very own chapel. Perhaps it is your intention to someday pray me to my grave."

Tiki walked to the chapel door and pushed it open, revealing a monk inside—Robel, with his yellow turban wrapped over his head and covering most of his face, a practice that was not uncommon when one was engaged in prayer or shielding themselves from the biting cold of the highlands that sometimes set in at dusk.

"And you even have your own priest," she mocked, looking down at the unidentified monk. "Aren't you doing well for yourself?" Then she addressed Robel directly in a condescendingly sardonic tone. "Go ahead, priest, monk, whatever you are. Preach me a sermon. Your Lady Mariam thinks I've done evil things. Please, cleanse my soul of all the evil."

Robel stood in place. He had his hands before him reverently and was staring at the floor, slightly bent forward as if physically cowering in fear of Tiki. Tiki enjoyed eliciting that sort of behavior in people. But Robel was simply hiding his face from his former wife.

"Look at me when I talk to you, monk!" Tiki then ordered, very serious now.

She was about to step closer to Robel when Commander Berhan spoke.

"My lady, we really have to go," he insisted. "One of your husband's men disappeared three nights ago, and we think the man in red is responsible. Until we find him, it is not safe for you to travel around these parts after dark."

Tiki stopped.

"Okay, monk," she said to Robel. "You owe me a sermon."

She stepped back, and along with Lady Mariam and Commander Berhan, began to walk towards the exit as Robel closed the chapel door behind them.

When they got to the exit door, she stopped.

"Give me what I want, and I may leave you alone," she said to Lady Mariam. "I will soon be sending you a reminder of just how perilous I can make things for you."

Then Tiki, Commander Berhan, and the rest of her escort began walking towards her waiting covered cart, leaving Lady Mariam at the door of her home. But then Tiki stopped. She turned around and looked back at Lady Mariam's house, a look of wonder and puzzlement in her eyes.

"Who was that monk in the chapel?" she asked Commander Berhan. There was something about him, perhaps something familiar. She could not quite put a finger on it, but there definitely was something uncomfortably familiar about the monk.

"Robel, my lady," Commander Berhan responded. "Just a peasant from somewhere west."

"Of course, you would know," Tiki said. "Are you still hoping to make Lady Mariam your wife and making it your business to know all about her affairs and associates? Then find a way to make her sign her land to us. Then maybe she'll have no choice but to turn to you for her survival."

"She is stubborn, my lady," Commander Berhan said.

"No, you are just a weak man," Tiki fired back.

She stepped into her horse-drawn cart, and she and her entourage marched off into the dusk.

Barely two days later, Tiki made good on her promise, with the appearance of more unwanted visitors to Lady Mariam's compound. They were the same men, then led by Mekonnen, who had shown up just days before and collected tribute from Lady Mariam. They had promised to be back, but Lady Mariam had not expected them back so quickly. Tiki and the Headman were tightening the pressure on her. Although Mekonnen was with them, they now had a new leader at the helm.

Robel was about to step out when he realized that he recognized the new leader of the group. He fumed as memories of Yohannis and his scouts came flooding back to him. He clenched his fists tightly as he remembered this man and his men plunging their daggers into his friends.

"Someday, Gebre," he muttered to himself. "Someday."

Gebre was the commander in Lord Groda's army who had been nicknamed Raw Meat.

Robel decided to stay in the chapel and watch from the window.

Gebre, Mekonnen, and their men did not dismount from their horses. The last time Mekonnen and his men had showed up to collect their tribute, they had had to wait for the produce to be brought to them. This time, Jembere and the servants were prepared. They already had a cart full of produce waiting. Lady Mariam had remained inside her home. She just wanted the goons to take the produce and leave.

The goons halted in front of the cart. Mekonnen glanced towards it.

"You have done well," he said to Jembere. "We did not have to wait."

"It is as you wish," Jembere said.

Mekonnen turned to Gebre, who trotted forward.

"Lady Mariam?" Gebre called. "I know you are in there. Come on out."

A moment later, Lady Mariam stepped out and stood before the goons. Gebre stared at her for a moment, taken by her dazzling beauty.

"I am Gebre," he announced.

"And that is a goat over there," Lady Mariam scoffed, leaning her head towards a goat roaming the yard. "So what?"

Gebre smiled. He was not surprised. He had heard of her stubbornness.

"You are a mouthy little one," he said, then looked at the produce in the cart. "I have come for my tribute."

"Sir," Jembere said, pointing at the cart, "it's right here, like we always have it, waiting for you."

"That is for the Headman, like you always provide," Gebre said. "I am now the leader of these men. Where is my share? What do I get for having to put up with you?"

"But we cannot afford to give you any more," Jembere pleaded. "The harvest is bad this year. There are families here that need feeding, too."

Gebre rode to the cart and kicked it over, spilling out all the produce.

"We will come back when you have double the amount," he said. "From now on, you pay the Headman's tribute and my tribute. And this time we come every week, not once a month. Every week!"

"But we cannot—" Jembere began.

"We will return in three days," Gebre warned. "If you do not have double the amount, we will take your entire harvest."

"This is not right," Jembere protested, getting down on his knees. "This is—"

"Get up!" Lady Mariam ordered Jembere. "We do not beg these devils!"

"Three days," Gebre repeated, then he and his goons began to trot away, first making sure their horses trampled over the produce from the overturned cart.

Tafari ran in front of the horses to try to stop them.

"In the name of Saint George and our Lord," he pleaded with them, holding his Bible before him. "Please, we—"

"Saint George has been dead for a thousand years, monk," Gebre said. "He won't help you.

Then from his horse, Gebre reached out with his foot and landed a skull-crashing kick straight at Tafari's head, sending the monk over to the ground, roiling in pain.

"You should not have done that, Gebre," Robel muttered to himself as he saw his friend hit the ground hard.

But the monk quickly stood up defiantly as Lady Mariam and Jembere ran to his side.

"I am okay, I think," Tafari said, robbing his forehead.

The goons disappeared into the surrounding hills, their exercise of intimidation for the day completed.

"What are we to do now?" Jembere cried.

Lady Mariam held his hand compassionately.

"We will continue to survive this, one way or another," she said.

She knew Tiki had set those men upon her, likely with the tacit encouragement of Commander Berhan. They wanted to ruin her, each for a separate reason.

CHAPTER 19

"Your hard work has helped to build this," Abba Mikael said to Robel and Tafari as they stared at another completed underground church. Painters were completing a huge mural on the side of the church depicting the Nine Saints, with the large, staring eyes typical of Ethiopian paintings that seemed to follow every move of admirers. "Before the king returns, there will be at least ten completed churches."

"We do our best, Abba," Robel said.

The grants from the king and donations raised from the faithful by Roha's churches and monks had come a long way.

"We have to go, Abba," Tafari said, "if we want to keep bringing in those donations."

Abba Mikael smiled.

Robel and Tafari hopped on their cart, with Robel driving.

"Help for the poor?" Tafari called out, followed by the ringing of the bell three times. "Help for the poor?"

When they arrived at the city center, they stopped, having already collected small amounts of silver, produce, and even a few gold crosses along the way. It was time for them to split up so they could cover more ground.

"I will see you in a few hours," Tafari said.

"Stay out of trouble, my friend," Robel said with an affectionate smile, his eyes drawn towards the small bruise left on his friend's head that resulted from Gebre's kick three days before.

True to his promise, Gebre and four of his goons were returning to collect their now vastly increased tribute from Lady Mariam. They had no doubt she had somehow found a way to put together the tribute, for she was a survivor and extremely resourceful. But they knew she could not sustain the amount they had demanded every single week. They were close to breaking her.

"If this works," Mekonnen said to Gebre as they rode past a group of pilgrims riding into Roha for the upcoming Genna celebrations, "Lord Groda may let you keep the farm."

"Do not get ahead of yourself, Mekonnen," Gebre warned. "Let's take things one step at a time. Lord Groda brought me all the way from Gojjam to handle this situation for a reason. He is not just going to give away the prize. I have known the man for a long time."

"Ho ho ho ho!" Mekonnen then called out to his horse, screeching to a halt along with the other men he was riding with.

There was a monk standing in front of them with his arms folded, looking at the ground, with part of his robe draped over his head and concealing his face.

"What the devil is this?" Gebre asked, looking at the monk.

Mekonnen and the others stood silently for a moment, a hint of fear and bewilderment gripping them.

"The man in red," Mekonnen muttered, a slight tremble in his voice.

Gebre laughed loudly and dismissively.

"So this is the man who you all fear," he jeered. "A monk? The one who has been killing your men? Are you serious?"

Then Robel raised his head and pulled back the draping from over his head, letting it fall over his back, and revealing his face. Gebre's horse jolted as he gasped in stunned disbelief, instantly recognizing the man before him.

"Satan's teeth!" he cursed.

"You know him?" Mekonnen asked.

"That is Lord Kiros!" Gebre said softly.

"Are you serious?" Mekonnen sputtered.

They had all heard of Lord Kiros before. Other than that he had betrayed Ethiopia and was dead or a fugitive, they also knew that he was one of the greatest swordsmen in the realm. And even more terrifying, they knew he had survived the bite of a black mamba many years before. A man like that feared nothing and was more dangerous than a hungry lion on the prowl.

"Do you want to die on your horses, or do you want to die fighting on the ground?" Robel asked the men calmly. "Either way suits me."

In a desperate attempt to increase his chances of survival in the impending fight, Mekonnen suddenly exploded forward with maximum speed towards Robel, with his sword raised high and ready to chop down the monk in one fell swoop. But with the speed of a striking viper, Robel reached underneath his robes and yanked out his sword from its sheath as he ducked backwards, narrowly avoiding the swipe from Mekonnen's sword as the rider bolted past him. As Robel stood back up, he used the hilt of his sword to strike at Mekonnen's horse, which whinnied and tumbled over with its rider about ten paces away. Before Mekonnen could fully get back on his feet to redress his failed attempt at killing Robel in a single daring and surprise attack, Robel was already sprinting for him. Intent on keeping the pressure on Robel, two of Mekonnen's men charged with their horses towards the monk. Robel, who had just reached Mekonnen, used his sword to knock the goon's sword from his hand, sending it flying high into the air above them. Without a moment to waste, Robel then sent his sword flying through the air towards one of the charging horsemen, which he immediately followed up by reaching into his robes, pulling out his dagger, and also sending it flying through the air towards the other charging rider. This action was so swift that both weapons seemed to reach the charging riders at the same time, with each one letting out piercing cries as they tumbled from their horses to their deaths.

Not letting up for even a second, Robel immediately returned his focus to Mekonnen, who at this time had retrieved his own dagger and was about to strike at Robel. But without even looking upwards, Robel raised his hand and snatched Mekonnen's sword from midair on its descend. He brought it down and thrust it forward, plunging it straight through Mekonnen's open mouth, with the tip protruding through the back of the goon's head. Mekonnen's body immediately went limp as the dagger in his hand dropped. His lifeless body slumped, supported only by the sword in Robel's hand. It was a short, straight, but very sturdy sword, similar to the ones Robel had seen in church paintings depicting the Massacre of the Innocents, the event when King Herod's soldiers killed thousands of babies in their vain attempt to kill a baby Jesus.

Robel stood there for just a short moment, looking at Mekonnen's body dangling from the sword. He wanted Gebre and the remaining goon to realize just how imperiled they were. He slowly turned and looked at them. He enjoyed seeing the terror in their eyes. Gebre's remaining accomplice, sweat dripping down his face, made a motion to turn his horse around and flee.

"Stay where you are!" Gebre warned, knowing that running away was useless. He knew there was nowhere for them to run to and be safe from Robel. Robel was the best scout and tracker he knew, and like a hunting dog, he could follow the scent of a hunted animal. He could track them down anywhere, no matter where they went. Their best chance of survival was to stand and fight, and hope to get lucky.

"For what it's worth, I never supported what Lord Groda did to you and your men," a frightened Gebre said in a pitiful attempt to save his miserable life.

He waited for a response, but none came. Robel simply stared at him.

"It was his idea the whole time," Gebre continued. "He first brought it up in Wukro. I asked him not to do it, but he threatened me."

Still there was no immediate response from Robel. The other rider was confused, unsure of what to do next.

Then Robel spoke. "You should not have hit my friend," he said softly.

"Your friend?" Gebre asked, at first unsure of who he was referring to, before it came back to him. "Oh, the young monk. Of course, I did not know he was a friend of yours."

Robel kicked Mekonnen's body from the sword and turned to face Gebre and his remaining goon directly. Gebre and his companion slowly dismounted from their horses, not wanting to meet the same fate as their accomplices who had been killed charging from horseback. Robel gave them a moment to unsheathe their swords.

"Is there anything I can say?" Gebre asked.

Robel slowly shook his head.

Then both goons charged at Robel with murderous intensity. They struck and he struck, and the clash of swords was loud. The clash had been Gebre's and Robel's. The other goon's sword had not even met Robel's. It had simply harmlessly swiped through the air as Robel had anticipated his move and ducked, avoiding it, while thrusting his own sword towards the man and then bringing it back towards his chest to stop Gebre's blow as he rose back up. He and Gebre then stepped apart in order to assess their next moves.

His gaze steady on Gebre, Robel did not even bother to look towards the other goon. Robel knew exactly what was coming next for him. Gebre, on the other hand, turned to look at him when he heard the man suddenly moan, drop his sword, and hold his chest. He was bleeding from a neat puncture wound that left a thin trail of blood over his white cotton vest. Gebre was shocked, but not surprised. He and Robel had been in many battles together on the same side, and he knew what the former scout leader was capable of.

The mortally wounded goon dropped. Keeping his eyes fixed on Gebre, Robel walked to the body of the goon from which his own sword was still sticking out. He dropped the sword he was holding, which had belonged to Mekonnen, and retrieved his sword.

"The sword of the last king?" Gebre asked.

Robel nodded.

"Forged in the fires of the black mountain," Gebre added,

Robel nodded again. Few weapons had had the distinction of being forged in the ever-present lava lake atop Erta Ale, a desert mountain east of the kingdom. Weapons forged in the flames from the lake of fire were believed to have added durability and fetched a high price on the market.

For this fight, Robel had to use a sword he was comfortable wielding, for he knew that Gebre was a fairly good swordsman in his own right. Robel had even respected him once, and it was unfortunate that greed had made them deadly enemies. But all the same, perhaps it was time that Gebre faced the punishment many thought he deserved. He was rumored to have once opened up his home to visiting pilgrims during the feast of Saint Mary several years before, only to have them killed with poisoned mushrooms and robbed of their belongings, a deed for which he had barely escaped execution due to lack of sufficient evidence.

Both men then charged at each other again, their swords clashing and clanging, blocking and skillfully avoiding each other's blows. Then they stood back, took a breather, and resumed. Gebre soon felt a sudden small but penetrating pain in his shoulder. He took a step back, touched it, looked at his hand, and realized he was bleeding. Then he made his fatal flaw—he got angry and followed up with a ferocious attack on Robel. He had let his emotion interfere with his skill. Robel waited for him to get close. Then he sidestepped at just the right moment and struck at Gebre with a wide swing of his sword. Gebre froze in place, then collapsed in a heap a moment later without a sound. There was a ghastly cut from his armpit to his torso, which while in the fit of rage, he had exposed for much longer than necessary as he had raised his arm higher than he should have in order to strike Robel.

Robel cleaned his sword on Gebre's clothes and re-sheathed it. He walked over to the body of the goon that had his dagger and retrieved it. Then he proceeded to search the bodies.

With Robel's back turned, a farmer carrying a bag of barley decided this was the best time for him to slip away unnoticed. The farmer stealthily crawled down the hill and disappeared behind it. He had secretly witnessed a monk in red single-handedly slay five of the Headman's men in combat.

"Help for the poor?" Tafari was calling from the spot in the butchers' section in the marketplace where Robel had left him. "Help for the poor?"

He soon looked up and saw Robel riding the cart towards him. He was, of course, dressed in his regular yellow robes of the Verenaian monks. His weapons and red robes were safely tucked under the cart.

"What took you so long?" Tafari asked Robel. "And your cart is mostly empty. At this rate, half the poor in Roha would starve to death and it would take a hundred years to complete a single church."

"Sorry," Robel said. "I got delayed by some very generous people who had a lot of gold and silver to part with."

Robel then presented Tafari with several small pouches, which he had collected after searching the bodies of Gebre and his men. Tafari opened them up and stared in amazement.

"Saint Verena be praised!" he exclaimed. "This is enough to feed 10 poor families for a month and complete the murals on the walls of Bete Amanuel church!"

"I know," Robel said softly.

"What made them so generous?" Tafari asked. "No one has ever donated this much before."

"I gave them quite an excellent lesson on a Bible verse," Robel said, helping Tafari load his donated items into the cart.

"Which verse?" Tafari asked.

"'The righteous will rejoice when he sees the vengeance; he will bathe his feet in the blood of the wicked,'" Robel quoted.

"From the Book of Psalms," Tafari said in puzzlement. "Good man, Robel. Good man."

The monks loaded the donations Tafari had collected into their cart and drove away, pleased with their take for the day.

Commander Berhan and all his 24 Riders of Roha rode into Lady Mariam's yard some days later. Something was seriously amiss.

"They seem afraid, my lady," Jembere said to Lady Mariam as they stepped out of her home to meet the riders.

"I see you have all your men with you?" Lady Mariam mocked Commander Berhan. "Worried something may happen to you? I hear someone is killing your friends."

"Gebre and his men were on their way here before they were killed," Commander Berhan pressed on Lady Mariam.

"There is a God," Lady Mariam said. "And he works in mysterious ways."

"What do you know about their deaths?" Commander Berhan asked, a stern tone in his voice.

"Do you think I had those men killed?" Lady Mariam asked. "I am surrounded by peasants who have never so much as held a dagger. Or perhaps you think I killed them myself?"

"If you know anything about what happened to those men, it is best you tell me before the Headman or Lord Groda himself takes charge of the situation," Commander Berhan warned.

"The Headman and Lord Groda taking charge?" Lady Mariam asked. "Aren't you the one the king left in charge of Roha's security? Every day I pray that you will find the courage to stand up for yourself and for what is right."

"This is no joke, Lady Mariam," Commander Berhan insisted. "I care about you and I fear for your safety. I truly do. I only want no harm to come to you."

"If you think I killed those men, perhaps it is your safety you should fear for," Lady Mariam responded.

"I came here just to warn you," he said. "I have done my duty."

"Your duty?" She laughed, then shook her head.

Commander Berhan said nothing. He grunted, turned his horse around, and hurriedly rode away with his men.

"They are afraid," Jembere said. "People think it is the same man in red."

"Whoever the man in red is," Lady Mariam said, "may God continue to protect him."

News of the killing of Lord Groda's men many days before in Roha had ruined the pleasant mood he was in after the relaxing holiday in the hot springs along the banks of the Gumara River that he and Tiki had just returned from. He, Tiki, Iskander, Mengesha, and some of Lord Groda's officials were having an urgent meeting in a library inside his fortress in Shire.

"People are beginning to spit at our faces," one of his men complained. "They don't fear us anymore. They say the man in red will kill us. No one is stepping forward with any information about him. And we have offered 20 pieces of silver."

"The merchants may stop paying us if we do not find this killer,"

Iskander said.

"Really, oh wise one?" Lord Groda mocked his nephew.

"All I am saying is that we have to get a firm grip on things around here," Iskander added, undaunted and determined not let his stupidity get in his way.

"You and your men cannot do a single thing right!" Lord Groda scolded his nephew.

"It was just bad luck that he slipped through our grasp," Iskander argued. "Do you think we planned to fail?"

"No, of course not, Nephew," Lord Groda said. "People do not plan to fail. They simply fail to plan."

Then Daga, Lord Groda's captain of the guard, suddenly burst in, dragging a peasant into the room.

"What is this?" Lord Groda asked.

"This man says he has information," Daga said. "He came all the way from Roha."

The room went silent as they waited for the man to speak. He was the farmer who had witnessed Robel kill Gebre and his four men.

"Tell Lord Groda what you told me," Daga instructed the man.

Cowering, the man nervously looked at Lord Groda.

"Well?" Lord Groda urged him on.

"Will I get the reward, my lord?" the man nervously asked.

"You'll have your silver," Lord Groda spat out. "Just get on with it."

"It was a monk, my lord," the man said. "A monk in a red cloak."

There was silence. Then everyone burst into laughter—everyone but Lord Groda.

"A monk?" Lord Groda asked.

"Yes, my lord," the man nervously answered.

"You are saying one single monk killed Commander Gebre and four men?" Lord Groda asked again.

"I saw it with my own two eyes, my lord," the man reiterated.

"He was a monk, so perhaps he had God on his side," Iskander laughed mockingly, followed reluctantly by Mengesha, who thought he had to follow his master's lead. But Mengesha stopped laughing abruptly after realizing that no one else was laughing, and Lord Groda himself was maintaining a deadly serious look. And Lord Groda was looking right at him.

Lord Groda stood up, fixed a gaze on his nephew, then walked closer to him.

"Moses had God on his side," he said to Iskander, "and he was able to part the Red Sea and drown a thousand Egyptian soldiers simply by desiring it. Do not make light of this."

Lord Groda had not forgotten his Bible. He had once wanted to become a priest and still bore some resentment for having been kicked out of the seminary as a young man. Despite his spectacular array of past and ongoing despicable deeds, he yet appeared to harbor a token dose of fear of the Almighty.

"What did he want, this monk?" Iskander asked.

"I do not know," the man said. "They spoke, but I did not hear them. But as God is my witness, it was a monk."

Lord Groda thought for a second.

"Get him out of here," he said, referring to the peasant.

Some guards grabbed the man and began to drag him out.

"Wait!" the peasant pleaded. "Please. What about my reward?"

Lord Groda thought for a second, then looked at one of his men and nodded. The man dropped a small pouch on the ground towards the peasant, who scrounged on all fours, scooped it up excitedly, and scrambled out of the room.

Lord Groda sat down again.

"Prepare my horse," he instructed his servants.

"Where are you going, Uncle?" Iskander asked.

"We are going to Roha," he said. "I will flush out this Red Monk of Roha."

CHAPTER 20

"Thank you for coming," Lady Mariam said to Robel as she walked out of her home.

"Not a problem, my lady," Robel responded. "You are the House of St. Verena's greatest benefactor. Abba Mikael said you needed help walking to church. I am happy to oblige."

It was the eve of Genna. The air smelled of incense. There was singing, and church gongs rang as priests and worshippers partook in Masses all over Roha and the realm. Small processions marched to the various churches with some singing hymns and some involved in subtle prayers. Some groups were led by monks, priests, or deacons, all armed with their hand crosses that the faithful continued to kiss in order to be blessed by God.

But Lady Mariam was a one-woman procession. She had requested her own monk, Robel, to walk her to church. This time she left her entourage behind, which usually consisted of Jembere and two female servants. For reasons she herself could not explain, she felt drawn to Robel and wanted to spend time with him—to get to know the man.

"The streets are not safe," she said. "You can cut the tension with a knife. I suppose you heard of the killing of five of the Headman's men. We were expecting them, but instead they wound up dead."

"People say the man in red may be responsible," Robel said.

"That's what they say," she said. "The Headman and his men are frightened. That makes them more dangerous now than they have ever been."

"They can threaten you," Robel said, "but they cannot touch you. They know that."

"The truth is that I am afraid," she confessed. "I am afraid to leave my house, but I have to come out. I have to show Iskander and Tiki that

I have no fear, even if it is not the truth."

"Why not hire guards to walk you wherever you want, like to church?" Robel asked.

"A few guards won't stop the Headman and his criminals," she said. "They'll simply chase the guards off. You know that."

"Lord Groda's men can do the same to me, my lady," Robel said.

"You are the only one I know who shows no fear before them," she said.

"I am just a man with nothing to lose," Robel said. "I only fear God and my mother—when she was alive."

Lady Mariam giggled, then looked at Robel for a brief moment in silence before speaking again.

"Somehow I just feel a lot safer with you," she admitted. "There is something different about you. Something that makes you different from the other monks. I cannot exactly understand what it is, but it is certainly there."

"My lady, I am but a poor peasant like many of my fellow monks," he said softly. "Whatever you see in me that you think different, I hope it is something good."

"I think I have only seen you show fear once," she said. "Of someone other than God."

"Now I am curious, my lady," Robel said, turning to her quizzically.

"I watched how you reacted before Tiki, Lord Groda's wife" she said. "You seemed shaken. You avoided looking her in the eye. You could not even speak when she spoke to you."

Robel felt his mouth instantly dry up. What had Lady Mariam found out? What did she suspect? He braced himself.

"If I did not know any better," she continued, smiling, "I would say you were smitten with her."

Robel smiled.

"I am a monk pledged to not concern myself with such matters, my lady," he said. "And Tiki is a married woman. It would be sacrilegious for me to even think of her in that way."

"Phew," Lady Mariam dismissed the comment. "Tiki's marriage to

Lord Groda is one of convenience. Everyone knows that. She wants access to his wealth and power, and he wants access to her title—and of course, she is a very beautiful woman. The snakes deserve each other. Theirs is a marriage forged in the deepest fires of hell."

"I have heard the rumors," Robel said.

"Most are true," Lady Mariam continued. "Her father's treachery caused her family to lose everything. So first she married another noble, Lord Kiros, hoping to regain her family's honor through him. It did not turn out well for either of them."

"You know Lord Kiros, my lady?"

"No. I only know of him. They say he betrayed his men and joined the Muslims to fight his own men. Some say he was killed in battle and some say he may still be alive—afraid of returning to his home in Shire. I do not know which is true."

"That is quite terrible, what he did," Robel said.

"If he joined the Muslims as some say," Lady Mariam added, "I find no fault in that. I have done business before with many local Muslims, a few Jews, and even some who do not worship anyone or anything in any way. I can tell you there are as many good men among them and just as many crooks as you will find among our fellow Christian merchants. My only quarrel with Lord Kiros is that he betrayed his men and took up arms against the kingdom—if that is what really happened."

"If, my lady?" Robel asked, his curiosity piqued.

"The story of what happened out there with him came from Lord Groda and his men," Lady Mariam explained. "He is about as trustworthy as a bucket of piss."

"Hmm," Robel mumbled.

"Lord Kiros, whoever he was," Lady Mariam continued, "must have stayed married to someone like Tiki only because of loyalty. He swore an oath to her during marriage, and I believe he intended to honor it. I think him to be dead, and I think Lord Groda is responsible, to get him out of the way so he could marry his wife. I do not put it past her that she planned the whole thing with Lord Groda."

"That is dangerous talk, my lady," Robel warned, having just instantly developed a new level of respect for Lady Mariam and her inclination to not rush to judgment over a man she believed she had never met. "If Lord Groda or Tiki hears of this coming from a noble such as yourself, the king's protection may not be useful any longer. Lord Groda might think it a necessary risk to rid himself of you."

"I do not care," she spat out. "I think they killed a good man."

"What makes you think he was a good man, my lady?" Robel asked. "You never met him."

"I do not need to have met him," Lady Mariam said. "All I know is that he stayed true to an evil snake of a wife till the very end even though he had nothing to gain from the marriage. To a man like that, loyalty is everything. That is something that is lacking these days—loyalty."

Robel was silent for a while, weighing Lady Mariam's words and letting them circulate in his ears, especially how accurately she had judged him even without actually ever meeting the real him—Lord Kiros.

"You seem to be a very good judge of people, my lady," Robel said.

"Except I cannot really read you," Lady Mariam admitted with a smile. "I could not tell if you were just smitten with Lady Tiki or terrified. If you were smitten, I wouldn't blame you. Many men are."

"Many men are also smitten with you, I have heard, my lady," Robel added. "Let's not give Lady Tiki all the credit around here."

"Maybe," Lady Mariam said. "But I think above all, many who claim to be taken with me also want the riches they think I have, and to get the access to the king they think I also have—if he ever returns."

"You are a lovely woman, my lady," Robel added. "Everyone knows that."

She was silent.

"I am sorry if I have offended you," Robel quickly added.

"No, Robel," Lady Mariam added. "You have nothing to be sorry about. And thank you."

Then there was more silence between them as they continued to walk to church, approaching the center of town where the supply of chickens, goats, sheep, and cattle was now more plentiful than ever. It was the best time of the year for the meat trade, and Lady Mariam herself had plenty of animals in the market being sold by her people.

This was because of the heavy feasting on meat that usually took place during the 12 days of Genna, to break the 40-day fast practiced prior to the festival.

It was also a time when vendors hawked and traded all kinds of goods, some real and some of questionable validity, like the man on a corner selling water he claimed came from Sheba's Bath, the lake in Axum said to have been used by the Queen of Sheba to bathe. It was supposed to have healing powers, capable of curing everything from headaches to old age.

"Tell me something, Robel," Lady Mariam abruptly requested. "Have you ever known love?"

"Love?" he asked, quite taken aback.

"The love of a woman?" she emphasized. "Have you ever felt the need to spend a lifetime with a woman?"

"Well—well, I—I—" he stammered, struggling for words and scratching his head.

Fortunately for him, he was suddenly interrupted by someone.

"Lady Mariam!" came the call in a harsh tone that clearly indicated it was not going to be friendly.

Lady Mariam and Robel stopped, turned, and looked. It had come from one of two men standing next to a workshop where two women were sifting grain using a giant sieve.

"You know them?" Robel asked Lady Mariam.

"No," Lady Mariam responded as the men began walking towards them, "but I have no doubt who they are."

Robel looked at the men and paid particular attention to the saber and dagger dangling from the waist of each of them. One of the men was significantly taller than the other. They were not approaching Lady Mariam for a pleasant chat, that was for sure.

Robel immediately stepped up to place himself between Lady Mariam and the approaching goons.

"Please, my lady," Robel whispered, "let me handle this."

Lady Mariam said nothing. She looked up at Robel's eyes as he spoke, and stepped even closer to him, feeling so safe and secure with him that she had to fight the urge to throw her arms around him and press her body against his.

The men stopped within feet from Robel, surprised at the daring of the monk to stand in their way.

"Okay, monk," the taller goon said, tapping his forehead in disbelief. "My name is Yesus and my mother always took me to church as a boy, so I may hesitate staining my sword with the blood of a monk on a Sabbath day. But my friend here, Gidey, is as pure a heathen as they come. He does not give a rat's behind about you or any of those grown men in church dresses, so do us a favor and get lost."

Robel did not budge. He simply stared at the goons and said nothing, standing with his arms held together with interlocking fingers below his torso and his feet slightly spread apart. It was a calm, blank stare.

"Did you hear what I just said, monk?" Yesus continued to threaten.

Robel continued to stare. Lady Mariam stood in silence. She was not afraid, not with Robel standing there.

A poet on a corner dazzling his audiences with his poetry, as well as traders, shoppers, and passersby in the street soon took notice of the brewing tension and began to quickly disperse lest they become the victims of the goons as well. They hid behind their shopping stalls and ran into nearby buildings from where they could still witness the unfolding situation without getting caught up in it.

Then there was a swoosh sound. It was from Gidey, partially pulling out his sword from its sheath, a gesture meant to frighten Robel.

Robel did not budge, but Lady Mariam grew concerned. She wrapped her hands around his right arm and inched much closer to him.

"Robel, please," she begged him in a soft, frightened voice. "Let the men say what they have to say and leave. Please."

Robel said nothing. His gaze remained focused on the goons.

"You best listen to the lady, monk," Yesus snarled. "She's got some sense in her."

Robel then turned his head towards Lady Mariam.

"My lady," he said calmly, pointing to a building. "Please go to that shop. I will handle these men. I promise you. Please."

"Are you serious?" Yesus barked, stunned by the monk's audacity.

"My lady," Robel insisted calmly. "Now, please."

"Okay," Yesus chuckled in disbelief, then said to Lady Mariam, "We will deal with you in a moment. Do as the monk says. I am now very curious to know just how he plans to handle us."

The goons parted to let Lady Mariam through, then they stepped closer to Robel.

Surprised and puzzled, Lady Mariam reluctantly walked to the building. Its occupants, many of whom had just been on the street moments before, eagerly opened the door and let her in, whereupon she immediately joined them by the window from where they could see, but not hear, the unfolding drama between Robel and the goons.

"Well, monk," Yesus teased, placing a hand on his sword so that Robel could clearly see it, "just how do you intend to handle us?"

"Any fool can have a sword," Robel said softly, "but it takes a wise person to know when to use it."

"Why don't you tell us then, monk, when to use our swords?" Yesus said.

Robel said nothing. He slowly separated his hands, placed a hand on his torso, then suddenly whipped back one of the flaps of his robes, revealing what was underneath it.

"A Bible," Yesus jeered, seeing the book dangling from a rope around Robel's waist.

Robel took up the Bible and lifted it up before the two men.

"I noticed that you two have been following us since we took the bend by the fruit seller," he said very slowly and deliberately so that the two goons could clearly understand him. "So obviously you have been sent by the Headman to bother Lady Mariam."

"Okay, smart one," Yesus laughed. "So?"

"It is the Sabbath," Robel continued, "and Lady Mariam just wants to attend Mass in peace, as do I."

"Get to your point, man, before my friend here begins to carve you up," Yesus said, pointing towards his companion, whose sword was still halfway out of its sheath.

"You want to frighten Lady Mariam," Robel said. "I cannot give you that satisfaction. But what I can offer you is the word of God."

Robel raised his Bible before the men.

"You can shove that in your behind," Yesus laughed. "You are—"

"If I were you," Robel insisted, inching closer to the man, "I would listen to me."

"You have a death wish, monk," the goon screeched, placing a hand on his sword hilt, about to unsheathe it. "You think we fear you? You do—"

"It is not me you should fear," Robel added quickly, unperturbed. "It is what you do not know that you should fear."

"Wh—what?" the goon stammered, his grip tightening around the hilt of his sword.

"Your friends are dying and disappearing," Robel reminded the goons. "No one knows who is killing them. Their killers could be out there right now, watching you harassing a poor monk and a woman just trying to get to church. And then they may come for you tonight."

The taller goon breathed in deeply as his friend shifted on his feet.

"Do you know who the man in red is, monk?" Yesus asked.

"No," Robel answered. "He has obviously gone to great lengths to hide his identity. But what I do know is that he could be out there somewhere, watching you right now, making plans for you." Robel paused as the goons turned their heads left, right, and back, quickly glancing around their immediate surroundings, just to be sure no one was really watching them. "The question is, is continuing the harassment of poor Lady Mariam worth the risk of having the man in red man come for you?"

"You play with fire, monk!" Yesus warned.

"That may be so," Robel agreed. "But I ask again, is harassing Lady Mariam worth the risk of having the man in red come for you?"

"You watch what you say, monk!" Yesus warned again.

Robel flashed his Bible before the goons again.

"You both may or may not believe in the God in this Bible," Robel said. "That is okay. I have a healthy dose of my own doubts about the man myself. But one good thing about this book is that it asks us all to treat others the way we would want to be treated. Now, you wouldn't want someone following you and harassing you on your way get your fill of tej, would you?"

"Monk—" Yesus began to stammer.

"It is the eve of Genna," Robel interrupted him. "Tomorrow we celebrate the birth of Jesus, your namesake. Your children and families will smile with you in the morning, or they will grieve for you in the morning. That will all depend on what you do in the next few seconds. I will say no more and I will stand out of your way." He pointed at the building where Lady Mariam was. "Now, you can go after her, or you can walk away." He pointed in the opposite direction.

There was silence. The goons stared with their eyes so wide they almost bulged out of their heads. Yesus scratched his head and took another nervous look at his surroundings.

From where she was watching, Lady Mariam stood as confused as everyone else who was with her, not having heard a word of what had transpired between Robel and the goons.

Then there was a swoosh sound of a sword. It was from Gidey. He had just fully re-sheathed his sword. Then both goons abruptly turned around and walked away without uttering another word.

Robel kissed his Bible and returned it under his robes. The tools of every monk were his prayer beads, cross, and prayer book. Robel had a fourth stored away in the monastery—his sword. He was thankful he had not been forced to use it this night. He turned towards the house where Lady Mariam was.

Lady Mariam and everyone welcomed the ease of the tension. They all returned to the street, with some people even patting Robel on the back and others asking for and kissing his neck cross.

"Thank you," one man said to Robel, who returned the gratitude with a nod and a smile.

"Lady Mariam," Robel called as she approached. "Mass starts soon. Those two will no longer bother you."

"What did you say to them?" she wondered aloud.

"I simply educated them on the virtues of Romans chapter six, verse 23, my lady."

"'For the wages of sin is death," she quoted the verse, "'but the free gift of God is eternal.'"

Robel nodded with a slight smile. Lady Mariam stared at him in stunned amazement for a brief moment, but said nothing else on the matter.

As they continued walking to church, random people began to smile and wave at them—at Robel, word having quickly spread before them of what he had just done. Talking down two of the Headman's goons and having them leave was not something that anyone had ever seen done before. The Headman and his goons feared and respected no one but the king. If only he was present! They would even spit in the face of Pope John VI, Bishop of Alexandria and Patriarch of the See of Saint Mark himself if he were to ride down from Egypt to try to reason with them. Yet a lowly peasant monk had somehow managed to talk sense into two of them.

Lady Mariam looked up at Robel. He was a man of unapproachable resolution and will. This was why she wanted him to walk her to church. This was why she wanted his company. Ever since that day when he had placed himself before her to stop Mekonnen from advancing towards her on his horse, she had felt herself inexplicably drawn to him.

She slowly placed her hand on his arm and held it as they walked. He looked down at her and put his hand on hers, then looked back forward as they continued walking. To Lady Mariam, his arm felt warm and strong. She wanted to lean against him, and yearned for him to place an arm around her. But they were in public. She did not want to embarrass Robel.

Too bad he was a monk.

CHAPTER 21

It was Genna day, finally. The only participants Genna was not particularly favorable to were the thousands of cows, goats, sheep, and chickens that were going to be slaughtered for the feasting to break the 40-day fast of Advent. Roha was blanketed by a sea of white clothed pilgrims and worshippers. Robel, Lady Mariam, and most of the faithful had spent the night in lavish ceremonies in the church, singing and worshipping for more than six hours. Every church was packed full, and deacons and officials were at their busiest. Thousands of lit tapers were carried by the faithful to illuminate the darkness over Roha, and to light the way as huge processions of priests and ululating congregations carried their church Tabot three times around their churches atop a priest's head. Even many of the unfinished underground churches commissioned by the king were being used, with many of the faithful regarding them as God's own houses.

It was Robel's first Genna as a monk.

"Thank God for Saint Yared," Robel muttered to Tafari, somewhat exasperated.

"Yes," Tafari said with some glee. "His hymns are the best."

"Not for the hymns, my friend," Robel said, "but the prayer stick." Robel rubbed the malwamiya, the T-shaped staff carried by many priests and monks, on which they could lean for support during very long church services. Robel had never used one until now.

After the church service, there was some period of resting in the early hours of the morning until mid-afternoon, when the monks and the throngs of faithful met again, this time for the event they were all really looking forward to—the genna game!

Roha and the monks of St. Verena had spent months preparing for this game. The monks of the opposing Debre Damo monastery had arrived the day before, participating in the worship and Masses with St. Verena. The game was taking place on a field outside the monastery of St. Verena.

Robel and his team of 20 players, including substitutes, felt more than ready to face the undefeated player-monks of Debre Damo.

"I hope you did not waste everybody's time with the practice sessions," Abba Mikael whispered to Robel.

"The outcome of the game will determine that, Abba," Robel asserted.

"We have to win," Abba Mikael said, taking a look over at the other team across the field with their abba, Abba Paulos standing with them, a gloating look on his face as if to say this was going to be another quick win for his team. "It will wipe that look off his large face."

The crowd assembled to watch the game quickly swelled to the thousands. To them, this was a welcome relief from the hours-long church sermons the night before. This was a chance to relax, eat, and enjoy a game where everyone was really a winner. The spectators supported both teams and just wanted to watch a good match. They generally did not take sides. Those monks not playing were collecting donations from the spectators, which were piling up in carts set up next to the church. There was gold, silver, crops, livestock, clothing, cooked meals, and even people who signed up to donate some time to work on the monastery farms or the underground churches that were still unfinished.

The only teams of real rivals here were the monks who were actually going to be playing the match. Monks were generally a peaceful lot who abhorred violence and avoided confrontation by all means. But if ever there was a time when there was an exception to this rule, it was during the genna games. It was a time when they put away their prayer books, Bibles, and pilgrims' crosses and replaced them with genna clubs, ready to beat the genna ball into the opponents' goal post—and occasionally ready to beat up each other with them. Sometimes it was as if the spectators came to the games not to actually watch them, but rather to watch massive fights and brawls among the monks that they hoped would take place. One such brawl fifteen years earlier had so raised the ire of the Bishop of Alexandria that he sent a representative from the Nubian kingdom of Alodia to mediate between the two monasteries.

There were drummers ramping up the spectators and the players. Just the day before, on Genna eve, they had provided a different kind of music—somber religious music to accompany church hymns. Now these musicians had transitioned, effortlessly producing the most trance-inducing wild and boisterous music, using a well-practiced artform which had taken each of them about four years to learn.

"They seem skillful," Robel said to Tafari, observing the players of the Debre Damo team. "But they still do not seem good enough to me."

"You haven't seen them play," Tafari cautioned, testing out his genna stick. "They are very skilled."

"One thing I have learned, my young friend," Robel said, "is that it is not the most skillful person who wins a game such as this. It is the fittest. We will find out just how fit they are."

Robel looked at his team. There was Mamo, a painter who maintained the paintings and frescoes that adorned the church walls of their monastery. There was Hagos, a skilled Tigrayan scribe who specialized in studying the lives of the Nine Saints and in copying liturgical works, providing his services to the newly built rock-hewn churches and other monasteries in the Tigray area. There was Emanuel, a monk who had given up trying to decode and translate ancient Mereotic scripts found in Roha and Axum and now maintained St. Verena's house of treasures. And there was also Tamirat, who taught mathematics, reading, and poetry in the monastery's schools. And of course, there was Tafari.

The sound of a horn blown by the referee signaled the start of the game. The Debre Damo monks played with great skill and quickly scored two goals, to the great disappointment of Robel and his players. But a short while later, it was becoming obvious that they were not going to maintain their scoring streak for much longer. Quickly tiring themselves out, they began to rotate out their most skillful players so they could catch their breaths. The monks of St. Verena, on the other hand, had barely broken a sweat and were able to keep their most skillful players on the pitch. Before long, they were outpacing the Debre Damo monks at every level, and soon equalized both goals. The crowd went wild. And shortly after, St. Verena scored a third goal, surpassing Debre Damo. The spectators howled as the drumming intensified into a riotous festive beat.

Abba Mikael winked across the field to Abba Paulos. Abba Paulos spat on the ground. Then the House of St. Verena bagged two more goals. There was no way Debre Damo was going to catch up to them now. The training and practice sessions were handsomely paying off.

Just when the House of St. Verena was about to seal their victory with a goal from Tafari, they were interrupted. Lady Miriam was one of the first to notice.

"Oh no!" she muttered, turning away from the game.

Then the rest of the spectators noticed it, and then the drummers, who slowly went silent. And then it was the players. The game came to a sudden halt as everyone turned their attention towards the road leading to the field. A slight commotion and fear swept through the crowd. Everyone froze. Lady Mariam and Robel looked at each other.

"Stay calm, everyone," Abba Mikael tried to reassure the crowd.

It was Lord Groda himself, riding at the head of about 40 of his men, including Commander Berhan and nine of his Rohan Horse Guard.

"What is this?" Abba Paulos asked Abba Mikael.

"That's Lord Groda," Abba Mikael responded, walking forward to meet the man. "All will be okay. I will see what he wants."

Lord Groda and Iskander brought their horses to a stop right in front of Abba Mikael, as the rest of their men took up positions to protect their lord and keep a vigilant eye on the crowd. Riding next to Iskander was, of course, Mengesha.

"Lord Groda," Abba Mikael called out to him, "I pray you are have having a pleasant Genna."

"Abba Mikael!" Lord Groda responded, slightly bowing in measure of some respect. "It's good to see all the monks outside the church. That is good, for I do not wish to desecrate any house of God with the blood of his servants. But I will not hesitate to do so if I have to."

Lady Mariam and all the other monks, including Tafari, stepped forward to better understand what was being said. Robel discreetly took a few steps back instead to conceal himself behind some spectators. He raised his turban to cover his head and reduce his chances of being recognized by Lord Groda or any of his men.

Abba Mikael took one look at Lord Groda and his bunch of characters before him and knew that he would have a hard time talking them down.

"Lord Groda," Abba Mikael said, "this is the house of the Lord. I ask that you please remove your men from these grounds."

Lord Groda chuckled then slowly inched his horse even closer to Abba Mikael so that its nose almost came into contact with Abba Mikael, who did not move.

"I will leave with my men, Abba Mikael," Lord Groda stated, "when I get what I want."

"And what is it you want, my lord?" Abba Mikael asked.

Lord Groda leaned towards Abba Mikael and said, "I want the monk who has been killing my men."

Robel's ears perked as he wondered how Lord Groda had found out that it was a monk killing his men.

"My Lord," a confused Abba Mikael protested. "I do not know what you speak of. All these men are monks. Violence is not their way."

"The man who killed my men—may God have them rest easy—was seen by a witness. The witness said it was a monk wearing red robes. There is no monastery but yours within three miles from where they were killed. So whoever that monk is, he must be one of yours, or you may know something about him. So, Abba Mikael, for everyone's sake, start talking."

"Lord Groda," Abba Mikael began to plead. "I swear we have no such monk among us. These men preach only peace and the Bible to all who would listen."

Lady Mariam glanced at Commander Berhan, their eyes locking with each other's briefly before he turned his head away in shame. How would he explain his cooperation with Lord Groda if the king returned from the wars?

Lord Groda began to ride his horse slowly before the crowd, observing it closely, as if to pick out the red monk himself. Robel made sure he was looking towards the ground when Lord Groda rode past him.

"Who among you is the red monk killing my men?" Lord Groda screamed.

No one responded.

"There is not a man among us capable of lifting a sword in anger," Tafari whispered to Robel. "Why does he think the killer is among us?"

"I ask again," Lord Groda continued. "Who among you is the red monk?"

No response. Robel knew that the jig was up. He knew Lord Groda, and he knew that his brutality knew no bounds, and that he would not leave until he had obtained what he wanted by any means necessary.

Lord Groda pulled out his sword and rode back to Abba Mikael, pointing it at his neck.

Tewodros, Commander Berhan's second-in-command, was quite startled and turned towards his commander, who was equally as startled at the dangerous turn of events.

Commander Berhan stepped towards Lord Groda, displaying a rare, albeit half-hearted attempt to constrain the man.

"My lord—" he blurted out.

"Stay where you are," Iskander ordered the commander, his permanent smirk on his face coupled with a grin that indicated just how much he was enjoying the situation and looking forward to having people killed.

Like a dutiful servant, Commander Berhan backed down instantly. Tewodros gasped but could do nothing but stand back and fume. His commander was letting them all down.

Lord Groda's attention remained on Abba Mikael, the priest's neck just inches away from the tip of his sword.

"Whoever you are, monk," Lord Groda announced, "you have until the count of ten to show yourself, or your abba here will lose his head. And then I will kill another monk, and another, until you show yourself or until you are all dead."

"You cannot be serious!" Lady Mariam protested. "These people have done no wrong to you!"

"And perhaps I will also start killing people at random," Lord Groda continued, undeterred and directing his words to Lady Mariam.

"I am prepared to die," Abba Mikael pleaded. "But please do not hurt anyone else."

"Then tell us who this red monk is!" Iskander yelled at the priest.

"There is no such monk among us, Lord Groda," Abba Mikael pleaded.

Robel's mind began to race. What could he do? People he cared about were about to start dying for something he had done. He knew Lord Groda and that insect, Iskander, were not bluffing. They meant every word they said. His weapons were, of course, not within his reach. Even if they were, there was nothing he could do. He was a good swordsman, but he certainly could not fight 40 men all by himself.

"One," Lord Groda began his count, his sword inching closer to Abba Mikael's neck. "Two."

Abba Mikael closed his eyes, at peace with himself and ready to accept his fate.

"No," Lady Mariam sobbed softly, tears streaming from her eyes.

Tafari tried to move towards Abba Mikael. He was going to offer himself. But Robel placed a hand on his arm, holding him back.

But what could Robel do now? If he revealed himself, Lord Groda and his goons were certainly not going to make the mistake of leaving him alive like they had after Bodera village. They were going to finish the job themselves this time. If he remained hidden, he certainly was going to watch his friends start dying before his eyes. But the monks seemed at peace and were prepared for death. He made a decision. He, too, was prepared for death.

"I am the red monk!" he blurted out.

CHAPTER 22

Someone had just admitted to being the Red Monk. Lord Groda and his men looked into the crowd before them but could not tell who had made the announcement. A murmur circulated through the crowd. The monks and many in the crowd had seen Robel make the claim. Tafari and Lady Mariam eyed him. He was a selfless man, willing to take the blame and sacrifice himself for everyone else so that their lives could be spared.

"Robel," Lady Mariam said softly to him, "do not do this."

"My lord," Abba Mikael addressed Lord Groda, "The monk only admits that to spare us all of your wrath. The red monk is not among us."

"Have your men look under the rocks by the stable," Robel said to Lord Groda, his face still concealed with the turban over his head.

At this, Tewodros and two of his men quickly dismounted from their horses and dashed towards the rocks by the stable. They began taking the rocks apart, then suddenly stepped back in shock. Tewodros lifted a small bundle wrapped in cloth and brought it to Lord Groda so all could see. He unfolded the bundle, letting the contents drop out.

With an audible gasp that ran through the crowd, without any doubt and before their very own eyes, red robes, a sheath containing a kaskara sword, and another containing a dagger fell out. A commotion swept through the crowd and the horses suddenly became skittish. Abba Mikael was speechless.

"The monk isn't one of you, you say?" a now angry Lord Groda snarled at Abba Mikael.

Lady Mariam took a step away from Robel. She needed a moment to fully ascertain what was happening.

"Robel, my friend," a shocked Tafari asked softly. "What is this?"

Robel turned towards his friend. "My name is not Robel," he said quietly.

"Not Robel?" Tafari asked, confused. "Who are you?"

Robel turned to face Lord Groda directly, who was expecting whoever had admitted to being the red monk to step forward and reveal himself. He slowly began to walk forward as the crowd before him parted to let him through. He got to the front and stood right in front of Lord Groda and his goons.

"So," Lord Groda addressed him, "you are the red monk?"

Robel slowly lifted up his head and pulled back his turban, revealing himself. This time the shock did not come from the crowd or monks. It came from Lord Groda and his men who recognized the monk before them. Lord Groda's jaw dropped. Iskander almost fell off his horse.

"What is happening?" Tafari asked Lady Mariam quietly.

Lord Groda ran his hands over his head, unable at first to say anything. He was completely dumbfounded. So was Commander Berhan. The simple peasant monk he had known as Robel was the killer he had been trying to find? Who was Robel, really?

Mengesha dismounted his horse, and with his hands on his sword hilt as a precaution, he approached Robel, very cautiously reached down below the monk's feet, and very wisely pulled away his sword and dagger to a safe distance away from him. He knew how destructive those weapons could be in Robel's hands. Mariam and the rest of the monks continued to watch the unfolding events in quiet disbelief. Who was this Robel that he inspired so much fear even among Lord Groda and 40 of his men?

"How dare you kill our men—" Iskander broke the shocked silence by starting to scream at Robel.

"Shut up, Iskander," Robel hushed Iskander dismissively, barely even glancing at the man.

Tafari gasped in sheer terror and wonderment, expressing the same feeling as the rest of the crowd at seeing the Headman—the most feared and dreaded man in Roha, interrupted while speaking, called by his name, and then hushed up so decisively by a mere monk. And most shocking of all, the Headman actually shut up as ordered by the monk, cowering in fear, even with all his men at arms with him.

Lady Mariam said nothing. Her fear and concern for Robel was slowly turning into anger. She had bared her soul to him, but he had been lying to her and everyone else all along. She felt betrayed.

"Lord Kiros," Mengesha addressed Robel, a slight quaver in his voice. "Step away from Lord Groda."

The crowd went wild as shocked whispers of Lord Kiros hissed out of their lips.

Lady Mariam squinted her eyes, a fiery look of rage burning inside them directed towards Robel—Lord Kiros.

"I am sorry, my lady," Tafari said softly to her. "I did not know."

"You have me, Lord Groda," Lord Kiros said. "Now let everyone else go."

Lord Groda was still in shock.

"How did you do it?" he asked Lord Kiros. "How did you escape the sultan?"

"I didn't," Lord Kiros replied. "Sometimes people just do the right thing when they know it is to be done."

"This time you won't get away," Lord Groda promised. "I can assure you. This will not be a very happy Genna for you."

"You have me, Lord Groda," Lord Kiros insisted. "I ask again that you let everyone else go."

"No, no, no, no." Lord Groda smiled, shaking his head. "It is not going to be that easy. Not for you, not for them"—he pointed at the monks—"and certainly not for her." He pointed at Lady Mariam.

"Lord Groda, you have no right—" Abba Mikael began.

Lord Groda turned and faced Commander Berhan. "In the presence of the king's representative in Roha, Commander Berhan," Lord Groda announced, "I declare the traitor and fugitive from justice, Lord Giorgis Kiros, captured and due for summary execution for his crimes against the kingdom of Ethiopia and Christianity. Seize him."

Commander Berhan nodded to Tewodros. Tewodros and two of his men drew their swords and seized Lord Kiros. He offered no resistance.

But Lord Groda was not done yet.

"And in the presence of the king's representative," Lord Groda continued, "I charge with treason Lady Mariam, Abba Mikael, and all the monks of the House of St. Verena for harboring and abetting Lord Kiros, a murderer and a fugitive from justice."

A commotion exploded among the crowd. Lord Kiros' association with Lady Mariam and the monastery of St. Verena had given Lord Groda an excuse to legally rid himself of Lady Mariam and claim her lands. Perhaps he could also now find a way to claim some of the lands of the House of St. Verena. Lord Kiros's reappearance was not as bad as he had initially thought. It was actually a stroke of good fortune.

"You are a snake!" Lady Mariam spat at Lord Groda.

"My lord," Commander Berhan protested. "Lady Mariam—you just cannot—"

"You will do as you are told, Commander!" Lord Groda ordered him.

"Yes, my lord," Commander Berhan acquiesced.

Commander Berhan then reluctantly ordered his men, "Seize them."

"No," Lord Groda said. "Not your men, Commander. My men will take them."

Commander Berhan's men backed down, uncertain of what to do. Some of Lord Groda's men then moved into place to seize Lady Mariam and the monks.

"No," Lord Kiros muttered to himself, realizing what was about to happen.

He knew Lord Groda well and knew what he was about to do to his captives. His declaration of the monks and Lady Mariam as traitors for harboring a fugitive meant they were subject to legal execution, and with Commander Berhan's inaction, Lord Groda could summarily carry out that sentence without much of a trial. Lord Kiros could not let that happen. He had to think fast.

Taking advantage of the commotion and panic sweeping through the crowd and even Groda's men, Lord Kiros elbowed the arm of one of Commander Berhan's men holding him. As the pain from the hit caused the man to release his sword, Lord Kiros snatched it up before it even hit the ground while simultaneously kicking the soldier away. Almost instantly the other soldier guarding him lunged forward with his sword, but Lord Kiros stepped aside and the sword swept past him harmlessly. He then spun around and knocked the sword from the soldier, stopping his attack instantly. The man stepped back as his sword dropped to the ground. He flinched, expecting Lord Kiros' sword to slash at him, but it did not. Lord Kiros ignored him and spun around to face three of Lord Groda's men who came charging at him. That did not end well for the three goons, as Lord Kiros quickly dispatched them all, sending them to the ground with mortal wounds.

Lord Kiros then reached for Commander Berhan. The Rohan commander immediately pulled out his sword to defend himself. However, always as quick as a striking viper, Lord Kiros expertly used his own sword to knock out commander Berhan's from his hands, then caught it with his free hand in midair as it flew off. At the same instant, Lord Kiros lunged forward with his own sword, straight towards Commander Berhan's neck.

CHAPTER 23

With death staring him in the face, Commander Berhan closed his eyes, expecting Lord Kiros's sword to puncture through his throat at any moment. But nothing happened. He quickly opened his eyes to find that Lord Kiros's sword had stopped just inches away, but holding the sword in place nonetheless. One little thrust and it would be then end for Commander Berhan. He froze, his life flashing before his eyes. Everyone else froze too. It had all happened so quickly that few had had the chance to react.

"Commander Berhan!" Lord Kiros said to him. "You are a commander of the Rohan Horse Guard, the best fighting men on horseback in the realm. For once, act like it. Show Lord Groda what you are made of. The king left you to keep order in this city, man! Do not let us down, Rider of Roha."

Lord Groda chuckled. Commander Berhan was his minion and took orders from no one else but him, with the price of disobedience being potentially very costly.

Commander Berhan stood silent, multiple thoughts racing through his mind. Recruited from his home in the small village of Gondar due to his skill on horseback, he had joined and had been training with the Rohan Riders since he was just a boy. He had served with them since then and had even saved the king's life several times during campaigns in the south to Christianize and expand the empire among nomadic tribes there. All officials knew he had tried and failed to persuade the king to move his capital from Roha to Gondar, believing its natural beauty and proximity to Lake Tsana to be a more ideal location for the king's New Jerusalem. The king had still trusted him with maintaining the peace in Roha in his absence even though he had taken almost all the Rohan

Riders with him to the front. So far, Commander Berhan had failed miserably in maintaining that peace.

Lord Groda's men slowly began to converge around Lord Kiros. There was no escape for him. He was a good swordsman, but he was one man against Lord Groda's 30 men and Commander Berhan's ten. Lord Kiros knew it, and he knew Lord Groda and Commander Berhan knew it too. Still, he held out hope as his sword remained pointed at Commander Berhan's throat, holding him frozen in place.

Lord Kiros then lowered his sword, stepped back, flipped Commander Berhan's sword, caught it by the blade, and offered it back to the commander, pointing the hilt towards him.

"I believe this is yours, Commander Berhan," Lord Kiros said.

Commander Berhan looked at Lord Kiros deeply, as if questioning his motives, then he grabbed the sword.

"Tewodros," he called to his deputy. "Place Lord Groda under arrest."

"Hmm?" Lord Groda mumbled, taken by surprise.

"I, Commander Berhan, representative of the king in Roha, am arresting you for planning the murder, robbery, and attacks of many good people in Roha, and of attempting on multiple occasions to subvert the authority of the king."

"You can't do that" Iskander interjected "You will—"

"I thought I told you to shut up," Lord Kiros coolly hushed Iskander again, who again backed down instantly.

"Kill them!" Lord Groda ordered in a feat of anger. "Kill the king's representative and all his men!"

Two of Lord Groda's dismounted men immediately attacked Commander Berhan, but to the surprise of everyone watching—except Lord Kiros—Commander Berhan expertly deflected the blows of his attackers and cut them down quite effortlessly.

"God knew why he never let you become a priest, devil!" Abba Mikael cursed at Lord Groda. "You are a disgrace to life itself."

Embittered, Lord Groda plunged his sword into Abba Mikael' torso.

The crowd gasped in horror. Lady Mariam let out a loud scream. Lord Kiros looked at Abba Mikael holding his chest in pain, then at Lord

Groda.

Abba Mikael grimaced. He was not surprised. He had expected no less from Lord Groda.

"God is not mocked," Abba Mikael said to Lord Groda, pain in his voice. "For whatever one sows, he will also reap."

Lord Groda smiled. "The book of Galatians," he mocked. "Chapter six, I think. I no longer believe in much of all that nonsense."

Abba Mikael closed his eyes and collapsed.

Lord Groda and his men then turned their wrath on Lord Kiros and the Rohan Riders as both groups attacked each other, their horses braying wildly as they galloped into combat. Lord Kiros immediately dropped the sword he was holding and picked up the belt containing his sword and dagger, still in their sheaths. He strapped it around his waist, and unsheathed his sword. He was prepared to unleash hell.

"Tafari!" he called. "Take Lady Mariam and the monks and hide!"

"Mengesha, get them!" Iskander screamed at his man, ordering him into the fray while he himself stood back, safely postured behind some of Lord Groda's men. Mengesha jumped into the fight, killing a Rohan Rider who had been knocked off his horse.

While the monks—for whom violence was against their way of life— were being led away from the fighting, many in the crowd turned against Lord Groda's men with anything they could wield—rocks, sticks, anything. This was their chance to rid themselves of the Headman and his people.

Lord Groda joined his men in the fracas, some mounted, but most not—as they had been pulled down from their horses. The men were being beaten and stomped on by the angry mob intent on vengeance against a group that had terrorized them for many months.

After engaging in a fight with two of Lord Groda's men that quickly ended with their faces planted to the ground, Lord Kiros was looking for Lady Mariam among the crowd. When he saw her, she and Jembere were being chased by Iskander, Mengesha, and two of their men. Lady Mariam was a target that was easy enough to compel Iskander to emerge from his relative safety to pursue.

"Don't let her get away!" Iskander screamed at his men.

Lady Mariam and Jembere were running towards the door of the south of the building. Lord Kiros was about to spring into action against Iskander when he heard several monks next to the stable screaming as they, too, were being pursued by three of Lord Groda's men on foot. The mob was not close enough to assist them, but Lord Kiros was. He wanted to save his fellow monks, but he also needed to assist Lady Mariam, a woman he had become quite close to over the months but had resisted pursuing due to his false identity as a chaste and pious monk. He did not have to pretend about who he was anymore.

He quickly cut down one of Lord Groda's goons who attacked him, then turned to Tewodros, who was still on horseback and fighting next to Commander Berhan. Tewodros had just mowed down one of Lord Groda's men, sending the goon flying off of his horse with a piercing scream. Lord Kiros grabbed Tewodros's leg, getting his attention.

"Take some men and—" Lord Kiros began to instruct Tewodros.

Tewodros spat. "I don't take orders from a traitor!" he fired at Lord Kiros, disdain in his eyes.

Commander Berhan had heard that. He immediately dispatched the man he was fighting and turned to face Tewodros.

"In the name of the king," he said to Teowdros, "I absolve Lord Kiros of any crimes he is accused of, until such time as they are proven by any accuser in a fair trial."

Commander Berhan immediately threw himself back into the fight after his declaration.

Tewodros then turned to Lord Kiros.

"What are your orders, Commander?" he asked Lord Kiros.

"Take some men and protect those monks!" Lord Kiros ordered, pointing at the screaming monks by the stable.

Tewodros nodded. He and three of his riders immediately galloped towards the stable, fighting their way through the mob as the battle against Lord Groda's men intensified.

Lord Kiros's attention quickly returned to Lady Mariam, who was still being pursued by Iskander and his goons. Fortunately, they had had to fight their way through the mob as well, significantly slowing their pursuit. Finding a path of least resistance, Lord Kiros sprinted towards the kitchen building. Upon gaining entry into the kitchen through the door at the northern end, Lord Kiros locked it behind him. He then dashed to the southern door and opened it, awaiting Lady Mariam and Jembere, who immediately ran in and were surprised to come face-to-face with him.

"Robel!" Jembere exclaimed, relieved.

"Lady Mariam!" Lord Kiros placed both arms on Lady Mariam's shoulders affectionately.

Lady Mariam said nothing. She was panting heavily. Lord Kiros turned to Jembere.

"Take her to the storage room," he instructed the servant.

"Okay, Robel," Jembere nodded, then gently took Lady Mariam's hand.

He was about to lead her towards the storage room, located at the left side of the room, when Lady Mariam paused, turned around, took a few steps towards Lord Kiros, then delivered to his jaw a loud and solid slap that connected so perfectly Lord Kiros thought his head was going fly off of his shoulders. He grimaced but did not reach for his jaw.

Then she turned to Jembere.

"His name is not Robel," she said. "It's Lord Giorgis Kiros."

Lord Kiros took the slap in stride. He deserved it.

"Do not come out of that room until I tell you to," he instructed Jembere.

"Yes, my lord," Jembere said, then led Lady Mariam into the storage room, where they closed the door behind them.

Lord Kiros remained by the side of the south door, waiting inside for Iskander and his three men. Within moments, all four came barging in, straight towards the north end without noticing Lord Kiros standing to the side inconspicuously. Iskander and his men stopped, realizing the northern door was locked from within, which meant Lady Mariam was still in the building.

"Search the building," Iskander ordered his men.

"Hey, goat face," Lord Kiros called.

Iskander and his men turned around to see Lord Kiros standing with his sword in one hand and rubbing on the cross around his neck with the other.

"Lord Kiros," Iskander called, smiling coyly but taking a few steps back to stand further behind his men. "You are a dead man."

Lord Kiros slowly turned around and locked the southern door, ensuring no one could escape the building. Known in monasteries as Bethlehem, the kitchens were also used for baking eucharistic bread for holy communion and for the preparation of wine for the congregations by specially appointed deacons. Lord Kiros wanted to avoid any bloodshed within it if it could be managed.

"Iskander," he began, "if you repent your ways and decide this moment to retire yourself to a monastery for the rest of your life, there is a chance I may yet let you live. I won't make this offer again."

Iskander, safe behind his men, laughed. "Kill the traitor," he instructed.

His three men, swords pointed forward, charged at Lord Kiros. Lord Kiros immediately killed one of the men with a jab to the heart while he blocked and sidestepped expertly to avoid blows from Mengesha and the other goon. Without easing up for even a moment, he sprang into Mengesha and the surviving goon, narrowly avoiding a thrust from Mengesha while taking a swipe at the other goon. The goon groaned then fell on his knees, with his head falling on Kiros's waiting sword, which went straight through his chin to the top of his head, finishing the job. Lord Kiros quickly pulled his sword out, letting the man's lifeless body drop. He then quickly stood up and blocked a blow from Mengesha, who had speedily recovered and attacked him again.

They both slashed and lunged for a moment, avoiding blows from each other and sending their own in return. Lord Kiros knew Mengesha was not a bad swordsman. A seasoned soldier who had fought for Lord Groda in many battles from the Lasta Mountains to Jijiga and Gojjam, it was the reason why Lord Groda had assigned him to watch over his nephew.

His fight with Lord Kiros went on for a few minutes more, sword clashing against sword as Iskander watched, guardedly confident that Mengesha would slay the man he had hated for a very long time. But his hopes were suddenly dashed when he heard a cry from Mengesha.

His bodyguard suddenly dropped his sword, drunkenly staggered backwards, and placed his hands on his side as he bled from a wound. With his last few moments, he turned to face Iskander.

"Run, Iskander," Mengesha instructed him with some difficulty. "Run!"

Then Mengesha dropped and drew his last breath.

Iskander froze. He stared at Mengesha's body, wanting to yell at it to wake up.

"But—but—" he stammered, his face suddenly covered in sweat.

"There is nowhere to run, Iskander," Lord Kiros said softly, sheathing his sword. "It all ends here, now."

"Wh—what about—wait," Iskander stammered. "I am—I am ready to repent of my ways."

"I'm sorry Iskander," Lord Kiros said. "You had your chance."

"What now?" Iskander asked, paralyzed with fear.

"You should draw your sword," Lord Kiros suggested. "All the time I have known you, I have never seen your sword."

Continuing to sweat profusely, Iskander feverishly unsheathed his sword and assumed a fighting stance.

"Boo!" Lord Kiros teased.

Iskander jolted and dropped his sword, which he quickly reached down and picked up again. Then in a fit of rage, and hoping to catch Lord Kiros while his sword was still sheathed, Iskander flew towards him in violent determination with his sword raised high, screaming like the devil himself. When he finally encountered Lord Kiros, who remained standing in place, there was no clash of swords. There was just a slight swoosh as Lord Kiros flashed his sword out of his sheath and then re-sheathed it, all done with fascinating and effortless speed. Then Lord Kiros started walking forward, not even taking as much as a glance behind him at Iskander, who stood frozen, facing the south door.

Lord Kiros walked towards the table before him and picked up a mango from a bucket of fruit. He grabbed a stool and turned around to face Iskander, who still stood frozen, with his back to Lord Kiros.

With fruit in one hand and stool in the other, Lord Kiros slowly walked to Iskander, who raised his eyes to look at the scout commander. Lord Kiros placed the stool before Iskander, sat down, crossed his legs, pulled out his dagger, and used it to start cutting chunks off the mango. He ate slowly and deliberately, watching Iskander, and savoring every mouthful just as much as he was savoring the site of Iskander dying before him.

Iskander had not really seen Lord Kiros's sword flash out and returned to its sheath. He had not seen what Lord Kiros had done with the sword in the brief moment it had been out. It had all been too fast for him. But Iskander had felt what Lord Kiros had done with the sword in that brief moment. That was why he was frozen. He tried to speak, but blood starting dripping from his throat, then his mouth. Lord Kiros had delivered an immaculately clean cut across the man's throat.

Iskander continued to struggle, his eyes widening. Lord Kiros was the last person he was going to see before he died, and he was really enjoying the moment, chewing on the mango and hoping Iskander was thinking of the murder of his fellow scouts at the mountain pass many months before.

Iskander soon took a last breath and fell to the floor, dead.

Lord Kiros dropped the remainder of the mango and re-sheathed his dagger. He had finally wiped off that smirk from Iskander's face.

Outside, Lord Groda sat on top of his steed, with his sword bloodied, watching as his men were dropping one by one. The situation had turned against him decisively. He had to get out of there while he still could. As his few remaining men coalesced around him to protect him, he began frantically searching for his nephew.

"Iskander!" he called. "Iskander!"

Then his eyes suddenly caught the south door of the kitchen building opening up. Out of it stepped Lord Kiros, Lady Mariam, and Jembere. Lord Kiros was dragging Iskander's body across the floor by its right leg, which he dropped once he noticed that he had gotten Lord Groda's attention.

Lord Groda fumed, seeing his nephew on the ground like a sack of yams. He turned his horse around and headed for the exit, hacking his way through the growing mob as his few remaining men kept pursuers at bay. In a moment, he was off the monastery grounds and fleeing on his horse to save his hide.

Commander Berhan was about to go after him when Lord Kiros stopped him.

"You won't catch up to him," Lord Kiros reasoned. "He's gone. Let us see to our wounded."

Commander Berhan understood. A few moments later, the swords fell silent. All of Lord Groda's men were either dead, wounded, or captured. But the screams continued—of the wounded, the dying, and the bereaved.

Abba Mikael was surrounded by monks of both the House of St. Verena and Debre Damo. Abba Paulos knelt beside the dying monk, holding him in his arms.

"We finally beat you," Abba Mikael chided Abba Paulos.

"The game was never finished," Abba Paulos disagreed with a smile.

Abba Mikael looked up and saw Lord Kiros.

"Don't you let Lord Groda have the last word on this," Abba Mikael warned, struggling to speak. "You must continue what you started."

Then Abba Mikael's eyes rolled back and his body went limp. Abba Paulos closed his old friend's eyes and sobbed.

Commander Berhan walked to Lord Kiros as Tafari, the monks, Lady Mariam, and other survivors were tending to the wounded.

Four Rohan Riders, nine civilians, and three monks, including Abba Mikael, lay dead.

"Lord Groda has about 50 more men in his fortress in Shire," Commander Berhan said to Lord Kiros. "He will be back, you know."

"I know," Lord Kiros responded.

"He will come after the monastery and Lady Mariam," Commander Berhan warned. "I do not have many men, but I must find a way to restore some semblance of law and order in Roha."

Lord Kiros walked over to Tafari, who was helping a woman apply a cloth bandage over her wound.

"How are you, my friend?" Lord Kiros asked him.

Tafari stood up and gave his friend a hug. "We have survived the day,"

Tafari said. "How are you holding up, Lord Kiros?"

"Better days have come and gone," Lord Kiros said, then paused briefly before continuing, "I owe you an explanation."

"No need, my friend." Tafari smiled. "You are a good man, Lord Kiros. But I'm afraid you do owe that explanation to Lady Mariam. You know women."

Lord Kiros looked over at Lady Mariam. She and Jembere were walking towards the exit. Lord Kiros caught up to them.

"Lady Mariam," he called.

"Lord Kiros," she responded. "I go home to bring medicines for the wounded. I would very much prefer it if you left me alone, if you do not mind."

"Please allow me to walk you home," Lord Kiros pleaded. "I promise I won't even utter a word if that would please you. I just want to see that you arrive safely. Lord Groda may still have some men out there."

"Like I said, Lord Kiros," Lady Mariam reminded him sternly, "I would very much prefer it if you left me alone. Please, I beg of you."

Jembere threw Lord Kiros a terse look and shook his head in disappointment with the man. Lord Kiros nodded his understanding, and Lady Mariam and Jembere proceeded with their walk home.

"Tewodros?" Lord Kiros called to the Rohan Rider who was walking by.

"Commander?" Tewodros responded.

"Send four men to walk with Lady Mariam to her home and back," he instructed. "They must not be seen."

"Yes, Commander," Tewodros responded, and immediately set about to accomplish his task.

CHAPTER 24

Lord Groda thanked his gracious goodness when he spotted the battlements of his fortress atop a mountain range in Shire across the horizon. He had ridden for two days and one night, changing horses several times in order to be able to return in haste and avoid the fate that had befallen his nephew and his men in Roha. The important thing for him was that he had survived. But that was not the end of it. He now had to destroy the monks, Lord Kiros, Lady Mariam, and even Commander Berhan and his men before the king returned from the wars. He would lose everything, and possibly his head, if his enemies remained alive to testify against him before the king. He galloped forward.

"Open the gates!" he was screaming at Daga, his captain of the guard who looked down at him from atop the battlements.

Daga's men parted the heavy corrugated iron gate as he rushed down to meet Lord Groda. He stared at his disheveled and bloodied lord in wonderment, who had ridden out of the fortress five days prior with 30 men, but had returned alone.

"My lord?" a perplexed Daga called to him as he dismounted his horse after riding through the gates. "What happened? Where are the rest of the men?"

"You won't believe it," he scoffed. "Where is my wife?"

"In her garden, my lord," Daga responded. "But what happened in Roha?"

"Send word," he ordered Daga, ignoring the question and storming off towards his wife's garden. "I want all our men. I'll double their fees."

"Okay, my lord," a still-confused Daga responded as Lord Groda dashed off.

"By Saint George, you look like a dog had you for dinner and then threw you up," Tiki spat out when Lord Groda burst into her garden, where she and a female servant were feeding fish in a small pond.

"We found the red monk," he blurted as Tiki took him by his hands.

"So, who was he?" she asked, affectionately leading him to a bench and laying him down. Then she turned to the servant. "A bowl of water and a towel."

The servant departed.

"He killed Iskander," Lord Groda lamented. "He killed him like some animal."

Tiki paused for a moment, then spoke. "Perhaps you are better off without him?" she said softly, gently rubbing her husband's cheek. "Now you are rid of him for good."

Lord Groda sprang up and slammed his hand on the bench.

"That was my late sister's son, woman!" he roared. "He had his faults, but he was still my nephew!"

"Shh, okay, okay," Tiki cajoled him somewhat apologetically. She kissed him, and gently pushed on his shoulders to lay him back down again as the servant arrived with the water and towel.

Tiki began to soak the towel in the bowl of water and use it to gently clean the bruises on Lord Groda's face.

"Why don't you tell me what happened, darling?" she urged him gently.

"The red monk is Lord Kiros," Lord Groda blurted out.

The towel dropped from Tiki's hand. Had she heard her husband correctly? She stood up and staggered back, then drew in a deep breath as her head seemed to start spinning. She turned to her servant.

"Get out!" she screamed at the servant, who did not need to be told twice. She turned back towards her husband. "Wh-what did you say again?"

"The Red Monk of Roha is none other than Lord Kiros, your former husband," he restated. "He has been living as a monk all this while in Roha."

"Hmm," Tiki breathed in deeply, letting it all sink in for a moment, before continuing softly. "I thought I spotted him in Lady Mariam's place."

"You did?" he asked

"But I convinced myself that it could not be him." Then, with a deafening yell, she said, "Because you said he was already dead!"

She then threw the towel at her husband, who sat up, knowing he owed his wife an explanation.

"How could I have known that fool of a sultan would let him go?" he said.

"So, husband," she continued, choosing to focus on resolving their problem at hand instead of revisiting the past, "what do we do now?"

"Don't you worry," he said. "I have plans for him and our enemies in Roha. They will rue the day they turned against me."

It took three days for calm to return Roha. The freedom resulting from the sudden absence of Lord Groda's goons and the ongoing celebration of the 12 days of Genna—combined with the celebration of the lives of Abba Mikael and those lost in the fight against Lord Groda—turned Roha into one giant party, teeming with the faithful and tej-full alike.

His identity now revealed, Lord Kiros had not returned to the monastery. He had moved into an abandoned hut at the edge of the city, which used to belong to a hermit monk who had passed on a few months earlier. All his efforts to meet with Lady Mariam had failed. She had utterly refused to see him.

Despite Lord Groda's defeat in Roha on Genna day, everyone in the city knew he would return, and that he would do so with blood in his eyes to exact the devil's due on a city that had turned on him. The city's only hope lay in the return of the king before then. Messengers dispatched by Commander Berhan and court officials to locate the king and relay urgent messages had not returned. Lord Kiros knew alternate steps had to be taken to prepare the city.

A few days later, Lord Kiros and Commander Berhan were in a building in Roha where the Rohan Riders were holding some petty criminals until their cases could be brought before a town judge. Lord Kiros and the Horse Guard commander had been discussing how to respond to

Lord Groda's eventual return, when Tewodros walked in.

"Commander Kiros," he called. "There are riders outside to see you."

Surprised, Lord Kiros and Commander Berhan walked out. There, seven mounted riders awaited. Their leader was someone Lord Kiros had least expected. He had to restrain himself from having the man pulled down from his horse and chopped to bits in the most frightening way possible. It was Daga, the ex-priest of questionable benevolence, and now a Lord Groda loyalist.

"You come to ask us to surrender?" Lord Kiros called to the man.

Daga dismounted.

"No, Commander Kiros," he responded. "We come to join you."

"What is stopping me from killing you where you stand?" Lord Kiros asked.

Daga sighed, then addressed Lord Kiros. "Commander Kiros," he began, "what Lord Groda did after Bodera to you and your men was wrong. I simply wish to make amends. I bring six good men with me. You will need us for what is coming."

"Why would we need you?" Commander Berhan asked.

"As we speak, Lord Groda is gathering a small army from here to Adigrat. By Timkat he will be here in Roha with at least 500 men. He will take no prisoners, Commander."

"Why have you turned against him?" Lord Kiros asked.

Daga took a deep breath and walked towards Lord Kiros. "Many of these men," he began, pointing at his men, "come from Gorgora as do I. But my people are the Oromo people, like some of your scouts were. Originally, we hail from the south. In the Oromo language, my name, 'Daga,' means 'one who does not forget.' I have never forgotten the many times you saved our skins and even Lord Groda's. I have never forgotten how you risked your own life many times when you could have just walked away. When word came that you still lived, it gave me a second chance to right what was wrong. And no man among us particularly cares for Lord Groda. The man is a greedy swine who only cares about the piles of land deeds he has seized from his victims."

"Surely, Daga, you must harbor a grudge towards us," Lord Kiros inquired. "I killed Iskander. He was your friend."

"He was a festering pile of manure," Daga spat.

All this time, since the murder of his scouts, Lord Kiros had played the scene over and over in his mind, of Daga simply standing by and doing nothing. Had the man truly had a change of heart, or was he a plant by the cunning Lord Groda, hoping to infiltrate Lord Kiros's ranks and be poised to strike at the opportune moment? There was no way for Lord Kiros to know, and even though it was a hard thing for Lord Kiros to do, he had to take Daga at his word. So he accepted the commander and his men into his ranks. If he had to help the monks and Lady Mariam survive Lord Groda's oncoming wrath, then they needed all the men they could get.

With the addition of Daga and his men, the fighters in Lord Kiros's ranks now numbered a miserable 32, including himself and 24 Riders of Roha, for a few more had just qualified and been recruited to the Rohan Horse Guard. How could they protect the monastery and Lady Mariam's place from Lord Groda and his more than 500 men expected to descend upon them?

"What about the king?" Daga asked Commander Berhan as they discussed the matter.

"Reinforcements won't get here for weeks," Commander Berhan said. "That is if the king can even send any."

"We are on our own," Lord Kiros said.

"We can evacuate the monks and Lady Mariam," Commander Berhan suggested. "But I do not know where to."

"It is no longer just about the land with Lord Groda now," Daga reminded them. "He wants the blood of the monks, Lady Mariam, and the people of Roha. He wants to send a message to those who dared to defy him. He is intent on butchery the likes of which you have not seen in Roha yet, Commander Kiros."

Lord Kiros was silent for a while, then an idea hit him.

"There is one place we can evacuate them to," he said.

"Pray tell," Commander Berhan said.

"And that will also draw Lord Groda away from Roha," Lord Kiros continued. "But we have to move fast."

"So where are we going?" Daga asked.

A short while later, Lord Kiros, Tafari, Commander Berhan, Daga, and Tewodros were meeting in St. Verena's assembly hall with Abba Kristos, who had replaced the slain Abba Mikael as abba of the House of St. Verena.

"So you want to evacuate over 60 monks to the monastery of Debre Damo in two days?" Abba Kristos asked Lord Kiros, not fully buying the idea. "It is a four-day journey to the place in the best of conditions, Lord Kiros."

"We don't have four days, Abba," Lord Kiros argued. "We will travel all night and all day, but we have to get to Debre Damo. It's the best place to protect you, the monks, Lady Mariam, Roha, and the men who will be fighting Lord Groda."

"I still think we should try to reason with Lord Groda," Abba Kristos suggested. "There may be some humanity left in him yet."

"You saw what he is capable of," Lord Kiros reminded him. "Unless you believe you are Saint Samuel with the power to tame wild beasts, I suggest we proceed with this evacuation, Abba."

"Do you not find this risky, Lord Kiros?" the abba asked. "Lord Groda may attack and destroy us while we are making this journey."

"The greatest risk will be to not take one at all, Abba," Lord Kiros said. "If we leave now, we can be in Debre Damo before word from his spies gets to him."

"And what will you do about this monastery and Lady Mariam's place?" Tafari asked. "Lord Groda will surely raze them to the ground when he realizes we are gone."

"Allow me to worry about that, my friend," Lord Kiros assured him. "With what I have in mind, Lord Groda will not waste his time to come here just to burn down a few buildings and kill a handful of ordinary Rohan citizens just out of spite. Other than you, Lady Mariam, and I, we will also have something in Debre Damo that he treasures above all else."

"And what is that, may I ask?" inquired Abba Kristos.

Some hours later, the monks of St. Verena were frantically loading supplies into mule carts, ready for their evacuation to the monastery of Debre Damo. Many had been reluctant to evacuate, preferring to stay and die with their flock of Rohans on the streets of Roha if need be. It took some convincing from Abba Kristos and Commander Berhan for them to come to reason. The evacuation was a hasty, panicked, but organized affair, with Lord Kiros and Commander Berhan assisting and urging the monks on.

Lord Kiros approached Commander Berhan as he directed the staging of some mule carts.

"Lady Mariam?" Lord Kiros inquired.

"She doesn't know it, but my men are still watching her," Commander Berhan stated.

"You know it falls on you to talk her into coming to Debre Damo with us," Lord Kiros said. "She still won't see me. God knows I've tried."

"I do not fault her for that, Lord Kiros." Commander Berhan smiled. "If I were her, you would not exactly be my favorite person right now."

"But we have to get her out of here," Lord Kiros said. "She cannot stay in Roha while we are all gone."

"She has a mind of her own, you know that. I cannot say she will listen to me, but I will do my best to reason with her."

"Do what you must, Commander. Just make sure she gets on the mule train."

Lady Mariam was in her home, painting scenes of the nativity on a wall in her bedchamber. Her mind was rankled with conflicting thoughts. The monk she had come to have strong feelings for had turned out not to have been a monk at all. At the time when she had believed him to be a monk, she had secretly wished he was not a monk. Now that he had revealed himself not to be a real monk, but was an army officer of a respected noble family, it should have made her feel good and hopeful about their prospects together. Only, it did not. She felt betrayed. She had opened up to him precisely because he was a monk—someone she could trust. She did not know how to feel now. She had really liked Robel. But now, surprisingly, she seemed to be in love with Lord Kiros, the most appreciated man in the city, who was now being referred to by all as the Red Monk of Roha.

Jembere walked into the room, providing Lady Mariam a reprieve from her thoughts.

"My lady, Commander Berhan is here," he announced.

Lady Mariam had had enough visits from Commander Berhan over the years in his vain attempts to convince her to marry him—the coward. But now he had proven himself to be anything but that, finally standing up to Lord Groda and holding him accountable for his deeds.

"Send him in," Lady Mariam instructed.

Commander Berhan walked in a moment later.

"Are you well, Lady Mariam?" he greeted her.

"Are your men done watching me?" she asked.

"You knew?" Commander Berhan asked, surprised.

"Since my father died, I have been the only woman in a business run by men," she said. "Many are the roughest bunch of men who did not think I belonged and wished me all sorts of ills. So yes, Commander Berhan, I have learned to watch myself and my surroundings."

"That is very worthy of you, my lady," Commander Berhan complimented her. "But now I will need you to gather what you need and prepare yourself to travel with me to the monastery of Debre Damo."

"Why are we going to Debre Damo?" she asked.

"You know Lord Groda will be coming for you—" he began to explain.

"And the monks and Lord Kiros," she finished his sentence. "You think he will follow us to Debre Damo, and that that is the best way to protect us all and the city, am I right?"

"Yes, my lady," Commander Berhan acknowledged, impressed. "We will stay there until the king's return to Roha with his army, or until we destroy Lord Groda and all his men from there."

"I am not going," she declared.

"My lady?" Commander Berhan asked.

"I am not going," she repeated. "This is my home. I will never run from Lord Groda. If I die, it will be in my home, not running like a scared little creature."

Commander Berhan breathed in deeply, rubbed his hand over his hair, and said, "My lady, it is no secret that I care about you deeply. So it will have to be over my dead body that I will let Lord Groda's people lay a hand on you. And since I do not exactly plan on becoming a dead body anytime soon, I will—and let me say again—I will drag you kicking and screaming out of here to Debre Damo if I have to."

Lady Miriam paused and looked into his eyes. He was not bluffing. She had never seen him be that assertive before. He was a different man now. She placed down her paint brush and sighed.

CHAPTER 25

Two nights later, Lord Kiros stood on the battlements of Lord Groda's mountain fortress in Shire, his dark red cloak blending in seamlessly with the moonless night that glazed over the mountain range. Lord Groda's guards could not see him. But he could see everything going on in the courtyard below. Lord Groda was talking to some men roasting a sheep on a spit by a bonfire. Lord Kiros wished he could swoop down and put an end to him. But the man was surrounded by at least 20 unsavory characters who looked like they had cooked and eaten their own mothers just for fun. Without a doubt, these were some of the men he was assembling to attack Roha. And more men kept streaming into the fortress, on promises of handsome rewards.

Lord Kiros knew exactly what he wanted that night. If he succeeded, he knew Lord Groda would abandon his plan to attack his targets in Roha and would attack the remote and very defensible monastery of Debre Damo instead. He would be unable to resist the urge of having the hated monks and Lady Mariam in the same location, and most importantly, to retrieve what had drawn Lord Kiros to his fortress this night.

A flame lit up a window in the room across from where Lord Kiros was hidden. His prize was in there. All he had to do now was bypass the guards along his way and get there. The most challenging part of his operation was complete, for he was already inside the fortress, having infiltrated it through a concealed drainage entrance and scaled the internal walls using extreme snake-like nimbleness to carefully avoid the guards. After all, he was a scout and could travel unseen, especially in the dark. He made his way towards the lit room. The window had been left open to let in the cool breeze. The guards did not see him.

He climbed through the window and leapt into the room. The woman who was inside jumped with surprise. She stepped back but did not scream after seeing Lord Kiros's unsheathed sword, which appeared to her to be a clear threat. Lord Kiros still had his face covered with a turban. He and the woman stared at each other.

Then Lord Kiros reach for his turban and unfolded it, exposing his face.

"Giorgis." The woman jumped back, even more startled.

"Tiki," he said softly. "You look—eh, not well."

"I—I—I don't—" she stammered. "I never wanted any of this to happen."

"Yet here we are," he said.

"What do you want, Giorgis?" Tiki asked.

"I'm here for something that is dear to Lord Groda," he responded. "Part of it once belonged to me. I have come to get it back."

"Lord Groda will hunt you down until he finds me," Tiki said. "And then he will see that you are dragged before him, begging him to kill you and end the pain he will inflict on you."

Lord Kiros sheathed his sword. He stepped up to Tiki and placed his hands on her shoulders. "Do not flatter yourself, Tiki," he said. "I am not here for you. Lord Groda can keep you. There is no longer anything about you that I could possibly want."

Tiki rolled her eyes. "What do you want then?" she asked.

Lord Kiros pointed at the metal chest behind her. Daga had told him it would be there. "Isn't that all that matters to you and your husband?" Lord Kiros asked.

"No, you can't," she protested. "It will ruin us!"

"You have ruined many others to get these," Lord Kiros said, brushing past her and opening the chest.

Inside the chest were stacks of documents written on antelope skin parchment—land deeds. They were the sources of Lord Groda's extensive wealth, most of them fraudulently obtained from nobles and even some peasant families over the years, from all over Roha, Shire, and even a few as far away as Axum.

"One peep out of you and I will slice off your tongue," Lord Kiros warned Tiki. "And not that you would care, but I would also gouge out the eyes of the first of your men who sets foot in here."

Facing Tiki to make sure she remained in his sight, Lord Kiros pulled a leather bag from underneath his tunic and began transferring the documents from the chest into it.

Tiki stood back, fuming in a mix of anger, surprise, and confusion. Lord Kiros emptied the chest into the bag but held one of the deeds in his left hand. He stood up, slung the half-filled bag across his back using his right hand, then stepped closer to Tiki, waving the document in his hand at her face.

"This is my family's land deed," he said. "For many years I did everything right and served Lord Groda so he would return it like he had promised my father. But the two of you had other plans. Tell me, Tiki, at what point did you decide that wealth was more important than us? When did you and Lord Groda decide my fate?"

Tears rolled down Tiki's face as she turned her gaze to the floor. "Giorgis, please," she said softly. "It was not supposed to happen this way."

Lord Kiros smiled, then sighed. "If Lord Groda wants these deeds back, they'll be in the monastery of Debre Damo."

Lord Kiros turned towards the window to depart, then stopped and turned back to face Tiki again. "You will never again set foot in Lady Mariam's place," he said. "Because the next time you do will be your last."

Then he turned to leave.

"You are not going to kill me?" a surprised Tiki asked.

"What for?" Lord Kiros asked. "You think I am angry with you? No, you are not worth the effort, Tiki. I am past that. There is a young monk in the House of St. Verena who has been my dear friend. I have learned many things from him. One of them is that I have come to understand that anger is a dangerous thing. Holding onto it is like drinking poison and expecting the other person to die. So no, I won't kill you. Live long and suffer."

With that, like a thief in the night—he was a thief in the night—Lord Kiros climbed out the window and disappeared into the darkness.

Tiki stepped back against the wall, leaned against it, dropped down to the floor, buried her face in her hands, and sobbed.

After two full days of hard riding, Lord Kiros arrived at the small village at the foot of Debre Damo, its residents having already evacuated to the safety of the surrounding hills, caves, and other nearby villages, knowing the trouble that was ahead. There was no time to lose. Lord Kiros knew Lord Groda's army was not very far behind him.

Commander Berhan met him and grabbed the reins of his horse, helping to bring it to a stop.

"I trust all is well?" Lord Kiros asked, dismounting his horse. "Lady Mariam and the others?"

"All's well, Lord Kiros," Commander Berhan responded. "Lady Mariam and the monks are well. A few bandits along the way saw a bunch of monks and thought they were going to be an easy target, but we quickly made the rogues come to see the error of their ways."

"Good man," Lord Kiros said. "Any word from the king?"

"Nothing yet," Commander Berhan said, then leaned in closer. "Is it as big as they say it is—Lord Groda's army?"

"It is," Lord Kiros said. "He's got at least 500 horsemen. They will be here in three days. It won't be easy fighting them with only 32 men. But at least his army won't be going to Roha." He tapped the bag of land deeds strapped to his horse. "He will want to have these back as soon as possible. He will come here and hit us with everything he has."

Commander Berhan smiled. "Excellent work, my lord," he said. He then nodded at one of his men who picked up the bag from the horse and threw across his shoulders. "It will be safe in the monastery."

"How can just 32 of us hold out against Lord Groda and his 500 men?" Lord Kiros wondered aloud. "I pray we can hold out until the king's men arrive."

"It is not much, but we have some help," Commander Berhan informed Lord Groda, leading him towards an encampment under an olive tree.

"Who are they?" Lord Kiros asked, looking at some seasoned men assembled before them under the tree, armed with spears and swords.

"These are some of my people—Jews of the Beta Israel clans in this area," Commander Berhan said. "There are 31 men. They are mostly hunters but are handy with the spear and sword and have served the armies of the kings of Ethiopia for many generations. Some come from Gondar, like me. They do not like Lord Groda's men. His bandits have made their hunting grounds unsafe. They just celebrated Sigd, so they made their atonement with God and are cleansed and will gladly take up arms against Lord Groda to help rid the world of him, even if it means dying."

"You are the Red Monk of Roha?" one of the men asked excitedly as they all stood up in amazement, looking at Lord Kiros.

"I thank you for coming," Lord Kiros addressed them. "We need help from good fighters. I pray we prevail."

"We will," said the first hunter. "We will, as God is my witness."

"And everybody else?" Lord Kiros asked Commander Berhan. "Where are they?"

"All safe, for now," Commander Berhan said, pointing towards a sheer cliff to the left.

Lord Kiros turned and took a good, long look at the cliff. It was so high he could not see the monastery said to be at the top.

"The monastery of Debre Damo," he muttered in awe. "Only heard of it, but never been here."

"It's quite a sight, eh?" Commander Berhan said.

"The monastery at the top was built by the Negus, Gebre Mesqel around 550," Lord Kiros said in awe. "It must have taken a giant pair of b—"

"I know," Commander Berhan said. "I have been here before."

"You have?" Lord Kiros asked, surprised.

"Not to worship, of course," Commander Berhan said. "This is one of the three Mountains of Princes, where male relatives of new ascendants to the throne are locked up until they are called to assume the throne themselves or die. I escorted some here when the king ascended the throne."

"So there are princes locked up there?" Lord Kiros asked.

"No," Commander Berhan said. "After the king returned from Jerusalem, he changed his mind about these things and decided to release the princes. I came back with my riders, and we escorted them back to the king's court or wherever else they wanted to go."

"I did not know of such things," Lord Kiros said.

"Of course not," Commander Berhan said. "Only those relatives who were a threat to the throne and their escorts ever knew about this place as a jail. This was something started by Queen Gudit almost 300 years ago. Those members of the royal family she overthrew whom she could not kill hid here. Rather than go after them, the usurper queen decided to simply have them contained. Her successors—and even the Zagwes who overthrew her dynasty—followed the same policy, except that they actually brought and kept possible contenders for their thrones here."

Lord Kiros looked again at the top of the cliff. It was a flat-topped mountain, but the monastery at the top could not be seen at all, not even from a distance. It was well-concealed. But despite that, Lord Kiros had another worry, something he had known all along but which was exactly what made this monastery the ideal defensive position for them to occupy until the king's reinforcements arrived.

"The cliff must be at least 50 feet tall!" he complained, gazing at the steep, vertical hill that looked more like a single giant rock with steep sides. It was even much higher than the five-story buildings he had heard of in Mogadishu and Axum, and almost as high as the magnificent Nubian pyramids he saw during his journey to Jerusalem with the king.

"Just how exactly do we get up there?" he asked.

"We climb," Abba Paulos said, emerging from a nearby hut with some of his monks.

"Abba Paulos," Lord Kiros addressed him, bowing slightly. "I thank you for agreeing to shelter us."

"It is what we do for one another, Lord Kiros," Abba Paulos said, returning the bow. "Abba Mikael would have done the same for us. He is missed."

"I know," Lord Kiros said, then quickly returned to the trouble at hand. "So how do we really get up there?" He pointed at the top of the cliff.

"Show him," Abba Paulos said to some of the monks who were with him.

One of the monks pulled out a horn and sounded it. Almost immediately, from atop the cliff, two ropes came flying down, dangling from the edge. The monks quickly grabbed the ropes and began climbing the wall, with no safety harnesses whatsoever. Lord Kiros watched in awe as the monks scaled the cliff almost as easily as if they were walking in a Timkat procession. If they made even the slightest errors, they were certainly going to plunge to their deaths, with their bodies smashing against the hundreds of sharp-edged rock outcroppings that blanketed the base of the cliff.

"That is a devil of a steep climb," Lord Kiros observed. "A lot steeper than I had imagined."

"It the best defense for the monastery," Commander Berhan said. "These and many churches and monasteries like it are spread across the realm."

"It is also one way to be closer to God in heaven," Abba Paulos said. "You know, the higher one goes?"

"I think it is also one easy way to meet God before one is ready," Lord Kiros said. "You know, by plunging to your death?"

"In my 48 years of climbing," Abba Paulos said, "I have never seen or heard of anyone plunging to their deaths from this cliff."

It took the monks mere minutes to scale the 50-foot cliff.

"They make it look easy," Lord Kiros said.

"One gets used to it," Abba Paulos said. "It is not as hard as it seems."

"You must be joking," Lord Kiros chuckled.

"There are 4,000 people who live in the surrounding villages," Abba Paulos added. "And many want to worship in the church up there. So they make the journey every Saturday and Sunday to attend. The old, the young, men, women, and even children."

"They all make this climb?" Lord Kiros asked, surprised.

"It is the only way to get to the church," Abba Paulos said. "There are 400 monks who worship in the monastery. Many of them live down in the villages, and they make this climb every single day, several times per day."

"Why?" Commander Berhan asked.

"For them and the worshippers who attend services here, this climb is also a test of faith," Abba Paulos said.

"That is a lot of trust to be placed in faith" Lord Kiros said.

"You think this church is high?" Abba Paulus chuckled. "Well, my friend, you haven't seen the Abuna Yemata Guh. It is more than a thousand feet high and sticks out of the earth like a needle towards the heavens. That, my friend, is a true chapel in the sky. It is an old church, even older than this one, but it is a beauty once you make it to the top. I was climbing to that church every week when I was but a boy."

"That's quite impressive," Lord Kiros said. "As a boy, the only climbing I did was up to church windows to watch the choir girls who were practicing singing."

Abba Paulos chuckled before continuing. "And even before that, my mother used to climb to church while carrying my three-year-old sister on her back while she was eight months pregnant with me. And when I was 40 days old, she carried me on her back to the top just to see that I was baptized there. I was seven years old when I made my first climb on my own."

"Even with all that, Abba," Lord Kiros said, "this is no easy climb. Now I see why Debre Damo used to win all the Genna games."

"We win because we are better players," Abba Paulos countered.

"Were, Abba," Lord Kiros corrected the abba. "You were better players. We made sure of that during the last game."

"But the game really never ended," Abba Paulos argued. "It was interrupted."

"That game was already over, Abba," Commander Berhan interjected. "There was no way you could have come back to win."

"Thank you," Lord Kiros said appreciatively.

"Okay, tough man," Abba Paulos said to Lord Kiros. "Let's see how good you can climb."

Moments later, more ropes were dropped from the top of the cliff, dangling from the ledge. Lord Kiros and the rest of the party each grabbed one. Each rope was made of plaited leather—sturdy and quite unbreakable. Scaling the sheer cliff also required tough and unbreakable courage and strength, Lord Kiros thought.

"This is not about strength," Abba Paulos warned as Lord Kiros grabbed the rope. "It's about faith."

Lord Kiros was not too sure about how much faith he had, but he was willing to take the chance.

A moment later, him, Commander Berhan, Abba Paulos, two of his monks, and the soldier who had carried the bag were scaling the cliff, while the bag itself was being hoisted up by the monks from atop the cliff. It was a tough climb, requiring nerves of iron, Lord Kiros thought. Each time he looked down, he felt his heart skip. He eyed the soldier with them. He was struggling. The soldier looked towards the top and sighed exasperatedly.

"Do not think about how much farther you have left to go," Lord Kiros advised him. "Think about how far you've come."

"Yes, my lord," the soldier responded.

Abba Paulos thought he had to distract the soldier to help him pass the time as they climbed.

"If you are in a race and you overtake the second person," he said to the soldier, "what position are you in?"

"You become the first person," the soldier said without hesitation.

"Wrong," Abba Paulos responded. "Think again, young man."

The soldier thought briefly, then chuckled. "I get it," he said. "You become the second person, because you overtook the second person but not the first."

"Good man," Abba Paulos said.

When they finally arrived at the top, with Lord Kiros, Commander Berhan, and the soldier panting like they had just escaped from a pack of highland wolves, Tafari was eagerly waiting for Lord Kiros. The monk reached out to his friend and pulled him up.

"Welcome to Debre Damo, my friend," Tafari greeted Lord Kiros.

"My God!" Lord Kiros exclaimed. "I thought being a monk in St. Verena was hard. But this—this is something else."

"Terrible times in the past called for difficult challenges," said a Debre Damo monk standing behind Tafari.

Indeed. Lord Kiros had heard of the story of the monk from Debre Damo, who during the destruction of churches and relics by Queen Gudit's forces centuries before, climbed to the top of a 108-foot ancient obelisk in Axum without the aid of ropes, using only his bare hands and strength. His aim was to prevent the sacred obelisk from being destroyed by the queen's men. They left it alone, for there were those among them who, despite being followers of the usurper queen, had no intention of endangering their souls by causing the death of a monk in toppling the obelisk.

"Is that it?" Tafari asked looking at the bag of land deeds that had already been hoisted to the top of the cliff.

"It is," Lord Kiros said.

Abba Paulos nodded at two of his monks, who took the bag of documents and disappeared with it into a building.

Lord Kiros turned back and looked behind him, first at the nearly 50-foot sheer cliff that they had just managed to scale, and then at the surrounding landscape of unending beauty they could now see from their vantage point.

"It is as if everything in the world is visible from here," Lord Kiros said in awe.

The dry land, with patches of acacia trees, and the engrossing scenery of the surrounding country was dazzling and mesmerizing to say the least. It was like staring into the heavens. Then he turned back around to examine his immediate surroundings atop the mountain. Equally as captivating, he was standing in a small, pristine village perched at the top of a flat-topped mountain. All the buildings were made out of finely-cut stone and richly-adorned masonry. There was a church, gardens, farms, living quarters, stables for livestock, and rock cisterns that collected water during the rains to sustain the community of monks for up to 13 months at a time.

"What is that about?" Lord Kiros asked, looking at a painting on the wall of a building that depicted a man on the back of a python. "What in God's name was a man doing on a snake?"

"That is Saint Aregawi," Tafari said. "One of the Nine Saints. He is the founder of this monastery. Legend says he first came up here riding on the back of a python."

"Really?" Lord Kiros chuckled, still panting from his climb. "He gets a comfortable and leisurely ride up here, but makes everyone else look death in the face by climbing up here?"

"Hmm," Abba Paulos muttered with a shrug of his shoulders. "Saints have their privileges. We are but simple mortals. What can I say?"

"Of course," Lord Kiros quipped.

"How about a quick tour of the place so you know what else you will be fighting to defend?" Abba Paulos suggested.

"Perhaps later, Abba," Lord Kiros politely responded. Then he turned to Tafari. "Lady Mariam—where is she?"

CHAPTER 26

A short moment after arriving at the top of the Debre Damo cliff, Tafari walked Lord Kiros into a garden of white roses and lilies. It was a place where the monks usually meditated and prayed. Lady Mariam was seated there with Jembere and a female servant. Lord Kiros approached Lady Mariam.

"Lord Kiros," Jembere greeted.

"Jembere, Adina," Lord Kiros returned the greeting.

Jembere and the female servant then departed to give Lady Mariam and Lord Kiros some privacy.

"It's good to see you, Lord Kiros," Lady Mariam said, clearly excited to see him, but struggling to conceal it. She was still upset with him.

Then they both rushed towards each other, but stopped just short of entangling themselves in a hug which they clearly and desperately wanted to give each other. Lord Kiros held back because he did not want to upset Lady Mariam. She held back because he had to know she was still quite upset with him. Lord Kiros simply placed his hands on both her shoulders and squeezed them slightly. She closed her eyes, feeling the comfort of his touch.

"I have missed you, Lady Mariam," he said as they stared into each other's eyes.

"And I you, Lord Kiros," she replied.

Like children spying on adults, Jembere and Adina were watching them from behind a pillar some distance away.

"Why don't they just kiss each other?" Adina wondered. "They both know they want to."

"Because until he renounces his vows, Lord Kiros is still a monk," Jembere said, "even if he does not dress as one now."

"The coming days will be difficult," Lord Kiros warned Lady Mariam. "Roha is spared, at least for now. If we stop Lord Groda here, then Roha will be finally free of him for good."

"You are a decent man, Lord Kiros," Lady Mariam said. "There are not many like you these days."

"My circumstances have forced me to be what I am now," Lord Kiros responded. "If we survive this, I hope—"

"We will survive this," she insisted. "I felt safe with you. Now all of Roha feels safe with you. Good will come out of this."

"I pray you are right," he said. "There are—"

"Lord Kiros?" Commander Berhan shouted his name from the edge of the cliff.

Lord Kiros turned towards Commander Berhan, a one-time persistent suitor of Lady Mariam. Did he still want her? Was he jealous at seeing them together? What was he thinking about the unfolding events?

"Come, my lord," he said to Lord Kiros. "There are men approaching."

Lord Kiros turned back to Lady Mariam.

"I must take my leave," he said. "Be careful. You will be safe up here."

Before he turned around, he paused.

"Wait," he said to her. "How did you get up here?"

"What?" Lady Mariam seemed upset. "You think I cannot climb because I am a woman?"

"No—well—" Lord Kiros stumbled for words.

"Okay," she said, "I was hoisted up here. You did not expect me to climb, did you?"

Lord Kiros smiled and shook his head at her. He took her right hand in his and gently rubbed it. She bit her lower lip as Lord Kiros slowly let go of her hand and walked backward a few steps away from her. He then turned around and walked back to join Commander Berhan and his party at the edge of the cliff.

They were observing dust rising in the distance, as men on horseback were riding in haste towards the cliff.

"What do you think?" Commander Berhan asked. "Lord Groda's scouts?"

"No." Lord Kiros shook his head. "About 20 to 50 men. There are too many of them to be scouts. Let's get down there."

"I want you to know, Lord Kiros," Abba Paulos said, "that we monks cannot fight to kill. But we will help you with anything else you need. This is not only your fight or the fight of the people of Roha alone."

"You have done enough for us already, Abba" Lord Kiros said. "We will take it from here."

Lord Kiros turned to Tafari. "Much of this fight will be down there," he said to his young friend, pointing below the cliff. "But Lord Groda is as determined as a hungry hyena. He will find a way to bring it up here, to us. You watch yourself, okay?"

Tafari nodded, then tapped his friend on the shoulder, wishing him good luck. Lord Kiros and Commander Berhan then quickly grabbed the climbing ropes and stepped to the edge of the cliff.

"We had better get used to this, people," Lord Kiros said, knowing that at some point they would have to climb back up the cliff—again.

When they arrived at the bottom, the approaching riders had gotten much closer. Tewodros, Daga, some of their men, and some Beta Israel fighters were already at the edge of the village awaiting the riders.

"Those are not Lord Groda's men," Daga said to Lord Kiros and Commander Berhan as the two joined him. "I have never seen that bunch before."

"They are Muslims," Tewodros said, recognizing their distinct robes and turbans. "What are they doing here?"

"I suppose we are about to find out," Lord Kiros said. He looked behind him to ensure that their roughly 60 men-at-arms were ready to face down the potential threat if needed. They were.

The Muslims got close and brought their horses to a halt before Lord Kiros and his men. Armed with bows slung across their backs and sabers strapped to their sides, the riders were dusty and fatigued, the result of days of hard riding through rough country and across the highlands. Their leader glanced over to Lord Kiros and his men, then dismounted and marched straight to the scout commander.

"The Red Monk of Roha," he said to Lord Kiros with tapered excitement. "So it's really true!"

Lord Kiros squinted his eyes. By Saint George, he recognized the man!

"Yahya!" Lord Kiros yelled out. "It is—You look well!"

"You remember, Lord Kiros?" he laughed. "Yes, it is me, Mohammed Yahya. The man you saved from Lord Groda at Bodera village."

"Yes, yes, of course," Lord Kiros acknowledged, truly happy that the former captive whom he had saved from Lord Groda survived after all. "What are you doing here?"

"I have come to repay my debt," Mohammed said. "I bring you 27 of the best bowmen west of the Danakil Desert."

"How did you—" Lord Kiros began to ask.

"My men and I are caravaneers, mostly from Harar," Mohammed began to explain. "We make our living escorting salt caravans across the desert from the salt mines of Danakil. We also escort men of my faith wishing to travel to Mecca, and sometimes men of your faith wishing to travel to Jerusalem. Lord Groda's men have lately made that somewhat difficult by attacking and pillaging some of the caravans, killing many. Everyone in Harar and Axum are afraid to go after him. But when we heard that a man in red was killing them in Roha—a man who turned out to be a monk—we thought it was a good thing. And then when we heard that that monk was Lord Kiros himself, the man who had stood up for me at Bodera—I knew I had to help finish his task and repay the debt I owed him."

Lord Kiros smiled and tapped Mohammed on the back. "You are a man of great courage, Mohammed," he said. "Your help is duly needed here, and your archers are just what we need."

"With these men, we now have over 90 men-at-arms," Commander Berhan said, grinning.

Later that day, Abba Paulos and his monks were finally giving Lord Kiros the tour of the monastery as they all walked the grounds, along with Tafari and Commander Berhan. Of course, Lord Kiros had had to make the climb back up to the monastery again. Of the men within his ranks, some made the climb up to the monastery as often as needed, while most chose to stay below, where they anticipated most of the fight against Lord Groda was going to take place anyway. They did not wish to challenge death any more than they needed to.

First, Lord Kiros and his party walked to the church, where everyone took off their shoes and sandals before entering through the main double doors that were supported by massive stone pillars.

"My God!" Lord Kiros muttered to himself as they stepped inside.

After skirmishing through the dry and nearly-barren landscape around the mountain, and gambling with his own mortality by laboriously scaling the death-defying sheer cliff that seemed to him like the closest thing to hell, stepping into the church truly felt to him like the nearest thing to being in heaven. Surrounded by the beautiful and colorful frescoes and murals—many of which were hundreds of years old—that adorned the walls and the ceilings, it was perhaps the only time in his life he had felt himself touched by any kind of holiness. These were the most beautiful paintings Lord Kiros had ever seen. There was the painting of winged angels on the left wall, created in colors so vivid and mesmerizing that for a moment Lord Kiros forgot the labors he had endured to get to the top of the cliff, and instead seemed to believe that he had been transported there on the back of the flying beings. There were murals of the Nine Saints, of the martyred Saint Mamas riding a lion, of Mary and her ascension to heaven, and most importantly, behind the alter, an intriguing fresco of Saint Michael, the guardian of the souls of martyrs and saints, suited for combat in plate armor and carrying a long sword raised above his head, ready to confront the devil on man's behalf.

"Beautiful," Lord Kiros muttered as he also gawked at the coffered ceilings of wooden panels of carvings depicting winged horses, crocodiles, rhinos, lions, antelopes, cheetahs, and other animals in the realm.

The party soon exited the church and continued their tour around the monastery, which consisted of around 200 buildings, some of them two-stories high. There was also an exquisitely-built stone bell tower that was used to signal meal time, prayer time, and other events. The 400 monks who called Debre Damo home were entirely self-sufficient and had everything at the clifftop that they needed to survive. They grew their own food in beautiful and well-tended gardens. They also maintained a poultry and a stable that raised goats, cattle, and sheep. They had no need to leave the mountain.

"This is our House of Treasures," Abba Paulos said as they entered a building that was surrounded by a stone wall.

From the look of it, Lord Kiros thought it made the House of Treasures of St. Verena look like a pauper's hut.

"Our isolation has enabled us to survive invasion, war, Queen Gudit, and even the plague of 840," Abba Paulos said. "But it has isolated us from the rest of the Christian world."

"Is that what I think it is?" Lord Kiros asked in awe, staring at a pair of manuscripts.

"Yes," Abba Paulos said. "The Garima Gospels. The monks of the Abba Garima monastery brought them here for safekeeping when the forces of the Shewa Muslims got too close to them."

Written in Ge'ez by Saint Garima around 350 AD, these finely-illuminated manuscripts—which showed among other things, beautifully illustrated and colorful scenes from the Gospel of Saint Mark—were the most beautiful illuminated manuscripts Lord Kiros had ever seen. Abba Mikael had even claimed that they were the oldest in the Christian world. After all, he had travelled widely and had seen many others, having visited Christian monasteries and churches throughout the Nubian kingdoms of Alodia and Makuria, Alexandria, Jerusalem, Syria, and even reportedly the Malabar Coast in a far-off place called India, to visit Christians there who were converted by Saint Thomas the Apostle in the first century AD. Abba Mikael always told of how he was surprised that more than a thousand years later his tomb remained there, revered by both Christians and Muslims alike.

The gospels were not the only ecclesiastical treasures in the House of Treasures in Debre Damo.

"This is a coin from the fourth century, during the reign of Ezana, one of the brother kings," Abba Paulos said, holding up a gold coin he picked up from a chest full of coins. "Do you know what makes this significant?"

"It has to be almost 900 years old if it is from Ezana's time," Lord Kiros said.

"Yes," Abba Paulos said. "But there is more. Look closer, and you will see that it has a cross."

"As do many coins, abba," Lord Kiros said, having seen crosses on Egyptian, Greek, and Arabian coins.

"But this is the first coin in the world to feature the Christian cross," Abba Paulos said. "That is what makes this different from all the others."

That made sense, Lord Kiros understood. Ethiopia was one of the first nations to make Christianity an official religion, under the brother kings, and therefore the first to place the cross on its coins.

During the next two days, everyone—including the 470 monks of Debre Damo and the House of St. Verena, Commander Berhan and his 23 Riders of Roha, Daga and his six fighters, Mohammed Yahya and his 26 archers, the 31 Beta Israel fighters, and Lord Kiros—worked together to build defenses mostly at and around the foot of the cliff.

"Should it come to it," Lord Kiros had explained to them all, "this battle will be one of body count, with our goal being to kill as many of Lord Groda's men as possible, to neutralize them as an effective fighting force and a source of scourge in this region."

The monks dug trenches and helped set traps by planting sharpened stakes in small, hidden holes around the field. Though not outright fatal, these traps were nonetheless capable of slowing down moving military formations by delivering ghastly injuries that could make a victim beg to be killed. The monks were committed to the Sixth Commandment of Thou shalt not kill, but the Ten Commandments said nothing about making the lives of one's enemies utterly miserable. So they had carried out their work with frightening dedication and precision, placing the sharpened stakes in strategic locations that Lord Kiros had identified as possible avenues of approach by Lord Groda and his forces.

Hidden in a valley nestled within a forest patch consisting of acacia, myrrh, and coriander trees within a field of scattered shrubs of wild khat, Lord Groda and his 500 men prepared for their assault on the Debre Damo monastery the following day. Sitting under a myrrh tree as some of his men busied themselves plucking leaves from the surrounding khat shrubs, Lord Groda was talking to a bearded man wearing a turban. The number of scars on the man's cheek that cut across his face indicated he had been in more than a few situations most people would rather avoid.

"I do not like this," the man warned Lord Groda. "This is not good ground to encamp. Lord Kiros and his people will learn of our presence if we stay here for another day."

Lord Groda chuckled. "Lord Kiros knows exactly where we are," he stated flatly. "There is no place where any army can hide to keep him from finding it."

"How can you be so sure?" the man asked.

"I worked with the man for almost 20 years," Lord Groda said. "There is no better tracker or scout in all of Ethiopia." He stood up and looked around into the surrounding hills. "He has been following us for two days now already, watching our every move."

"Two days?" the man asked, surprised.

Concealed within a stretch of wild white roses on a hill a short distance away from Lord Groda's encampment, Lord Kiros, Daga, Commander Berhan, and Mohammed Yahya were watching Lord Groda's army.

"So who is he?" Lord Kiros asked, referring to the battle-scarred man Lord Groda was talking to.

"Ibrahim al-Ghazi," Mohammed said. "We have fought his bandits before."

It made sense. Everyone knew of the notorious Somali, Ibrahim al-Ghazi the brigand. He was an Islamic sheik whose bandits consisted of Muslims, Christians, Jews, and even pagans. He did not care. If you wanted gold, silver, and treasure, and were willing to kill and pillage for it anywhere, then you were exactly what he was looking for.

"Why would Lord Groda ally with him?" Daga asked. "He always hated the man."

"The walls of Harar," Lord Kiros responded.

"Harar?" Commander Berhan inquired, unsure of what the fortified, walled Muslim city of Harar in the eastern part of the Ethiopia had to do with it.

"Seven years ago," Lord Kiros explained, "Al-Ghazi and his men laid siege to the whole city and somehow were able to scale the walls and overcome its defenders. The city was only saved after the king sent reinforcements to drive out al-Ghazi and his men. Lord Groda hopes to use the experienced climbers of al-Ghazi's men to scale the cliffs of Debre Damo."

That explained it. Ibrahim al-Ghazi was known to all by name, a notorious brigand wanted in Nubia, Ethiopia, the Mogadishu Sultanate, the Shewa Sultanate, several pagan chieftains, and even other brigands in the fringes of Ethiopia.

"This is not a fight we want," Lord Kiros said. "We must avoid it if we can until the king returns, for the odds are not in our favor."

"But what can we do?" Commander Berhan asked.

"I'll need you to take a message to Lord Groda," Lord Kiros said.

A moment later, Commander Berhan mounted his horse. Lord Kiros handed him a small package wrapped in cloth.

"Will Lord Groda know what it means?" Commander Berhan asked.

"He will," Lord Kiros said. "All those years spent trying to become a priest? He must have learned a thing or two about the history of this realm."

Commander Berhan smiled, then sprang off on his horse towards Lord Groda's encampment. A short while later, carrying the package in one hand and leading his horse by the other, he was brought by sentries before Lord Groda, al-Ghazi, and their men.

"Commander Berhan," Lord Groda called. "Lord Kiros has my land deeds. Why do you and his people fight for what no longer belongs to them?"

"I assure you, Lord Groda," Commander Berhan began, "we do not fight you for just the lands. We fight you to protect the security of society—to rid this land of you and your vermin."

"You finally found the guts you were missing, I see," Lord Groda mocked.

"I bring a message from Lord Kiros," Commander Berhan stated, ignoring the insult and handing the small package to Lord Groda.

Lord Groda took it and unwrapped it, revealing a bundle of ten arrows tied together with a string. He chuckled. "Your Lord Kiros is a funny man," he said.

"What is your response to him, my lord?" Commander Berhan asked.

Lord Groda dropped the bundle, pulled out his sword, and with a single strike, shattered all of the arrows.

"That is my response to him," Lord Groda said, pointing threateningly at Commander Berhan. "Go back and tell him."

Commander Berhan bowed his head slightly towards Lord Groda, turned around, mounted his horse, and galloped away.

"So what was that bit all about?" Ibrahim al-Ghazi asked Lord Groda.

"Ever heard of Augustus Caesar of the Romans?" Lord Groda asked.

"Of course," al-Ghazi replied.

"More than a thousand years ago, after many battles between the Romans and Nubians over some business disputes, Caesar sent his legions into Nubia to try to force them to pay taxes to the Romans. A one-eyed Nubian warrior queen they called Amanirenas sent the Roman commander a bundle of arrows just like these." He paused.

"What did it mean?" al-Ghazi asked.

"It was a message," Lord Groda said. "'If you want a war, keep these arrows, for you will need them.' That was her message to the Romans."

"What did the Romans do?" al-Ghazi asked.

"The Roman commander must have returned the arrows, because the legions immediately withdrew and Caesar again never bothered the Nubians."

Al-Ghazi paused for a second before speaking. "They say you used to want to become a priest," he said. "Surely you must have some reservations about killing all those monks."

"God himself has few reservations when it comes to killing," Lord Groda said. "In our Bible, there is a story of a prophet named Elisha. He was bald, you see. One day 42 children laughed at his bald head. He wasn't too happy about it. So do you know what God did for him?"

"Made his hair grow?" al Ghazi guessed.

"No," Lord Groda said. "He sent bears to tear the children apart and eat them. So I have no qualms about killing those monks. Even God destroys those who bruise his ego."

"But Lord Groda," al-Ghazi cautioned, "you are not God."

CHAPTER 27

It was the 12th day of Genna. It was a quiet day in Debre Damo. Twenty-one men from Shire had joined Lord Kiros's ranks after learning that he was still alive, and a chieftain from a small and little-known village of Bahir Dar had sent 15 men. His goal was to help end the seasonal raids against his village by al-Ghazi's men. But most significantly, some Rohan nobles, with what little wealth they had left, had equipped a small force of 125 volunteers composed mainly of ex-soldiers and hunters. They had wisely turned down hundreds of ordinary Rohan volunteers, determining that their lack of any type of military or combat experience whatsoever was going to make them a liability rather than an asset to the fight against Lord Groda in an organized battle.

Lord Kiros now had 251 men-at-arms, facing more than twice that number in Lord Groda's 500 men. Lord Kiros and his men were under no illusions that they were all going to survive the day. They knew Lord Groda's men were only a few hours away, and so began to prepare their souls for the worst possible and likely outcome.

Lord Kiros and many in his ranks were in the Debre Damo monastery church, with Abba Paulos presiding over a special Mass for the repose of their souls should they meet their end against Lord Groda that day. Lord Kiros had declined to take communion because he did not think himself pure enough, having joined the monastery in deceit, and most importantly, having broken the sixth commandment multiple times in the previous few weeks.

At the bottom of the cliff, Commander Berhan had joined the Beta Israel fighters to build a makeshift temple under an olive tree, where a Kahen was now leading a Jewish service they were all attending. In front of the abandoned village, Mohammed Yahya and his men were prostrated on finely woven carpets, facing east towards Mecca, as they conducted their morning prayers to Allah. And lastly, in the middle of the village and in the monastery atop the cliff, were some of Daga's men and several Rohan Riders, Shire men, Bahir Dar men, and Rohan volunteers, wondering what on Earth the fuss was all about, over God, Allah, or Yahweh. These men just lived their lives without a care in the world for any kind of spirituality.

"You do not care for where your soul goes if you should fall today?" Commander Berhan later asked one of his soldiers who had not taken part in any kind of prayer.

"What does it matter, Commander?" the soldier replied. "If I should die, my soul would go to wherever souls go. If no such place exists, then I would just be dead and that would be it. I think I have lived life as a good person to those around me. That is what really matters to me."

Moments later, as Lord Kiros, Daga, Mohammed, and Commander Berhan were inspecting the defenses, they noticed some of their fighters doing something rather peculiar. One of them was ripping pages from the Bible and handing them out to his companions, who proceeded to chew and swallow the pages.

"What are they doing?" a confused Mohammed asked.

"They believe swallowing the pages will keep them from getting killed," Lord Kiros said. "It is a practice that started during the plague of 849, when people thought it was God's punishment on the land for expelling a bishop. People ate Bible pages to help them ward off death. People ate so many Bibles that some churches had to close their doors because they couldn't find enough to conduct Mass."

Mohammed looked petrified. Then he turned his attention to some other soldiers who were on their knees, their swords and spears nearby, muttering some words to themselves.

"And these ones?" Mohammed asked.

"They are performing the Wudase Mariam," Daga said. "Prayers to the Virgin Mary. Do you know who that is?"

"'O Mary! God has chosen you and purified you,'" Mohammed quoted. "'He has chosen you above the women of all nations.'"

"Ah," Daga exclaimed, surprised. "You know the Bible? Though I must confess I have never heard that quote before."

"That is because it is not from the Bible, Daga," Mohammed said. "It is from the Holy Quran"

"The Quran?" Daga asked.

"Of course," Mohammed said. "We Muslims believe in much of the same things that Christians and Jews believe in. The Quran talks of Jesus more times than any other person. And then of Moses. Together they are mentioned more than 200 times. Mohammed himself is only mentioned five times."

"It is fascinating," Daga observed, "to have Christians, Muslims, Jews, and heathens from Roha, Gondar, Shire, Bahir Dar, Gorgora, and Harar, put aside their spiritual differences to fight for a better tomorrow. If only our kings and chieftains could do the same."

Just then, Tewodros rode by with his scouts.

"Lord Kiros," he reported. "Lord Groda is just over the hill. We should prepare."

A short distance away, Lord Groda, riding at the head of his mounted column together with Ibrahim Al-Ghazi, was ecstatic about their chances of complete and total success. His scouts had reported an opposing force of less than half the size of his army.

"So is it really as they say," al-Ghazi asked, "that this Lord Kiros survived the bite of a black mamba?"

"It is as they say," Lord Groda responded. "I was there, in the southern forests when he was bitten."

"How do you know it was a black mamba?" al-Ghazi asked.

"Because he caught the snake," Lord Groda responded. "The thing is, he refused to kill it. He said it was not the snake's fault that it was a snake, so he released it, even as he believed he was going to die. He became violently sick for a few days, but then miraculously recovered."

"A man like that fears nothing," al-Ghazi said.

"That is true," Lord Groda said. "That sometimes makes him reckless."

"I hope you are right," al-Ghazi said.

"Thirty-two years it took me to build what I have," Lord Groda complained. "And he wants to wipe it all away in a few days."

"You never knew when to stop," al-Ghazi said. "That is your problem. You kept pushing and pushing, and now your enemies are fighting back."

"Oh, but I can push back harder," Lord Groda asserted. "That is why you are here."

"As long as you pay me in solid gold," al-Ghazi reminded him. "That is why I am here."

And then there was a sudden anguished and piercing cry from the left flank of the column. It was quickly followed by another, then by several more.

"Archers! Left flank!" one of Lord Groda's men yelled.

Lord Groda looked left, then across the hill, where ten archers, belonging to Mohammed's detachment, were letting fly volley after volley of arrows towards his men.

"They are trying to slow us down," Lord Groda said to Ibrahim. Then he turned to Moas, one of his commanders who had been riding next to him. "We keep moving forward, but send some men after those archers!"

Moas immediately spun around, and within moments, he and about 30 men began charging at the archers at full gallop. The archers withdrew immediately, but Moas and his men continued after them, getting caught up in the excitement and making the deadly mistake of chasing them down a narrow gap between a hill and a cliff. By the time the riders realized their tactical blunder, they found themselves canalized in a pass and surrounded by the ten archers and 50 riders led by Lord Kiros himself. They had been waiting. The slightly heavy chainmail armor that many of Lord Groda's men wore made maneuverability more difficult for them than it did for Lord Kiros's men, whose armor—if it could even be called that—consisted mainly of thick and padded cotton cloth that they wrapped around their torsos to provide some degree of protection. Lord Kiros's men quickly and mercilessly cut down most of Moas's men as they panicked and engaged in a confused and scattered withdrawal.

Only Moas and two of his men made it back to their lines, whose right flank was now also under attack by five of Lord Kiros's archers.

About twenty of Lord Groda's men were already charging at them at full gallop as well. These also repeated the tactical blunder of chasing their adversaries through a narrow pass. This time, they were met and surrounded by Commander Berhan and about 40 men. They, too, were slaughtered, down to the last man.

It took another similar ambush of 17 of Lord Groda's men, this time slaughtered by a detachment led by Tewodros, for Lord Groda to realize that chunks of his army were systematically being separated, cordoned off, and neutralized.

"We keep pushing forward," Lord Groda instructed Moas and his commanders. "They want to slow us down because they know time is not on our side."

The next attack from archers, this time coming from the left flank, was ignored. Lord Groda's column just kept on riding forward at full speed, hoping to escape the gauntlet of death by getting to the cliff of Debre Damo and exacting a punishing vengeance.

From the safety of some bushes, Mohammed watched Lord Groda's men as they ignored the archers and avoided taking the bait again. Mohammed addressed one of his men standing next to him.

"The red monk was right," he said to the man. "Lord Groda won't always take the bait. Send the signal."

The man next to Mohammed sounded a horn, sending a signal down the line along Lord Groda's path and the avenue of approach to the monastery. Small groups of archers along the path started emerging from their hiding spots and began shooting arrows at Lord Groda's men, bringing down many as they tumbled from their horses. Lord Groda watched the unfolding carnage and ordered his men to increase their speed. He had to take the fight to their stronghold and force them into a pitched battle before he lost all his men.

In the rear of Lord Groda's column, Lord Kiros and his men from the first ambush were giving chase, with the archers releasing volley upon volley of arrows while galloping at full speed. Lord Groda's men did not stop to fight. They knew in doing so, Lord Kiros's men would just withdraw and disperse into the surrounding hills. Their only chance was to get to the monastery as fast as possible, make a stand there, and attack the monastery at the same time.

When Lord Groda's army finally reached the cliff, his hopes were renewed.

"Finally," he exclaimed. "We will take no prisoners!"

But then he realized that many of his horses were tumbling over, their riders with them.

"What is this?" he screamed in anger.

"Traps, my lord!" Moas explained. "They have them all over the field."

Lord Groda watched in horror as little holes dug in random places over the field, camouflaged with dirt and leaves, served as a traps for his horses. Their riders plummeted into hidden pits with waiting sharpened stakes to finish the job, impaling the men and sometimes the innocent, unfortunate horses.

"Surround the cliff!" Lord Groda ordered Moas.

In a pincer movement formation, Lord Groda's men split into two, veering in opposite directions in an attempt to surround the base of the clifftop monastery.

Lord Groda again watched in bewilderment as the front ranks of the left side suddenly screamed at the same time as sharpened stakes buried in the ground suddenly sprang up, impaling several of the riders and knocking them off their horses. They had triggered trip wires. This threw the formation into complete disarray as the ranks behind them slowed down and tried to go around, only to be met with more stakes that knocked off the first rows as well, deepening the consternation within their ranks.

Just when it could not get any worse for Lord Groda's men, at the top of the cliff, a Rohan noble in command of Rohan volunteers and some of Mohammed's archers waited eagerly to repay Lord Groda for all his treachery. With itchy fingers on the strings of their bows, they realized Lord Groda's men were now well within range of their arrows.

"Waste them!" he yelled at his men.

Standing at the edge of the cliff, his men now began raining down deadly accurate volleys of arrows at the bedraggled attackers.

"We were supposed to be fighting a bunch of monks!" Lord Groda screamed in frustration.

Many of his men deployed their shields, with some effect. Others were simply taken off guard, while others may have believed themselves to be immune, a notion that was soon dispelled once 15-inch arrows started sprouting from their bodies.

"My lord," Moas called to his commander, riding from the rear of formation, "we are losing too many men!"

"And you will lose your head if you do not press the men on," Lord Groda threatened.

A frustrated Moas ran back into the formation to press the men on. "Forward!" he yelled. "Keep moving!"

Now firmly established at the base of the cliff, Lord Groda was where he wanted to be. His men stood their ground, and a detachment turned to the rear to face the attack from Lord Kiros and the rest of his men. He deployed his own archers to face the threat from their rear and from above. Now it was his turn to punish the defenders. They unleashed pure hell, dropping many of Lord Kiros's riders and overwhelming the archers at the top of the cliff, with many plunging to their deaths.

Lord Groda liked what he was seeing. Now he was ready to deploy the men most critical to this operation.

He turned towards al-Ghazi, smiled, and then instructed him, "Send up the climbers."

CHAPTER 28

Al-Ghazi had just received instructions from Lord Groda that validated the single purpose for why he had been hired for the operation against the defenders of the monastery at Debre Damo. He turned towards his commanders standing next to him, and nodded. Several men then dismounted from their horses and pulled down some bags that were strapped to the back of their horses. They opened the bags and took out climbing ropes with four-pronged grappling hooks attached to them. With archers ready to defend them, the men got to work.

"Now!" their commanders ordered.

The archers shot arrows at the defenders at the top of the cliffs, forcing them to duck for cover, giving their climbers a significant fighting chance to do their work. With the hooks at the end of the ropes tied to arrows, the climbers shot the arrows towards the top of the cliff, at areas that could be used as anchors. Once that was done, they pulled on the ropes to ensure they were hooked and secured. Within seconds, they had at least 20 ropes dangling from the cliff, providing multiple points of entry into the monastery.

When the defenders at the top of the monastery realized what was happening, they became frantic.

"Cut the ropes!" their Rohan commander urged his men.

Many pulled out their daggers and began hacking at the ropes, while at the same time, Lord Groda's archers from below were relentlessly targeting them.

Many of Lord Groda's men were already on the ropes, eager to get to the top in anticipation of getting their hands on the abundance of coin and treasure Lord Groda had promised were stored in the monastery.

The fight for the cliff soon became a duel of archers, as those on both sides began targeting each other. It was an epic contest to the death, with each side relentless in its pursuit of dominance. Men cried on both sides as each met his end, many falling from the cliff as they were hit by arrows or had their ropes cut. Lord Groda's men, with their abundance in numbers, seemed to be replacing the ropes on the cliff faster than Lord Kiros's men at the top of the cliff could cut them off.

So far, it was going according to plan for Lord Groda. He would soon have his men at the top of the monastery and inside it to recover his stolen documents.

The fight was relentless and brutal. But despite the bravery of the defenders, their numbers were simply not large enough to hold out the seemingly endless number of climbers and their archers. Before long, some of the climbers made a foothold atop the cliff, forcing the archers to divert resources towards combating in brutal hand-to-hand engagements. This in turn relieved the pressure on the other climbers, many more of whom were now able to mount the ropes and make it safely to the top.

At the monastery itself, sheer panic soon ensued.

"Quickly, let's go!" Tafari screamed at Lady Mariam, her servants, and his fellow monks from St. Verena, asking them to follow Abba Paulos to an underground hideout. "They're here!"

As they snaked through a dark, narrow, underground passage, Lady Mariam approached Tafari.

"Any word on Lord Kiros?" she asked in a whisper to avoid disturbing the frightened silence they were all experiencing. "Is he all right?"

"Nothing heard, my lady," Tafari said. "But our people continue to fight. Therefore, their leader surely continues to fight with them."

Many of Lord Groda's men, by force of numbers alone, were now established atop the cliff. In a euphoric orgy of wanton destruction, they began toppling statues, breaking down doors, and wreaking as much destruction on the monastery as possible, hoping to find hidden treasures somewhere. Three monks who stood by defiantly to protest the attack were mercilessly cut down.

But just before Lord Groda's men broke into the main entrance of the church, the door suddenly flew open, and out came Tewodros and about 30 fighters, including several Riders of Roha on foot. They had been stationed there for just this purpose, to serve as a last line of defense. They tore into the wave of Lord Groda's 25 men who had managed to make it this far, completely taking them by surprise and throwing them off their guard.

Back below the cliff, Lord Groda's men continued to try to make their way forward while still facing some minor resistance from the archers at the top. The rest of Lord Kiros's men continued to battle Lord Groda's men below, in bitter fighting on horseback.

"Ah!" a man screamed next to Lord Kiros.

It was Daga. He collapsed from his horse with an arrow just below his throat. His death was instant. There was nothing Lord Kiros could do for him. Daga had fought and died for what he believed in. Lord Kiros made a quick sign of the cross towards his body.

He immediately continued with his assault, his men pushing Lord Groda's men closer and closer to the cliff, the plan being for the archers atop to continue picking them off.

Then he noticed that Lord Groda and al-Ghazi, who were now themselves dismounted from their horses, getting ready to mount the ropes themselves and ascend to the monastery.

"The scoundrel!" Commander Berhan muttered to himself, having observed Lord Groda and al-Ghazi as well.

"To the cliff!" he ordered the men under his command.

Many of those men immediately broke from their current engagements where possible and raced for the cliffs, where they quickly dispatched the fewer numbers of Lord Groda's men who were left fighting.

Lord Kiros picked up a spear dropped by one of Daga's slain men. Constructed for perfect balance and precision-aiming by blacksmiths in Shire, it consisted of a wooden shaft inserted into an iron spearhead. At the end of the shaft was a heavy iron ring designed to provide balance to assure steadiness in flight. Lord Kiros raised the spear, took aim, and let it fly. One of al-Ghazi's men, who was about a quarter of the way to the top of the cliff, screamed in agony and let go, plummeting to his death with the spear stuck in his back. Lord Kiros mounted the rope and began climbing, as did Commander Berhan and many of their men. Often, these men were forced to fight against Lord Groda's men to get control of the ropes. Above, many of Lord Groda's men noticed that Lord Kiros's men were mounting ropes, too. One of the men tried to cut down a rope mounted by Commander Berhan.

"Don't!" another of Lord Groda's men stopped the cutter. "We need these ropes too!"

The cutter immediately mounted the rope next to it and began to descend, his sword at the ready, to face Commander Berhan. Both men met midway, with their swords clashing. Commander Berhan emerged victorious, with Lord Groda's man screaming as he took a cut to the shoulder and plunged to his death below.

Having regrouped and re-organized the archers by splitting them into two groups, one dedicated to targeting Lord Groda's archers, and another to targeting his climbers, Lord Kiros's archers were exacting a frightening toll on the enemy. This made the ropes a death trap for Lord Groda's men and lessened the burden on Lord Kiros and his climbers.

Finally catching on to this, Lord Groda's archers turned their attention to Lord Kiros's archers, leading to the archers on both sides turning away from the climbers and focusing on each other in a violent effort to neutralize the threats posed by the other.

"At last, it's just you and me now, Lord Groda," Lord Kiros said with a rare smile as he and Lord Groda met, swinging from ropes next to each other.

"You give me what I want, and my men and I will leave," Lord Groda said.

"Your word is about as trustworthy as that of a hyena guarding a chicken farm," Lord Kiros said.

Then they both went at each other, each man proving his skill in swordsmanship despite using one hand to dangle from the ropes. Known for having been a champion long-distance runner back in his younger days, Lord Groda proved to be a formidable opponent, matching Lord Kiros for skill and endurance, despite being 20 years Lord Kiros's senior.

In the midst of their duel, Lord Kiros noticed another attacker coming at him from above. The momentary distraction allowed Lord Groda to break contact, and he quickly climbed upwards while Lord Kiros faced off the new attacker. By the time he was done with the unfortunate man, Lord Groda was already at the top.

Before Lord Kiros made it to the top, he watched with satisfaction as Ibrahim al-Ghazi screamed and took a plunge to his death, with an arrow stuck on his side. Good riddance, Lord Kiros thought. Ibrahim Al-Ghazi had cemented his reputation as a brutally effectively raider and someone who knew how to scale heights. It was only fitting that he should meet his end on one.

Lord Kiros finally reached the top of the cliff and was surprised to see that Lord Groda and a few of his surviving men were surrounded by the surviving Rohan archers and Tewodros and his men, who had succeeded in holding off the assault into the monastery itself. There was no hope now for Lord Groda, and he knew it. His attack on Debre Damo had simply fizzled out in the face of the overwhelmingly superior tactical and strategic defensive maneuvering implemented by Lord Kiros and his commanders. All was lost. Lord Groda was desperately fighting now for his life. He had raced to the top of the cliff completely unaware of the situation on the ground there.

"Stop!" Lord Kiros yelled out.

All the fighting ceased instantly.

There was silence. Even below, much of the fighting seemed to have stopped, with most of Lord Groda's men killed, wounded, captured, or fleeing for their lives. Lord Kiros looked at Lord Groda, then looked behind him. More and more men began climbing to the monastery from below. They were all Lord Kiros's men.

"Your army is annihilated," Lord Kiros said to Lord Groda.

Lord Groda looked around earnestly.

"No, no, no!" he mumbled, not understanding how it had all come to this. This was a battle he was supposed to have won easily. He couldn't believe he had just lost 32 years of hard work in just a few hours. Panic soon kicked in.

"Fight!" he urged his surviving men in a desperate plea. "Fight!"

Wanting to save their own lives and knowing that there was no use in continuing to fight, the men ignored him. He grabbed one of the men and pushed him towards Lord Kiros. Lord Kiros simply shoved the man aside. The man then turned towards Lord Groda, looked him straight in the eyes, and dropped his sword. The rest of Lord Groda's men did the same, dropping their swords, spears, and bows.

In desperation, Lord Groda picked up one of the spears and offered it back to the man who had dropped it.

"Here," he cried, offering it to the man. "Keep fighting. This isn't over yet! Fight on!"

When the man ignored him and simply looked down, he offered it to another man.

"Fight them!" he pleaded. "I'll give you more gold and lands than you have ever dreamed of. Keep fighting!"

When the man ignored him too, he tried to offer it to another man, who also looked away. None of his surviving men were willing to die for him.

"Lord Groda," Commander Berhan called. "No amount of land or gold can be of any use to a dead man."

At this time, Lady Mariam and her servants, and all the surviving monks—having been alerted that the fighting was over—had emerged from hiding and were watching the scene before them.

When Lord Groda realized his efforts were useless, it dawned on him that all was really lost. He dropped the spear and his sword, collapsed to the ground on his knees, and started panting like a dog, looking all around him. Lord Kiros was enjoying every single moment of Lord Groda's humiliation and desperation. A smile flashed across his face. He wanted this man to suffer like he had made hundreds of others suffer.

"How does it feel?" Commander Berhan asked Lord Groda. "Was it all worth it?"

"Please," Lord Groda begged, crawling to Commander Berhan, "I will follow the king's laws. I will." Then he crawled to Lord Kiros. "You will get your lands back—more lands back. I promise." Then he turned to Lady Mariam. "You too. You will keep everything. And I will give you more!"

Lady Mariam scoffed. They were all ignoring Lord Groda's pleas.

"You!" Lord Groda turned to Mohammed, crawling to him. "I spared you! I let you live! Show mercy!"

"He remembers me," Mohammed said with a smile, then kicked Lord Groda away from him.

"You once told me a story about a leopard and an antelope, and how the antelope had to die for the sins of the father," Lord Kiros addressed Lord Groda. "Well, now I will tell you one about a tortoise—a very greedy tortoise."

Lord Groda remembered the story he had told Lord Kiros when he had betrayed and left the scout commander to die at the hands of the Shewa sultan.

"It was only a story," Lord Groda pleaded. "I meant nothing by it."

"Once," Lord Kiros began, "there was a feast in the sky for all the animals that could attend. The tortoise wanted to attend, but the problem was that he could not fly. So the birds loaned him some feathers. He used them to fly to the feast. When they asked him what his name was, he said his name was "Everyone." It was an unusual name, but they let it be. A few moments later, just before the feasting started, the tortoise publicly asked the host, 'Who is this food for?' The host replied, 'It is for everyone.' The tortoise then claimed that because his name was Everyone, the food then belonged to him alone. He therefore sat there and ate it all himself. All the other animals were angry, especially the birds. When it was time to return, they refused to loan him their feathers again. As a result, the tortoise had to simply jump from the sky to the land. He did so, but shattered his back. That is why to this day the tortoise's back remains cracked, to warn the everyone else of the dangers of greed."

Lord Groda got the message. He fell back, then slowly stood up, giving in. He was not going to find any help or mercy from this crowd. He knew what was coming. He slowly walked to the edge of the cliff, his eyes watering slightly.

"Like the tail of an animal, regret comes at the end," Lady Mariam muttered, seeing the anguish in Lord Groda's eyes.

Lord Groda took one last look at Lord Kiros, perhaps expecting a last-minute reprieve of sympathy. But Lord Kiros kept his eyes fixed on Lord Groda, then spat on the ground to his left.

Knowing they wished him hell, Lord Groda took a step over the cliff and plunged down. He did not scream or cry as he fell. However, a moment later, they heard a loud scream as he landed with a heavy thump. And it continued. He had not died!

Lord Kiros and his people ran to the edge of the cliff and peered over to see him. Lord Groda had not landed at the bottom of the cliff. He had landed on the branch of a small sycamore tree growing on the side of the cliff next to a cave opening.

The very tiny cave with barely enough room to hold a man had been used by a hermit bahitawi monk, who for 67 years never left its confines, choosing to maintain only minimal human contact and dedicating his life to meditation and praying for God to forgive man's sins. Living off the figs of the sycamore tree and the occasional food and water brought to him by the faithful who could reach him, he had been dead for five months before his remains were discovered just a few days prior to the battle.

Now Lord Groda hung dying in the most excruciating pain close to the cave, paying for his sins on humanity. He was hanging upside-down, impaled and held in place by a branch sticking through his thigh.

"I think, my lord," Commander Berhan said, "unlike the tortoise, Lord Groda has got more than just a cracked back."

"Even nature wants him to suffer," a Rohan volunteer added.

One of Mohammed's men raised his bow and nocked an arrow to finish off Lord Groda.

"No," Lord Kiros said, stopping the archer. "We cannot kill a wounded man. That would be murder. Let's leave him to God. But it is a good thing he will stick around to think about all the misery he heaped on others."

CHAPTER 29

Lord Kiros, his men, and the monks spent the next several hours and the following day providing aid to the wounded, both friendly and enemy alike, only interrupted by continuing agonized screams from Lord Groda, who was still hanging around. To many, Lord Groda's cries were music to their ears, but to the monks it was distressing. They attempted to climb down to assist him, but the soldiers and fighters declared the move to be a security risk and forbade it.

By the end of the second day, Lord Groda's screams had ceased. Just to be sure, Lord Kiros took a peek over the cliff and realized Lord Groda was doing some good after all. He was feeding vultures—not by choice, of course. He was very unlikely to emerge from that venture in one piece. He was done for, his litany of misdeeds finally at an end.

Of the 251 combatants on Lord Kiros's side who had engaged Lord Groda's men, 92 had been killed and 112 wounded. Few had emerged unscathed. It was not a miracle that his side had emerged victorious against overwhelming numbers. It was the skillful use of terrain and an effective strategy by Lord Kiros and his commanders that had earned them victory.

The threat from Lord Groda's men to Roha and the surrounding regions had been destroyed, and as an added bonus, the notorious brigand Ibrahim Al-Ghazi and his band of cutthroats had been annihilated as well. Roha was finally free of Lord Groda's thugs. Lady Mariam could now safely return to her home. The St. Verena monks were now safe. Many families who had lost properties to Lord Groda could now reclaim them. Most importantly for Lord Kiros, he too could now reclaim his lands, return to Shire, and live a life as a lord again.

The Beta Israel fighters, Mohammed Yahya's Muslim caravaneers, the men from Shire and Bahir Dar, and the Rohan volunteers all returned to their homes soon after the fighting. They had all come together to help neutralize a common threat that hampered their way of life.

Commander Berhan and his men had to leave soon as well to ensure that order was maintained in Roha. They were going to take Lady Mariam, her servants, and the monks of St. Verena back with them. Lord Kiros was to depart with them as well, to settle his affairs in Roha before returning to his lands in Shire.

The St. Verena monks and most of the surviving Riders of Roha were assembled at the bottom of the cliff in their mule train, ready to depart. Lady Mariam and her two servants waited at the top of the cliff to be lowered to the bottom by monks. But Lady Mariam soon noticed that Lord Kiros had not emerged to join them. She walked over to Tafari.

"Where is he?" she asked.

"You should have a talk with him," Tafari responded. "He is in the church."

Lady Mariam walked to the church, took off her shoes, and walked in. She saw Lord Kiros standing in front of a painting of the Virgin Mary holding the baby Jesus. He was just staring at it, deep in contemplation. But what struck Lady Mariam even more was that Lord Kiros had ditched his soldier's garb. He was back in the robes of a monk.

"Lord Kiros," she called as she walked close to him.

He slowly turned around to meet her and smiled. "Lady Mariam. You are looking well."

"The danger to you is over," she said. "Your innocence is proven. Why do you return to hide as a monk?"

He stood quiet for a moment before responding. "I do not hide in these garments as a monk any longer, Lady Mariam," he said. "This is who I am now, a freer man than I have ever been."

"But your lands," she said. "You have wanted them back for many years."

"I no longer have a need for them," he said. "I have learned these past months that there is a lot more to this life, and other ways for one to find fulfilment. It is not always in land and wealth."

Lady Mariam looked to the ground, tears rolling down her cheeks. Lord

Kiros gently touched her chin and lifted her head up so that their eyes met.

"I am deeply sorry, Lady Mariam," he said. "Were we at different times, and were the circumstances different, perhaps we may have walked the same road forward. But now we have to walk separate paths."

Lady Mariam kissed Lord Kiros's hand affectionately. She understood him. She had been around the Church long enough to understand that phenomenon where men and women who felt a calling from that invisible power beyond their control followed their hearts and never looked back. She had seen it time and time again. Every monk and priest had had that calling.

"The caravan will soon be leaving for Roha," Lord Kiros warned Lady Mariam. "You should be with it."

"Without you coming with us, I'm not sure how I could manage," Lady Mariam said.

"Commander Berhan is a good man," Lord Kiros said. "His wishes for you are sincere."

"Yes, he is a good and decent man," Lady Mariam said. "He has proven that these past few days. I have admired him for a long time and he has pursued me for a long time as well."

"Then what has been the problem?" Lord Kiros asked. "Why have you not given him the chance he has always wanted?"

"He does not believe in Christ," she said. "He follows the Jewish religion. How can we manage a household so divided?"

"Christian, Jewish, Muslim," Lord Kiros said. "Those are but words devised by men. It's all the same God, isn't it? And besides, was our Lord Jesus Christ himself not a Jew?"

Lady Mariam smiled, wiping the tears off her face. "But why are you staying here?" she asked. "Your monastery is in Roha."

"I have much to answer for," he responded, "for the things I have done that I cannot be proud of. Penance here at Debre Damo will help me see through some of that. Then I will return to the House of St. Verena."

Just then, Commander Berhan stuck his head through the door of the church to see Lady Mariam and Lord Kiros, who was still holding her face affectionately.

"My lady," Commander Berhan addressed her gently, not really wanting to interrupt them. "It is time. We have to go. I'll be waiting out here."

Lord Kiros and Commander Berhan then looked at each other. Commander Berhan nodded at him, and he nodded back, completing a quiet goodbye between friends who were grateful to each other. Commander Berhan stepped back to wait outside.

Lord Kiros then looked back at Lady Mariam, took her right hand in his, brought it to his face, and kissed it.

"You must go," he said. "Commander Berhan awaits. He is a worthy man and is true to himself."

She smiled at him. He let go of her hand and she turned around.

"Be well, Lady Mariam," he said to himself as she walked outside, though he knew she could not hear him.

Outside, Commander Berhan was waiting by the door, looking towards the cliff edge. When Lady Mariam emerged from the church, she stopped and looked at him. They eyed each other. He held out his hand to her. She accepted his hand in hers, and he led her down the stairs. When they got to the bottom of the stairs, she did not let go of his hand as they walked towards the cliff edge. Instead, she leaned against him, placing her head on his shoulder.

"So, Commander," she said to him. "Tell me about this little village of Gondar you keep talking about."

Two weeks later, the king returned from the frontiers, victorious over his enemies and having added more territory to the realm. Having been brought abreast of the events in Roha by Commander Berhan and Rohan court officials, he re-certified and returned the land deeds seized by Lord Groda to their rightful owners and heirs. Commander Berhan also saw to it that the families of Lord Kiros's scouts who were treacherously murdered by Lord Groda received the death benefits they were due, most of it seized from Lord Groda's estates.

As for Lord Kiros, after he subsequently returned to the House of St. Verena, one of the first things he did was visit the blacksmith workshop in St. Verena, where Abba Mikael's apprentices still worked. He handed them a bundle wrapped in cloth. They opened it up, revealing his sword and dagger.

"What do you want us to do with these?" one of them asked.

"Melt them down and turn them into crosses," Lord Kiros said.

Lord Kiros had his lands restored as well, but having found a way to free himself from the wants of this world, he continued to live as a monk. Instead, he donated all of his estate to the Church to help complete the rock-hewn churches and feed the needy on the streets of Roha.

With Commander Berhan's persuasion, the king's court confiscated Lord Groda's estate to help pay for recompense to some of those he had wronged. This, of course, deprived Tiki of his wealth. Ever one to want to better her lot by any means necessary, through a court official she ingratiated herself with, she claimed to the king's court that her marriage to Lord Groda was not legal and therefore she was still technically married to Lord Kiros, who had never divorced her since she had believed him to be dead. The king's court sided with her and declared that as the wife of Lord Kiros, she was entitled to part of his property, and that he was still responsible for her upkeep even though they were no longer living together. But the amount of this upkeep on Lord Kiros' income. And since he had donated all his lands and had no income other than two or three meals per day from the monastery, he was only required to provide her one meal per week, which amounted to the equivalent of a mango.

Tiki never showed up to claim her entitlement. She passed away of cholera four months after Lord Groda's death in a hut in her ancestral village, destitute.

The Timkat festival following the battle against Lord Groda had been especially meaningful for Lord Kiros. As he dipped himself into the baptismal pool of St. George's cross-shaped rock-hewn underground church, he felt himself truly reborn like he had never felt before.

Although many praised Lord Kiros for having given up his worldly ways for the life of a monk, he was always quick to point out that every monk used to be something else. He was by no means the first to make such a drastic and radical change. There was the well-known Moses the Black who was also known as Moses the Robber. Living in Egypt about 900 years before Lord Kiros's time, he was a notorious Ethiopian bandit, who after seeking sanctuary with a group of Egyptian monks to escape the authorities hunting him down, decided to remain a monk after the danger had passed. He died in 405, sacrificing himself for his fellow monks in order to save them from a band of raiding bandits. His fame was so renowned that his relics remained in the Paromeos Monastery in Egypt. Even a monastery in faraway Syria, Deir Mar Musa al-Habashi or Monastery of Saint Moses the Abyssinian, was named in his honor in the sixth century. But all of that paled in comparison to the conversion of Ethiopia's sixth century King Kaleb, who after his successful battle of Najran in Arabia during his crusade to protect Christians, gave up his throne, sent his crown to the church of the Holy Sepulcher in Jerusalem, and went to the Abba Pantalewon Monastery built at the top of a rock in the Ethiopian Highlands, where he lived the rest of his days as pious monk.

Giorgis Kiros spent the remainder of his long life in the service of the needy of Roha and was fortunate to live long enough to see his friend, Tafari, eventually become the abba of the House of St. Verena.

EPILOGUE

In all, 11 rock-hewn underground churches were built in Roha in an attempt to create a New Jerusalem as a refuge for Ethiopian Christians no longer able to travel to Jerusalem after it was captured by Muslims from the Crusaders. After the king's death, the city of Roha, Ethiopia's capital at the time, was renamed after him—Lalibela, a king of the Zagwe Dynasty. Today, Lalibela draws hundreds of thousands of faithful annually, seeking fulfillment in its churches and sacred springs. Many of the land grants and deeds issued by King Lalibela 800 years ago survive to this day.

After almost 300 years in power, the Zagwes, who were regarded by many simply as stewards of the throne, were forced to abdicate in an arrangement brokered by Ethiopia's most revered saint, the bearded and wise Takla Haymanot. This also paved the way for the installation of a new Negus—king of Ethiopia, reintroducing the Solomonic dynasty to power and beginning the Second Solomonic Age, an event known in Ethiopian history as the Return of the King.

Years later, following an initial move by a Solomonic king named Minas, his descendants officially establish a new capital of Ethiopia at Gondar in 1635.

The Second Solomonic Age lasted for 700 years until it was disestablished in 1974. The Tewahedo Church remains the most influential non-governmental body in Ethiopia today.